Forgive And Remember

Family Bonds Generational Saga

Reem Kashat

PINKISH BOOKS LLC

Copyright © 2024 Reem Kashat and Pinkish Books LLC.

ALL RIGHTS RESERVED

This is a work of fiction. Names, characters, organizations, places, events, and incidents are either products of the author's imagination or are used fictitiously. Any resemblance to actual events, locales, or persons living or dead are entirely coincidental.

No part of this book may be reproduced, or stored in a retrieval system, or transmitted in any form or by any means electronic, mechanical, photographic, recording, or otherwise without the expressed written permission of the publisher.

Contents

1. Dedication — 1
2. Chapter 1 — 2
3. Chapter 2 — 13
4. Chapter 3 — 30
5. Chapter 4 — 40
6. Chapter 5 — 45
7. Chapter 6 — 59
8. Chapter 7 — 70
9. Chapter 8 — 80
10. Chapter 9 — 97
11. Chapter 10 — 104
12. Chapter 11 — 113
13. Chapter 12 — 121
14. Chapter 13 — 132

15.	Chapter 14	143
16.	Chapter 15	149
17.	Chapter 16	158
18.	Chapter 17	176
19.	Chapter 18	192
20.	Chapter 19	213
21.	Chapter 20	217
22.	Chapter 21	227
23.	Chapter 22	241
24.	Chapter 23	251
25.	Chapter 24	260
26.	Chapter 25	273
27.	Chapter 26	280
28.	Chapter 27	291
29.	Chapter 28	296
30.	Chapter 29	305
31.	Chapter 30	310
32.	Chapter 31	316
33.	Chapter 32	325
34.	Chapter 33	335

35.	Chapter 34	345
36.	Chapter 35	357
37.	Chapter 36	366
38.	Chapter 37	372
39.	Chapter 38	376
40.	Chapter 39	393
41.	Chapter 40	399
42.	Chapter 41	406
43.	Chapter 42	420
44.	Chapter 43	434
45.	Chapter 44	439
46.	Chapter 45	448
47.	Chapter 46	458
48.	Chapter 47	467
49.	Chapter 48	479
50.	Chapter 49	488
51.	Epilogue	498
52.	Acknowledgments	507
53.	About the author	509
54.	Asher and Mariam	511

55. Asher and Mariam   512
56. Family Tree   513

Dedication

To my family: Mom, dad, brother, sister, aunts, uncles, and cousins.

With your continued love and support through the good and the bad - you have shown me the truest meaning of the word family.

Love you always and forever!

Chapter 1

ASHER

"Twenty-six years of service flushed down the drain." Ragheed banged his head into his hands and scratched his buzzcut scalp—a familiar tell of his turmoil.

One. Two. I examined each cream ceramic floor tile from the office door to the window with each stride of my legs. *Thirteen.* "Don't be dramatic. It's going to be fine." *Fifteen.* I turned on my heel and echoed my steps. *One.* I noted the gray specks of glitter that sparkled

CHAPTER 1

against the cream surface of the tiles, each pattern identical. *Four.*

"Asher."

I glanced up from my inspection of the floor and met his exasperated stare. He pinned me with a "fuck you" glare and rolled his eyes.

"You're scared too, or you wouldn't be in a one-man parade."

I had a tell of my own. Pacing. In my mind, I was able to move stalled time with the forceful stride of my legs. *Six. Seven.* The porcelain clanged with each step beneath my combat boots. Every footfall reverberated through my entire body and kept time with the thump of my heart. "I have to believe it's going to be fine."

"It's Jones's word against ours," Ragheed said.

"Akhi, it's cool. We'll explain what happened. The lieutenant commander will understand," I said.

My phone vibrated in my hand and the letters *HOME* appeared on the screen just as the office door opened. Since I'd enlisted in the Navy and moved to San Diego, my parents' phone calls were always both persistent and at the wrong time. With a sigh, I silenced the ring and stuffed my phone into my pocket.

Ragheed and I stood at attention. It took every ounce of my self-control not to grab the sorry excuse of a human, Jones, and slam him into a wall. He flashed me a smug smile before he sauntered down the hallway toward the elevator.

"Senior Chief George, Senior Chief Jarbo. At ease." Lieutenant Commander Martin was the kind of man who radiated power and authority. He was built like a brick house, had beady blue eyes and a hooked nose that flared with his no-bullshit attitude, but during sea and shore duty under his command, I quickly learned he was a man of utmost integrity.

"Have a seat, Charming, Peter Pan."

Martin had been a petty officer when I started my naval career, and he had been the one who'd given us the nicknames that had followed us throughout our careers. He had known Ragheed and me for a long time and should realize this allegation was bogus. I hoped the years we'd served with him were enough for him to see through Jones's lies.

Electricity pumped through me as I wandered about the office, my eyes fixed on a photo of my sea duty in 1997. Martin was in the center surrounded by Ragheed, Kal, Bash, and a few other seamen who had started out with us that year. We'd studied our asses off and underwent critical specialized training to become Electronics Technicians in the Nuclear Power Field. We'd built a career just to have it possibly taken away and tainted by a jaded prick out to salvage his pride. I just couldn't let that happen.

"Have a seat, son, you're making me nervous." Martin's tone was flat, but I heard the sincerity in his voice.

I sighed and fell into the chair beside Ragheed—my body losing all fight and relaxing into the leather seat.

"We are going to speak off the record first—since I want very candid answers from you both." Martin's blue glare fixed on Ragheed. "Then I will have to take an official statement for the Captain's Mast."

"Captain's Mast?" I nearly leaped from my seat. A disciplinary review from the board could end my career. "Lieutenant Commander, sir, you can't be serious!"

"Jones is a lieutenant, and he is claiming that Charming held him down while you hit him. He's got a black eye to prove it. He is looking for consequences for your actions."

Anger rolled through me, but I worked hard to keep my cool. "Sir, that's not what happened."

"Jones is an egotistical prick. I'm sure he deserved that black eye, but you violated the UCMJ and we don't condone assault in the Navy, son."

"Sir, *he* assaulted the bartender. Ragheed and I were going out the back door and we heard a woman scream in the bathroom."

"She actually gave him the black eye." Ragheed's voice showed a hint of admiration for the bartender's courage. "Asher just pushed him off the girl, and we left."

"Right. And we told his buddies to get him out of there before he caused any real trouble," I said.

"Do you think you could get the girl to file a formal complaint?" The lieutenant commander asked.

"I don't know—I asked her last night, and she was dead set against it. She doesn't want any trouble."

"Well, it's your word against his." The lieutenant commander sat back in his chair and pulled out a cigar. He never lit it inside, but he rolled it between his fingers while he mulled

CHAPTER 1

over the situation. "It's not the first time his integrity has been questioned. You two, on the other hand—these are the first serious disciplinary charges made against you."

"So what should we do, sir?" Ragheed said.

"Well, Charming, I recommend you both give a truthful statement, and in two weeks you can charm the Captain's Mast into believing you and Peter Pan here. But until then, effective immediately, I want you men on leave until the hearing. You each have a shit ton of leave time, so use it. I don't want you anywhere near Jones or this base until the hearing."

"What are we going to do for two weeks?" I asked. I'd never had any real time off without traveling somewhere. Sitting around with a black cloud over my head—I didn't think I could handle the pressure.

"You should go home for a while. See your family but be sure to be back by July eighth."

"Home?" I gasped. "No, maybe a little time at the beach, sir."

"That's right, Peter Pan doesn't like to go home." Martin winked.

Ragheed chuckled. "Even the lieutenant commander knows you avoid Michigan."

It seemed like it took a lifetime, but we finally finished giving our official statements, and then our entire lives were on hold for fourteen days. I checked my phone as we made our way to Ragheed's car, and the missed call from my family home glared at me in bold red writing. With my entire life's work in the firepit, I didn't have the emotional capacity to call back. At least, not until I took the edge off the despair that settled in the pit of my stomach.

"I need a drink." I sighed.

"Maybe we could convince Sally to make a statement if she knew that our careers are on the line," Ragheed said.

"Maybe, but I honestly don't blame her for wanting to stay out of it. She might get some flak from his minions if she did come forward."

"I agree." Ragheed ignited the engine of his black '67 Mustang.

Another call came through from HOME, and this time I just sent it to voicemail.

"You should be nicer to your parents," Ragheed said in Arabic.

"Mind your business," I retorted. He didn't understand my relationship with my family. Besides, I wasn't in the mood for their complaints about my bachelorhood and lack of children. I just needed one shot of whiskey first.

Ragheed groaned beside me. "Where are the guys?"

"Khalid took a few days off for his cousin's wedding in Michigan, and Basher—you know how he is—probably at Sycuan Casino, hugging a slot machine and calling it baby," I said.

"Can you believe we've all been together for over twenty years?" Ragheed asked.

"Time flies when you're having fun," I said.

"What the hell are we going to do?" Ragheed turned the Mustang into the parking lot.

"I don't know."

"I've debated retiring." He ran his fingers through his trimmed hair. "But not like this...I wanted it to be on my own terms." He parked the car and slammed his hands on the steering wheel.

"What else would you do?" I was baffled. I couldn't imagine my life without the Navy.

"I'm forty-four. I should have a mortgage, wife, and kids, but I always thought I had more time. And I should be closer to my parents. They're old and anything can happen."

"Not an option for me."

"That's a choice, sadiqi."

"Absolutely. And my choice is hell, no."

Marriage and family? No, thank you. I didn't believe in love or the sanctity of marriage anymore, and I wasn't equipped to be anyone's father. I was selfish, I wanted to live life on my own terms and not be obligated to anyone else. The only factor in my life choices was my own happiness.

"Don't you want to have a kid? A legacy—a little you that lives on?"

"The world couldn't handle another me. Just ask my father." The laugh on my lips was bitter to my own ears. "I'm a disrespectful son and an all-around horrible human."

"That's not true, and you know it, sadiqi."

I flashed him my phone screen with the message from home and opened the car door. "I think this would say otherwise."

We had only made it a few steps to the bar entrance and my phone buzzed again, but this time the name on the screen halted my steps. *Niles Shammas.*

"Hang on...it's Niles."

"Your brother's best friend?"

"Yeah." My stomach dropped. Niles wasn't the chatty type, so his reaching out to me after the calls from home made the acid roar in my

CHAPTER 1

abdomen. I doubled back to the Mustang and clicked the green button on my phone screen. Mouth dry, I answered with a hesitant, "Hello." I couldn't help the tremble in my voice.

"Ash..."

"Yes, it's me. What's wrong?" My heart slammed against my ribcage.

"You have to come home...it's—" Niles choked and the rest of his words were muffled.

"It's what? My parents? My mom? What?"

"Bass...Bassam." Niles's voice quivered.

"What about Bass?" The blood turned to ice in my veins and I struggled with my own words. "Niles, where is my brother? Aetini akhi. Let me talk to him."

Muffled sounds only answered me. My pulse hammered in my ears, and a cold sweat covered my skin.

"Niles!" I shouted into the receiver.

"Asher, this is Mariam. You must come home." A woman's voice sounded on the other end. A calm, soothing tone that was familiar and foreign at the same time. I gripped the phone tighter.

"Mariam?" I swallowed hard. This had to be a cosmic joke. There was a time I dreamed, hoped, and prayed she'd be on the other end of the receiver asking me to come home, but in this moment, I dreaded those words. Feared the phrase that would follow her request to return home.

"There's been an accident," Mariam said.

"Who?" I couldn't manage more. I just needed to know why my brother wasn't the one calling me. Why *she* and her brother were on the other end of this call.

"Bassam and Lydia were in a car crash and...and...they didn't make it..."

My knees gave out and I fell back against the car. The wind was knocked out of me, and my heart cracked open. Sorrow gripped my entire body. A jagged "no" tore from my lips, and my body shuddered as the tide of tears threatened to drown me. Everything else she said didn't register. Ragheed placed his hand on my shoulder and took the phone from me.

Bassam was gone.

Chapter 2

Mariam

Only a few things brought me joy in this world—my beautiful daughter Tamara, a flavorful meal, and the Books and Bites bookstore. The doorbell chime lightened my mood, and the scent of parchment and pastries brought a smile to my lips. The store was buzzing with customers, and I was glad I'd pre-ordered my books online.

"You look like shit." Zaynab, my childhood best friend and the owner of my happy place, stood behind the counter organizing a display of bookmarks. We met in elementary school and bonded over Narnia. She held all my adolescent secrets and indiscretions, and I had photo evidence of her juvenile transgressions. We were linked for life.

"I heard Asher's voice for the first time in like twenty-six years."

"How?" Zaynab leaned against the counter and grabbed my hand. I was sure she was on her tippy toes. She was a tiny thing, only four-foot-eleven with a boyish figure, big brown eyes, and long, wavy brown hair.

I swallowed hard. "I had to be the one to tell him his brother and sister-in-law died in a car crash."

"Holy moly. I'm so sorry. She squeezed my hand. "That must've been horrible."

My stomach hardened at the memory of Asher's anguish and grief through the phone line, and I eased my hand away from her grasp. "Niles called him, but he couldn't utter the words, and it fell to me to deliver the horrific news to Asher."

"I can't even imagine what he and his family are going through right now. I haven't been able to shake the heaviness in my chest since you

CHAPTER 2

texted me yesterday." She did the sign of the cross with her right hand and kissed the white gold rosary necklace around her neck. "May they both rest in peace."

I averted my gaze and turned to the stack of books on the table beside the register. The back of my throat stung, and sweat trickled down my back. I was going to see Asher again. After twenty-six years. My heart swelled, but my mind was filled with dread.

"How do you feel about seeing him again?" Zaynab sensed my turmoil.

I rubbed my face with both hands. "The last time I laid eyes on him, he gave me a death glare and walked away." I chewed on my bottom lip. "I'm freaking out. Why does he still have such an effect on me?"

"You loved him."

"I did, but it's not that." I groaned into my hands. "It's what he represents for me."

"Your first orgasm?"

I smacked her hand lightly, and she recoiled. "Mind out of the gutter."

"Sorry, it's an illness." She shrugged. Her gaze found mine, and her expression softened. "I think he represents everything you gave up when you got on that plane."

"Yeah." A warm tear slid down my cheek, and I breathed in a jagged breath. "I gave up me."

"I've watched you give up on all your hopes and dreams."

"My life has been a cycle of taking care of everyone, making sure they are all content. I want the same satisfaction for myself. I need joy that doesn't revolve around my daughter. I've been on autopilot from the moment I got on the airplane to Iraq and married Nabil. And after hearing about the tragedy last night, I realized life is too short. I need to find my happiness."

"Hey, look at me."

I peered up at her big brown eyes.

"What would make you happy?"

"Doing something I love—something magical." I picked up a book from the display case on the checkout counter. "Slay dragons and save the world."

"Mariam, be my partner. Let's expand the bookstore."

I reared back at Zaynab's words. The paranormal romance novel I'd been investigating tumbled from my fingers and hit the sales counter with a loud thump. I opened and shut

CHAPTER 2

my mouth. Imaginary worlds and stories were my fixation, but running a lucrative business like Books and Bites was outside my capability.

"I just came into the store to buy my weekly haul."

"That used to be the dream when we first met. Remember? We were going to own a bookstore. But better than the one at the mall because they didn't have enough books."

"We were ten years old."

Her smile was pure sunshine, and she steered its full radiance on me. "This place." Her arms stretched over her head like fairy wings. "Could be half yours, and together we would make it a readers' haven."

"I could loan you the money. I'd love to see what you could do with an expansion."

"I can't take your money."

"Why not? You know how much this store means to me. Let me help you make your vision for this place come true."

She crossed her arms and surveyed me. "Nope. Besides, I want a partner, someone to share in the responsibility. It's a lot to manage all on my own—especially if it were expanded."

"Partner?" I shook my head. "No, I can't. I don't know the first thing about running a business like this." My heart and mind weren't on the same page. Warmth spread throughout my body. The offer was heavenly. I could be immersed in faraway lands happily ever after, the scent of ink and paper as a career. My stomach fluttered, and my pulse raced.

"That I can teach you, but you already had wonderful ideas that worked to grow the business. The kids' nook was your suggestion, and now it's always overflowing with little readers. You have passion for this store and love it as much as I do. I couldn't trust anyone else like I trust you to be my partner."

My mouth went dry, and I chewed on my lower lip. Could I do this? Take a chance and do something I loved instead of just working out of necessity like I did in my current career as a hairdresser? Risk my retirement fund on a whim?

"The building next door is still for rent." Zaynab tapped her fingers on the wooden counter and cocked her head at me with a mischievous grin.

"Is it?" I leaned in closer. With Tamara nearly out of college, a mortgage-free home, and a steady, lucrative income from the salon, it was now or never.

CHAPTER 2

"Yup." She picked at her fingernail. "I would still have to keep my job until Tamara is working full time."

"That's fine." A smile tugged at her red-stained lips. "Is that a deal?"

My hand trembled in her grasp, but I squeezed my eyes shut and let the answer come straight from my heart. "Deal."

"Yay." She clapped. "Really?" Eyes wide and glowing, she skipped around the counter and tackled me in a bear hug.

I nodded, and her glee echoed in the small space. "I'm so excited."

"I'm excited too. Scared to death, but you have given me something to feel happy about."

The alarm on my phone chimed, bringing real life into focus.

"That's your work-in-ten-minutes alert?" Zaynab returned behind the counter and retrieved my packaged online order. "Here you go. And you know, you really make me angry when you pay for the books online instead of letting me give you a friends-and-family discount."

I grabbed my bundle of books. "After we are officially partners, I'll consider it."

Zaynab took me by the shoulders. "Thank

you." Tears welled in her eyes. "And I know I kind of bullied you into this so if you change your mind when you wake up in the morning, no hard feelings."

"I don't think I've been this thrilled about anything in a long time." Filled with adrenaline, I promised to touch base in a few days and headed to the salon.

Saturdays at the Beauty Squad Salon were always busy, but during wedding season it was a war zone. I longed for my comfortable chair in the sun with my head in one of my new novels from the bookstore. Instead, my day stretched into one vast blur of hairstyles, colors, and cuts. By the time lunch rolled around, my mouth watered at the scents of garlic and spices. I unfolded the impeccably wrapped wax paper and inhaled deeply.

"Hello, gorgeous." It wasn't just a sandwich. It was a magnificent creation of perfectly shredded and seasoned chicken, zesty homemade pickles, and velvety garlic sauce that made my tastebuds rejoice.

"Mariam, you gonna make love to the sandwich or eat it?" Farrah teased with a mouth full of her own lunch. "We only have a few more minutes before the next set of appointments."

"I like to savor my food, not devour it."

When she laughed, her silky platinum blond bangs fell over her big gray eyes, and I noticed her dark brown roots. "You're going to need a touch-up soon."

"Girl, I already put myself on your schedule for Wednesday—I'm your last client."

"Right, because you're going to spend the weekend with that boy," I mocked.

"There is nothing about him that's a boy—he is all man. And his name is Khalid—but his friends call him Kal," Farrah said.

"What are you going to tell your family this time?"

"I've got a client flying me out to do her makeup and her entire bridal party in San Diego. It's a half-truth—I am doing his cousin's makeup and her bridal party, but it's in Bloomington Hills at the Golden Hotel."

Nearly forty, Farrah lived with her parents and had to date behind their backs. I couldn't picture having to sneak around at her age, but unfortunately, it was the norm for unmarried Chaldean women with old-school parents to live two separate lives. Despite the fact she was more than capable of supporting herself and helped her family, Farrah had a curfew and had to come up with elaborate schemes just to spend a few nights with a man. It infuriated me it was considered dishonorable and disrespectful for an unmarried Chaldean woman to leave her family's home before marriage, but some families, like Farrah's and mine, acted like we still lived in the villages of Iraq with their old traditions and values. I swore a long time ago I would never treat my daughter that way.

"What if someone sees you around town if you're supposed to be out of state?" I could only imagine the fallout from a relative telling her parents she was seen at a hotel in Bloomington Hills or a surrounding neighborhood.

"They won't." Farrah made the sign of the cross. "You're so lucky you don't have to lie. I'd give anything to move out and not get disowned."

"I didn't move out. I had an arranged marriage and now I'm a widow with a daughter in college. Different circumstances, my friend."

"Yeah, sorry, I always forget since you tend to live like a nun."

I rolled my eyes. "I'm not living like a nun."

"When was the last time you had sex?"

CHAPTER 2

I knew where the conversation was headed and wasn't interested. My chance at romance and happily ever after had been ripped from me when I was just out of high school. My husband and I were complete strangers who were forced together by our families. We had nothing in common. To make matters worse, for the better part of sixteen years, our marriage was a stream of hospital visits and illness. The only delight throughout all those years was our daughter, Tamara. And the bookstore. I didn't realize it before, but the possibility of owning the store lifted my spirits in more ways than I could count. As the day progressed, the dream of going into business with Zaynab had flourished in my mind.

"You're still counting, aren't you?" Farrah teased.

"I remember, I'm just not telling you."

My marriage lacked in many ways, including the bedroom, and never truly inspired the swoon or the excitement described in my romance books. We were blessed with our daughter at the start of our marriage—a honeymoon baby. He fell ill shortly after our failed attempts to have another child, causing him to withdraw and become sexually uninterested.

For years, the specter of loneliness dominated my marriage. Then, he was gone. Now, I was free, and I dictated my own path.

"Anyway." Farrah rolled her eyes. "I want to fix you up with one of his friends. I told you they're all Navy men, Chaldean, and all so freaking hot."

"I'm not interested in a relationship." I was interested in a booty call, but military men were out of the question. The uniform alone would remind me of Asher. I wanted something no-strings. Just sexual chemistry and random hook-ups. *Navy men.* A cold chill danced up my spine. Could Asher and Kal be friends? I hadn't made the connection before today, but they were both in the Navy, stationed in San Diego, and originally from Michigan.

"I'm sure any of the dudes in his group thingy would be up for a no-strings agreement," Farrah said.

"Do you know the names of the guys in his group? Have you met them?" I chewed on my bottom lip.

"I've never met any of them in person, but I've seen pictures. They all have cute nicknames from cartoons. But I don't know their real names. Why?"

CHAPTER 2

"No reason." I swallowed hard. Farrah was a good friend, but my history with Asher was something I only shared with Zaynab and my diary.

"Don't you miss having a significant other in your life?"

"Mom, your next client is here." Tamara, the light of my life and our part-time salon receptionist popped her head into the break room and saved me from answering Farrah's question. I was too embarrassed to admit that even though I had been married for many years, I never truly had a partner. I was trapped in a loveless marriage filled with loneliness.

"Thanks, honey. Have Hannah show her to my chair and tell her I'll be right there."

"Wait, Tamara." Farrah wiped her mouth with her napkin. "Help me out. I'm trying to set your mom up with one of Kal's Navy buddies, but she's trying to ignore me."

"Farrah," I warned.

"What? She thinks you need to start dating too." She stood and made her way to the trash can, and I couldn't help but admire the trendy way she styled her torn jeans and off-the-shoulder T-shirt compared to my basic black long-sleeve shirt and leggings.

"She's right, Mom, you've grieved enough for Dad and shouldn't have to spend the rest of your life alone."

When had she grown up? It was only yesterday she was a little girl with her hair in braids. Now, she was a fully-grown woman with wild curly hair that flowed down her back, perfectly applied eyeliner framing striking black eyes, and a whole lot of wisdom. But how could I tell her that I never really grieved her father's death? Guilt washed over me. I was a horrible woman for not even shedding one tear for my dead husband.

"I'll leave you two to talk." Farrah eased past Tamara and out the door.

"It has nothing to do with grief. Has it occurred to you I might not want to be in a relationship with anyone, ever again?" I asked.

Tamara sat across from me and covered my hand with her own. "That would be incredibly sad, Mom. You deserve to be happy. I don't think Dad was capable of showing anyone actual love."

Tears pooled in my eyes when I noted the sadness on Tamara's face. "I'm sorry, honey. He loved you very much." My lunch soured in my stomach, and I was unable to savor the last bite of my favorite sandwich.

"I know he loved me, but I think he was so wrapped up in his own head most of the time, he couldn't see past himself. We deserved better."

"Maybe. But I'm content on my own for now." Tamara's declaration about her father had unsettled me. I knew Nabil loved her, but I hadn't known she observed the lack of attention I received from her father. I patted her hand. "Anyway, I have big plans brewing and I just want to focus on me for a while."

"What kind of plans?"

"I'm going into business with Zaynab, and we will be expanding the bookstore."

"Really? That's amazing." She leaped from the chair and wrapped her arms around my neck. "Wait, does that mean I get free books?"

"When was the last time you paid for a book?"

"Never. There's a free library in my living room."

"Don't worry, that won't change. Now let me wash up so I can get to my client."

She nodded. "I have this fun project—I need to create a family tree and take DNA samples from everyone in the family for my genetics class. It would be interesting to compare the DNA match percentages since your ancestors married first cousins." She shuddered and made a gagging sound.

"Not everyone married their first cousins." I suppressed my own shiver and tossed my trash before heading to the sink to wash my hands.

"Whatever." Tamara followed me to the sink. "I know your side will be okay with it, but I don't think it's appropriate timing to ask Amoo George and Auntie Juliette for Dad's side of the family."

"Probably not. Their grief is heavy now."

Tamara's voice trembled. "I can't believe they're gone."

"Me too. We should probably see if they need help with Bassam's kids, especially during the funerals."

"I already offered to watch them along with Jordan and Jaxson. Khalu Niles is bringing them all over before mourners start going to Amoo George's house this evening."

"That's very kind of you, I'm sure they'll appreciate it."

"Yeah, Asher seemed grateful for the offer to babysit tonight."

CHAPTER 2

"Asher is here already?" My stomach fluttered.

"Yeah, he caught a red-eye and flew in this morning. He was with Khalu when I called to see what time I should expect the boys."

I gripped the countertop. My vision went fuzzy, and a wave of nausea rolled through me. Asher was home, and it was only a matter of time before I would be face-to-face with my past.

Chapter 3

TAMARA

Tamara's legs trembled up the long, wonky staircase to the attic. She hadn't made the trek up those steps since she'd moved a few of her father's belongings up here ten years ago. Her mom had donated most of his clothes and things but had saved a few CDs, pictures, and other keepsakes she'd thought Tamara would want to keep in remembrance of her father. But in truth, Tamara hadn't wanted any of it. There was a time when she had been

CHAPTER 3

Baba's little girl, the apple of his eye, but one day everything changed. She was twelve years old, nauseous and feverish from flu, but the memory of the paramedics driving away with her father inside the ambulance in a flash of red lights and blaring sirens was forever etched in her mind.

When he returned home, he had been a completely different person. He was never cruel or abusive—but it was like one day she was his favorite person, and the next, she was a stranger. She pretended it hadn't affected her in front of her mom, but just like he'd become distant with his wife, he had done the same with his only child.

Her throat tightened. She'd lied to her mother today. Tamara didn't believe her father loved her. Deep in her heart, she knew he couldn't love anyone but himself. She groaned. She dreaded reevaluating all these conflicted emotions, but she needed pictures for the family tree and knew they would be in the attic.

Palms sweaty, stomach churning, she bit back the nausea as the door to the attic swung open. The odor of musk and dust prickled her nose, and she was sure a sneezing fit was not far behind. She examined the space that had held all the things her mother would consider family treasures and wondered why it intimidated her so much. It was a normal-looking attic with oak walls, flooring, and a tiny window at the peak of the roof that served as the only source of light. Since it was summertime in Michigan, light blazed through and warmed the otherwise cold place. Boxes, bins, and all kinds of wooden chests were scattered around the space. Tamara resented her mother's lack of organizational skills and her horrible packrat tendencies. The plan was to just grab her father's pictures, but she had no clue where they'd gone. A ton of boxes had been added since the last time she'd come up here.

With a sigh, she grabbed the first box and rummaged inside, but it was a box filled with Christmas decorations. The next was a lot of the same, more home décor, seasonal china, Halloween decorations. Besides being a packrat, her mom decorated the house for all seasons and holidays, so the décor—from bedroom comforters to kitchen china—changed with each holiday and season. The woman was a fanatic. They had decorations for Easter, spring and summer, Halloween and fall, and of course Christmas and winter.

CHAPTER 3

The next box was filled with little pumpkins of all shapes and sizes. Tamara recognized them from last fall when her mother had them scattered about the house. Beside the box was a huge bin with three large light-up pumpkins that had decorated the front porch last October. She shook her head and moved on. The next three boxes were filled with fake Christmas flowers. One box had white crystallized roses, the next bejeweled holly, and the other filled with pink velvet amaryllis. Tamara vowed to organize this space one day. It was impossible to find anything in the swarm of boxes and bins.

"Tam?" Cross's raspy voice called from the stairway.

"Up here." She glanced at the time on her Apple Watch. She'd already spent nearly an hour in the attic and was nowhere near finding any of the boxes with her father's things.

She heard Cross's thunderous steps as he entered the attic and flinched at his tone. "Why is the front door unlocked again and you're home alone?"

"I must've forgotten to lock it after I picked up the mail."

He wrapped his big, strong arms around her

and kissed her cheek. "Babe, it's not safe. What if someone followed you in?" His delicious scent of spice and sandalwood covered her, and she breathed in her first relaxed breath since she made it up those steps.

"Then I would work my boxing on them." She jabbed him in the stomach with her elbow, but he chuckled when she cringed at her elbow colliding with his abs of steel. He spun her around and clasped her waist.

Cross was beautiful. Chiseled jawline, plush lips, golden-brown boy-band hair, and auburn eyes, she was captivated by him—how could she not be? The intensity in his stare always stole her breath, tangled her words, and set her on fire.

"Bosa for your man?"

"Yes..." Her voice was husky and breathy like the heroines in the movies. Cross asking her for a kiss was completely foreign and a dream come true. She'd secretly crushed on him since the eighth grade, but she was too prideful to admit it. One summer he'd gone from a gangly boy to a man with hard muscle and broad shoulders overnight.

She still hadn't wrapped her mind around it—only a few months ago, he had been her

CHAPTER 3

childhood best friend, and now they were dating. She and Cross were together, as in boyfriend-girlfriend, and sex. There was lots and lots of sex. Heat pooled in her belly. She'd lost her virginity to her best friend. How many people could say that?

She wrapped her arms around his neck and pulled him flush against her frame—then kissed him like he was the air she needed to breathe. His hands cupped her backside, and she nearly climbed him like a tree.

Somewhere outside a car alarm beeped, startling them apart.

"I thought we were babysitting tonight?"

She made her way over to the window to make sure the coast was still clear—the last thing she needed was her uncle, the kids, or her mom finding them lip-locked or even worse, in a more compromising position. She hadn't told her mom about the shift in their relationship yet, which wasn't like her. Normally Tamara couldn't keep anything from her mom. Yet, if her mom knew the dynamic between them had shifted or that her perfect daughter wasn't a virgin or saving herself for marriage anymore—like she had—she might take her to a monastery. Her mom pretended to be cool and worked hard on being less like her overprotective parents, but Tamara had noticed her discomfort in breaking cultural traditions.

"They should be here soon. Jordan had a soccer game tonight, so I thought I'd start looking for pictures for my genetics assignment until they get here."

"Find anything yet?"

"Nope." She picked up a box filled with beautiful hardcover stories of faraway lands with princes, princesses, and evil stepmothers.

"More books. Why am I not surprised?" Cross said.

"She's saving these for her grandbabies." She snickered.

"How many are we going to give her?" He pulled her flush against his hard chest, his strong arms warm and safe around her waist. He tugged on the hem of her shirt and traced the skin with his fingers. Tremors slid up her spine.

"We just started dating and you're already talking children with me, Mr. Bahri?" She rested her head against his pecs.

"Yeah, I've already started our five-year plan. We get engaged after you finish your stu-

CHAPTER 3

dent teaching. One year later, we get married. Then we start our family. I'm thinking two kids, a boy and a girl?"

Her pulse raced, and she wasn't sure why. Excitement, fear, or a dream realized—she couldn't quite figure it out—but her chest ached, and she pulled away from his embrace.

"At least we have a plan." She did her best to hide her unease, but Cross had been her BFF before he was her boyfriend, and he knew her better than she knew herself most days.

"What's going on in that beautiful mind?"

"I'm not sure. All those plans kinda freaked me out."

He took her hand in his. "It's just stuff I've thought about. I'm not pressuring you. We did just start dating and if you are having second thoughts about us, tell me. I'd rather be friends than have you hate me later."

Her heart shattered a little at his words. She couldn't imagine life without him. "Plans freak me out. I'm not sure why, but I don't think it has anything to do with the fact that the plans are with you. I know without a shadow of a doubt that I'm in love with you. I love you, Cross. I've never been happier."

"Good, because I'm crazy about you." He

kissed her fully on the lips and lingered just for a moment before pulling away, leaving her panting and wanting so much more of him.

He started opening boxes in the corner of the attic and let her stew in the heat that radiated through her body. They worked in silence for a while and she finally found the box of her father's things, but before she could rummage through it, the doorbell chimed with five consecutive rings.

"The monsters are here."

"Before you get the door, did you know your mom used to keep diaries?"

She walked over to the boxes he probed. Leatherbound journals filled an entire box to the rim. "Yeah, she's kept them as long as I can remember."

"This one is dated September 1997."

"That's the year she married my dad." A little curiosity tugged at her brain. She was curious about her parents' experience marrying strangers. Her mom once said it wasn't anything she wanted for Tamara and rejected the idea the moment Jidu attempted to "find a match for her," yet she'd always seemed resigned to the fate she'd been dealt.

The doorbell chimed again, even more per-

CHAPTER 3

sistent than before. "That's Jaxson. He's going to break down the door, and this is why I don't lock it."

"I get this logic." Cross smiled.

She handed him the box with her father's things. "Can you bring down this box for me while I run to get the door? Also, put the journal back where you found it. I don't want to make my mom think we violated her privacy."

"Only if you promise to make out with me after the monsters leave."

"Of course." She blew him a kiss and ran for the stairs.

Many things plagued her, but she knew she was the luckiest girl in the world to have someone like Cross in her life. But would he always love her the way he did now, or would he one day change his mind?

Chapter 4

Nuha

"Where's my black tie?"

Sitting at her dresser trying to hide her tired eyes with concealer in the way her granddaughter had taught her, Nuha observed her husband of fifty-two years move about the room in his long johns searching for yet another thing right in front of him that he could not see.

"Manni, it is on the bed beside your shirt, pants, and blazer that I pressed this morning."

CHAPTER 4

"It's not there."

Fury flashed through her. What else did he want her to do, dress him? Put labels on each article of clothing with instructions on where they should be worn on his body? She dropped the makeup sponge, stomped over to the bed, and snatched up the black tie.

"You seriously didn't see this?"

She was struggling with controlling her emotions today. It was all the stress of the past few days. The constant crying and prayers. Late nights comforting a distraught friend—her patience drained, her heart broken, and she didn't have it in her spirit to baby a grumpy old man.

"It's the same color of the pants. I didn't see it." He grabbed the tie from her hand and placed it beside his shirt.

He went ahead to put on his pants over his long johns. How the man could stand the layers of clothing in this heat stumped her.

It was a hot sticky afternoon in July and she nearly considered not wearing a silk slip, but she heard her mother's voice in her head. *"A lady must always wear her undergarments beneath her dress. It would be scandalous if the outline of your legs showed from beneath your dress."*

"The girls better be coming to the funeral. Niles too," Manni said. "They better not disrespect us by not paying their respects to George and Juliette."

"Of course. Niles and Bassam were like brothers. And yes, they're all coming to the funeral and bringing food."

"Where are my black dress shoes?" Manni had strolled over to the closet and was just staring into the atmosphere.

"They are right next to your feet."

"What are they doing there? They are normally in the shoebox."

"I took them out for you."

"How was I possibly supposed to know that?"

She sighed. "Well if you open your eyes for once—"

He whipped his head and glared in her direction. "Your tongue is becoming as sharp as your daughters'."

"My daughters are the most respectful children any parents could have." She matched his stern expression. "You should be more grateful for your daughters and son—today more than any other day."

CHAPTER 4

"Don't be ridiculous. You don't love our children more than me."

"I wouldn't dispute that," Nuha said, "but maybe you need to start treating them as the adults that they are."

"Of course I treat them as adults, but I am their father. I can say whatever I damn well please."

"No. You can't. I will no longer allow you."

"Is that so?" He moved toward her, but instead of Nuha's normal cowering, she straightened her back and lifted her chin. "This tragedy has taught me one thing. Life is too short for regrets, and I have many of them with my children already. I will not have any more."

For the first time in their marriage, Manni was speechless. It was like he was seeing her for the first time. She left him standing open-mouthed and strutted into her walk-in closet to get dressed.

Watching her best friend, overwhelmed with worry about what lay ahead for her three small grandchildren, grieve the loss of her son and daughter-in-law, something inside Nuha had cracked. It was as though through Juliette's loss, a realization hit Nuha. Life was too short, and in the blink of an eye, God help her, she could easily be the one grieving a child. A cold shiver crawled up her spine, and she said a quick prayer to Mother Mary to protect her children.

Chapter 5

MARIAM

The screeching cry pierced through the quiet chatter of St. John's Church and forced the hair at the nape of my neck on end. I knew the unpleasant sound and braced myself for what was coming next.

Ameera Asmar, the community's black cloud, prepared her lungs for the melody of death. The woman was skilled at making a room filled with grown men and women cry like newborn babies. It was a song she personalized for every funeral. She used the skillful craft to pick at the scabs of the mourners' pain.

"Juliette. Juliette. Juliette, Lydia and Bassam are gone. Your oldest boy has been called home by his maker." This *song* was supposed to be a mournful hymn in Chaldean, but she sounded more like a dying cat than anything that resembled lovely. Her words cut through the air like diamonds on mirrored glass.

A cold chill seeped deep in my bones. The memories of my late husband's funeral and Ameera's chanting slammed into me like a ton of bricks. Tears welled in my eyes, and I remembered the dreary day when Ameera bellowed my name the same way she called on Juliette. It had been ten years ago, but the bubbling weight of the guilt and despair seemed like only yesterday.

Ameera's plump body was bathed in the rainbow rays of sunlight beaming through the mosaic windowpanes. Her chubby, flabby arms flew in the air and pointed at the ceiling of the modest church, and she swayed in the wooden pew, basking in the spotlight. "Lydia. Bassam. You left your babies. Those poor children are orphans now. Orphans. They will never again see your faces. Hear your

CHAPTER 5

voice. Gain your wisdom," she continued in Chaldean.

The mothers of the dearly departed sat in the front of the church facing their women family and friends, as was tradition in the Chaldean culture. The sight of the two moms sitting so small sliced at my broken heart. Lydia's mother, Aster, rocked with the anguish of the *song*, her pale face blotchy and streaming with tears. The poor woman hadn't seen her daughter in seven years because they lived oceans apart and had limited funds, but she had flown in from Germany to say goodbye to her daughter. Bassam's mom, Juliette, tiny already, dissolved in her chair with silent cries, her face not visible through the curtain of black hair.

Funerals in general were horrific, but a double funeral of spouses leaving three children behind was beyond devastating, and this woman relished in the pain of these inconsolable mothers. I couldn't understand the need to increase the grief of the mourners by stabbing at the wounds of the brokenhearted.

Bile burned in my throat, and my stomach threatened to reject my breakfast. My mother's warm hand gripped my trembling fingers.

The air grew thin. I inhaled a jagged breath. *Exit.* I needed to exit.

"You better get out of here before she sees you," Mom said.

Another syllable from that woman and I would fall to pieces. Not because I'd lost my husband—until this day, I never was able to shed one tear for that man. But because her words picked at my struggles and the sadness I witnessed in my daughter's eyes.

I shot up from the chair like it was on fire, but getting my hips through the tight benches and the sea of women in black caused more commotion than I'd intended. Just as I rounded the aisle, I stilled at the sound of my name being repeated over and over in a melodramatic way. Like a deer caught in headlights, I couldn't get my legs to move toward the door.

"Mariam knows the heartache of loss. She lived through the loss." I stilled and closed my eyes, praying for the floor to open and swallow me up. "She had to raise her pretty Tamara all on her own. Even years before he was called by his maker, she was burdened with the responsibility of caring for her sick husband..."

The familiar words licked at my wounds and paralyzed me back in time.

CHAPTER 5

"Enough," a rich, velvety male voice commanded in Chaldean, and a wave of silence washed over the murmuring of sobs.

Asher. I snapped out of my spell of humiliation to thank my savior but nearly didn't recognize the man standing before me. I wouldn't have if it wasn't for the Navy uniform. Good God, he looked spectacular in the white shirt against his olive complexion. The dress blue coat hugged muscular arms and a broad chest, and gripped his frame like it was a second skin. The many service badges, ribbons and stripes fastened to his blazer emphasized the air of authority around him.

"We need to cry. This is a funeral," Ameera explained like she was reciting the law of the land.

His intense stare bored into mine. My legs were transfixed by the power that radiated from him. I swallowed hard. The sun beamed through the stained glass windows and bathed him in its shimmering light, making his eyes glimmer like black onyx. I couldn't peel my eyes away from him. His black hair was no longer long and curly but buzzed short to his scalp, highlighting his angular jaw and the small hook in his nose.

He was the first to break eye contact and turned his attention to Ameera. "We are in a church. Pray for the souls"—his voice cracked—"of my brother and his wife." He stormed away with powerful, long strides, and my heart tumbled into my gut.

The air was knocked out of me. I hadn't laid eyes on him in quite some time, and I resented the way my body came alive the moment our eyes met.

"Our Father," my mom's voice interjected in Chaldean, and she started to pray the rosary loud enough to command the room. The rest of the flock followed, and the room erupted in the murmur of steadfast prayer.

Needing air desperately, I made my way out the double doors of the church and to the garden the Sunday school kept. The sweet, flowery scent surrounded me, and the freshwater scent of Bloom Lake wrapped around me like a much-needed hug. The church was a few blocks away from the lake, but the freshness still radiated through the entire town of Bloomington Hills.

"Hey, sis." Niles's shadow appeared beside mine, and the scent of tobacco polluted the air.

"I thought you quit," I said.

CHAPTER 5

"I did." He exhaled rings of smoke and held out the green pack of Newport cigarettes.

"Nah, I'd rather not pick up that habit again." I turned to take a good look at Niles. Green eyes that were a couple shades deeper than my own were bloodshot red, and the traces of sleepless nights were clear in the circles beneath his eyes. He and Bassam had been groomsmen at one another's weddings, and the shock of his untimely death showed on my big brother's face.

"You, okay?" I whispered.

"No. But I will be." His wide shoulders unyielding, he turned and stared into the distance. "You okay after the attack of the black cloud?"

"You heard that all the way from the men's side?"

"Her lungs are like a blowhorn. You good, sis?" He placed a strong, warm hand on my shoulder.

"Yeah. Did you see Ash go toe to toe with Ameera?" I changed the subject, not willing to allow the turmoil bubbling up inside to explode.

"Yeah. Not many people have the chops to stand up to her."

"I'll have to thank him for being my hero."

"You used to like him." His tone was matter-of-fact, not a question.

My heart sank. "No."

He exhaled a puff of smoke and turned to face me. This time, his sadness was masked by a teasing grin. "He has the prettiest curly black hair. And God, that accent..." His tone was a pitiful attempt to mock my teenage voice.

"You read my journal." Heat crept up my neck, and I swatted his shoulder.

"It wasn't at all as exciting as I'd hoped."

"Jerk face." I exhaled, relieved he never got to the exciting parts of my journals.

"Dorkface." He shoulder-bumped me. "He's still single."

"That was a long time ago. I'm not the same silly girl in love with the boy next door."

"He loved you, Mariam."

"No. He didn't."

The lie burned like acid on my tongue, and the nausea from earlier rolled over me like a windstorm. Memories of two sweet teens spending hours at the lake talking about any and everything, laughing, joking, and dreaming about their futures... It was a long time ago. From time to time, the what-ifs would creep

CHAPTER 5

into my heart and mind. I would daydream about what my life could have been if I had disobeyed my parents' wishes and lived the life I always dreamed of instead.

I always came to one conclusion: I wouldn't have Tamara, so for that reason alone, I couldn't be sorry I had followed the course my parents had laid out for me. But I could always play the what-if game. Like would I have been a hairdresser still or would I have gotten my degree and become a teacher? Would I have been happily married to a man I loved and not widowed in my thirties?

"Bass." Niles shook his head, and the mourning shined in his eyes. "He told me Ash left for the Navy because you were going back home to get married."

The weight of his words nearly knocked me off my feet. It wasn't like I'd had a choice. My marriage was arranged. Back then, it was still a thing, and my father was as traditional as they came. The night of my high school graduation, he informed me that he had secured me a good marriage match and that we were leaving for Iraq to meet my fiancé in a few weeks' time. He even rush-ordered me a passport. All my plans of going to college were postponed, all my choices taken from me. I could have fought more for my freedom of choice, but in the end, I learned Asher's true feelings for me and still, I hadn't been strong enough to combat my father. Going along with his plan was just the easiest.

"Well, it was a long time ago," I said.

Niles stepped on the cigarette butt and picked it up off the ground. "Believe what you want."

"Jerk face."

He shot me another mischievous grin. "You still getting the boys for me?"

"Yeah, I promised them a beach party."

"Thank you for spending so much time with them since *she* left."

She was his ex-wife, who'd run off and left him with two little boys without so much as a backward glance.

"I love hanging out with them."

"You're their favorite." He shoulder-bumped me again. "Don't tell Rena and Sara. And Mary already knows she's not their favorite."

"My lips are sealed."

He walked back to the church, and I followed, debating if I should make a run for the car instead, then remembered I'd come with my sister Rena.

CHAPTER 5

When we returned to the church, lunch was in full effect, and the U-shaped table that wrapped around the church cafeteria was covered with rich Chaldean dishes. Dolma, curry, chicken and beef kebabs were just a few of the dishes I recognized from scents alone. They permeated the air, but instead of my usual gusto for this food, acid burned in my stomach.

"Eat, I made the dolma," Ameera ordered. She handed me a white paper plate filled with rice and beef-stuffed grape leaves, while Nabila, the owner of Taste of Iraq, scooped a spoonful of qouzi, her famous spiced rice with lamb, and plopped it next to the dolma. But as much as I loved food, and her food in particular, I couldn't eat a bite.

"I know you love my qouzi." Nabila's big brown eyes sparkled with pride, and she moved on to Niles.

"Auntie Nabila. I love your qouzi." Niles flashed me a grin and rubbed his belly. "What else do you ladies have to eat?" While the rest of the women fawned over him, I shifted away and found myself face-to-face with Asher. Well, face to chest. He must've shot up at least another four inches from the last time I stood this close to him. He had at least a foot over my five-foot-one-and-a-quarter-inch height. His cold stare chilled me to the bone.

"Asher. Hi, I'm ahh..." I stammered. "I'm so sorry for your loss."

"Thank you." His voice was clipped, and the look of something—anger and/or dislike—had me stumbling back. I couldn't find anything reminiscent of the tenderness that had once greeted me in his eyes, but maybe it was grief and I was self-projecting.

He turned to leave, and I clasped his arm. "Hey, and thanks for stopping Ameera for me."

His cold stare darted to my hand on his arm and then pierced into my eyes like daggers. "I didn't do it for you."

I jerked my hand as though I'd just touched an open flame. My face burned hot, and I struggled to catch my breath. "Well, thanks, anyway."

I turned on my heel and made it to the far edge of the room in record time. My heart raced a million beats a minute. My blouse stuck to the sweat trickling down my back, and I couldn't get my breathing to ease.

"Hey, ready to go?" Rena said. "I have to pick up Scarlett from daycare before we get the kids from camp." Rena was nearly fourteen years younger than me and more like a daughter than a sister. She had the prettiest yellowish-green eyes, and instead of the mud-brown hair like the rest of the Shammas children, her hair was the color of spun gold. She was my parents' "oops" baby. My father would always joke and say she was the milkman's child, though she was a carbon copy of him.

I nodded. "Your timing couldn't be better."

"What did I miss?"

I glanced in Asher's direction. He was sitting at the opposite end of the room with his broad arms propped on his knees and his scrunched-up face staring at the floor.

"Nothing important."

"Good, I have a question—" She shot a worried glance over her shoulder. "Who is that woman with the black hair next to Mom?"

I followed her gaze to a thin woman with a pointy nose, big wide eyes, and legs for days. "I think she's Lydia's cousin, why?"

"I think"—she glanced again—"I've seen her before, at Jon's office."

"Does she collaborate with him? Maybe a healthcare rep, or possibly a patient?" My brother-in-law was a doctor, a general practitioner. Several people were in his office all the time for many varied reasons. As though the woman sensed us talking about her, our gazes met from across the room, and I gave her a small smile before averting my gaze. Just before I did, I noticed her expression seemed almost malicious, and when I glanced again, she had engaged in conversation with my mother. Maybe it had been my imagination or the conversation Rena and I were just having, but unease settled in my gut about that woman. I kept that feeling to myself for the moment, though.

"Are you ready to go?" I whispered.

"Do we have to say goodbye to Auntie Juliette?" Rena bemoaned.

"No, we'll see them all again tomorrow."

Chapter 6

ASHER

Sitting on the complete opposite side of the room where all the males had gathered, I couldn't take my eyes off Mariam Shammas. She had the same flawless oval-shaped face, big bright eyes, and sinful curves that had only gotten better with age. But her smile—that smile would bring a roaring lion to its knees. She'd manipulated the entire community into believing she was some sort of a saint, but I knew better. I learned a long time ago that she was a wolf in sheepskin.

Mariam's big green eyes robbed me of my soul with just a flutter of her eyelashes even after twenty-six fucking years. A shitshow of emotions exploded all at once, and my adolescent insecurities crashed into me like a runaway train. For fuck's sake, I had sweaty palms, and my shirt had adhered to my skin. My mouth was dry, and I was seeing spots. I was sure my heart was going to leap out of my chest and land at her feet. Once again, I was the pathetic bastard who'd fallen for a green-eyed siren disguised as an angel.

Her warm hand had brushed my arm, and all the pain she'd caused me all those years ago turned my blood cold. It was like a switch was flipped inside of me, and all the rage of the past and my present grief bubbled into white-hot fury.

"Akhi, you want me to bring you a plate?" Ragheed had come home with me after the call about Bassam, and I was grateful. I'm not sure how I could have made it back here without him, but he had been a mother hen ever since.

"I'm not hungry." My gaze was still fixed on Mariam.

CHAPTER 6

"Okay, I'll make you a kabab sandwich." Ragheed patted my shoulder and left me to stew and glower in peace.

In retrospect, it had been crazy and stupid to spend hours writing a letter in a language she couldn't read, but English was my second language, and I couldn't properly express my sentiments any other way.

I hadn't slept a wink the night before graduation in apprehension of giving her the letter to go along with the gold earrings I'd gotten her as a thank-you gift for tutoring me throughout our high school education. I'd worked odd jobs and helped my father at the family photograph business all summer to save up for the gold heart studded earrings. In truth, I didn't need the tutoring sessions after sophomore year, but I was so enthralled with her that I'd held on to them as a lifeline to Mariam. Then, senior year, she'd wanted me to teach her to read Arabic, and I'd gotten the bright idea to tell her the letter was her last homework assignment from me.

My entire body trembled at the memory of entering the gymnasium all those years ago. I'd wiped my sweaty palms on my graduation gown and tried to steady my jagged breath.

The excitement around me from the other students celebrating their liberation from childhood only served to accelerate my anxiety. The small velvet gift box trembled between my fingertips, and my pulse raced while searching for her. I finally found her long, dark ringlets in the sea of emerald-green caps and gowns, sitting on the bleachers with her beautiful face hidden inside a book. The room buzzed around her, but it was like she was on a deserted island. I wasn't surprised. Mariam was rarely seen without a book at the bridge of her nose. The tension in my ribcage loosened and my soul smiled at the sight of her. She'd always had the ability to calm me, my anchor in turbulent seas...

It was do-or-die time. Somehow, my wobbly legs made it across the gym and up the bleachers beside her. Her bright green eyes peered over the pages of the book, and my stomach surpassed the fluttering of butterflies. It was more like two fighter jets thundering at takeoff.

"Ash...We did it." She beamed, and my heart soared. That smile with the matching dimples and beauty mark on her right cheek did something wicked to me.

"Yes." I swallowed hard. "What are you

CHAPTER 6

reading?"

She flashed me a cover that featured a half-dressed man and woman titled *Love of a Highlander*.

"More romance?"

"What can I say? I'm in love with love." She bit her glossy lower lip, and I suppressed a moan. The look of longing danced in the depths of her eyes, and the words, *I'm in love with you* almost tumbled out. Almost.

"What's that?" She pointed at the black velvet box, and my nerves shifted into high gear again. I'd forgotten I was clutching it between my fingers.

"It's for you." My face burned hot.

"Me?" The surprise in her tone was not lost on me and I braced myself for rejection.

"Yeah, it's a thank-you gift...for being the best tutor ever." I tried to conceal my trembling voice to no avail and placed the box in her warm hand. Our fingers touched, and I savored the feel of her soft skin beneath my fingertips a moment longer than I intended.

"You didn't have to..." She tilted her chin and glanced at me beneath heavy lids, a beautiful shade of pink kissing her cheeks.

I closed my hand over hers and relished in

the contact of her skin. "I wanted to."

"Can I open it?" Her signature dimpled smile illuminated her face, and I had to remind myself to breathe.

"Yes." My attempt to sound cool was nearly convincing.

She opened the box and gasped. "Ash, wow."

"You like them?" I whispered.

"They're beautiful." She made quick work of taking off the dangly things she was wearing and replacing them with the gold hearts.

"Not as beautiful as you."

She wrapped her arms around my neck, and I let her scent of ocean breeze and coconut wash over me. Her soft lips lingered on my cheek, and I bit my own lip to muffle a moan. "You're very special to me, Ash," she said.

I tightened my grip on her, and she tucked her head in the crook of my neck. So many things I wanted to tell her at that moment, but I didn't trust myself to verbalize them. That was why I'd written the letter.

"You too, Mariam." My fingers entwined in her soft locks, I wanted to hold on to this moment forever. "There's a note in the box. I—I wrote it in Arabic. It's your final assignment to decode the letter." She peered up at me, but

CHAPTER 6

her arms stayed locked around my neck. The emotion in her face mirrored my own feelings, and hope clung to my chest.

"What is it?"

"You'll have to translate it to find out." Her rosy lips were so close to mine that I stared down at her mouth. The need to taste her was all-consuming, and I inched closer.

A flash of light followed by a "Hey, Ash" pulled me from my dreamscape and back to reality—inside a gymnasium where everyone could see us. Bassam was standing at the foot of the bleachers with a camera clutched in his hands. She pulled away just before Niles walked over, thank God. I didn't want the shit beaten out of me on my graduation day. But I would do it again and again if it meant that I could hold her.

Bassam beamed. "We're here to take a few pictures of the two of you."

"Yeah, get your asses down here," Niles said.

After that one perfect moment, the graduation celebrations shifted into high gear, and we didn't have another moment alone. I did manage to tell her to call me after she'd completed her assignment, and she'd promised she would.

The entire next day I waited by the phone, but she never called. The next day was more of the same. Nothing. On the third day, I was jumping out of my skin and couldn't wait around anymore. I went to her house, but she wasn't there. I tried her family party store, nothing. Frustrated and wallowing in my desperation, I somehow made the ten-minute walk down the pathway toward the alcove beside the lake. It was the place she'd brought me to when we'd first become friends and now, I considered it our special place.

As I walked the path I always took with Mariam, I found her sitting on the shore watching the ripple of the lake.

"Hey." I let my body plop down beside her. My chest hammered so loud I was sure she would hear it.

She acknowledged my arrival with a soft "Hey." But her eyes never left the water. Her massive mane danced around her soft, creamy shoulders and the heart earrings glistened in her ears. A little hope ignited inside me.

"I haven't heard from you." I hated the sound of misery in my voice.

"I've had stuff going on at home." Her voice was so remote and distant, and the celebratory

CHAPTER 6

glow from graduation was completely gone.

"Are you okay?"

"Listen, I have to go." She got to her feet. The pit in my stomach widened, threatening to swallow me whole. She was avoiding me. Had she read the note and didn't feel the same way? Was she avoiding me because of those stupid impulsive words? She must have read the letter and now she couldn't bear the sight of me.

"What about the assignment?"

"What?"

"The one in the box." My tone escalated with every word I spoke.

"Oh." The vacant look in her eyes faltered. "I—I don't know what happened to it."

My heart cracked open. "You don't know?" My voice trembled.

"No. After our party, I don't know what happened to it," she said.

She tilted her head, and for the first time since I sat beside her, I noticed her face. Dark circles rimmed her bloodshot eyes. I clasped her shoulders and stared into their depths, the illumination I found in them gone. "Tell me what's wrong."

Tears streamed from her eyes. "My father…"

She looked down at her feet.

"Is he okay?" I felt horrible—something was wrong with her dad, and I was being a self-absorbed jerk.

"He and your dad arranged a marriage for me to your cousin, Nabil, back home..."

"Nabil?" White-hot fury raged inside me. I dropped her shoulders like she'd just burned me. "And you've agreed?"

"I really don't have a choice...I wasn't asked. I was told. You know how my dad is, Mary and Sara were married the same way."

"You don't have to agree. You could say no," I insisted.

"I can't...go against my whole family. I can't tell my father no."

"You can't or you won't?"

"Both, I guess."

"You want to marry him?" The mere thought of her wanting to marry another man made me want to throw up. *My* Mariam wanted to marry Nabil. The boy who used to piss his bed at night was going to take my girl away from me.

"Of course not. I don't even know him." She fell back onto the sand and covered her face. I got to my knees in front of her and wrapped my arms around her.

"Mariam, habibi, tell them no. Stand up to your family."

"You don't understand. I can't disobey my dad. I just can't."

"You can. You just won't." I stood and roughly wiped the sand off my shorts. My father had arranged this bullshit, maybe I could get him to break it off. If he knew my feelings for her, maybe he would help me undo this mess he'd created.

"Wait."

"What?" I balled my fists and crammed them into my shorts before staring into her eyes.

"What was in that letter, Asher?"

My fucking heart. "Nothing. Just a thanks."

Chapter 7

Mariam

"Ama. Ama. Are we going to the beach?" Seven-year-old Jordan leaped out of his chair in the old cafeteria of Landover Elementary School and hugged me around my waist. Next to being called Mom, nothing was more glorious than when the boys called me Ama. It was just "dad's sister" in Arabic, but it made me melt like hot fudge.

"Hey, kiddo." I hugged him back. "We sure are."

CHAPTER 7

"Yes." Jordan tossed his arms in the air in celebration. "Jaxson, let's go," he ordered.

It was like looking at a miniature adult with nut-brown hair that wasn't curly or straight but still naturally unruly and untamable when it was time for a haircut, puppy-dog big brown eyes, and double-trouble dimples on both cheeks. Though Jordan favored his mother and looked nothing like my brother, he had the same "I'm the boss" persona and attitude with Jaxson that Niles had with me growing up.

Jaxson's face lit up when our eyes met from across the cafeteria, and he ran over with a colored picture in his outstretched hands. He was only four, but I was sure my little man was the next Michelangelo. Landover Elementary had an excellent summer program that was created by the school's art teacher and immersed kids in all forms of art.

"Ama. I drew you a new picture." This blond-haired, green-eyed kiddo was the opposite of his brother in looks and demeanor, and except for the blond hair, he was Niles's miniature. Jaxson was a little charmer and dazzled everyone with his lopsided grin and dimples. I lifted him into my arms and admired the piece of art. He was getting too big to carry, but I didn't have the ability to decline when he ran into my arms.

"You got some serious talent, young man."

"It's a picture of our beach day."

"I see that. That me, you, Jordan, and Tamara?" I pointed at each stick figure by height and hair color.

"Yes." His little finger pointed at a blonde woman and baby in his drawing. "I drew Scarlett and Ama Rena in my picture too." Jaxson's R's were pronounced like W and his S's were just swallowed so that it sounded like he'd said *Carlett* and *Wena*.

"Ama Rena and Scarlett are in my car waiting for us," I said.

"Really?" Jaxson smiled and flashed me his baby teeth.

"Yup. Let's grab your things and go see them."

"Awesome." Jaxson leaped from my arms and ran for his things.

The door of the cafeteria opened, and I squinted my eyes to avoid the sun that poured in and framed Asher. My heart skipped a beat, the blood rushed to my ears, and it felt like I'd dunked my head underwater. I intended to

CHAPTER 7

turn away but was transfixed by the sight of him. His brooding stare found mine and immobilized me.

The air crackled with tension, but the sound of a little girl crying broke the spell between us. We both searched for the source of the tears and found that the panic-stricken voice belonged to Bella, Asher's four-year-old niece. With a sigh and a glance up at the ceiling that looked more like a plea for heavenly help, he made his way past me toward his niece.

Jaxson shook my arm. "Ama, do you know him?" He pointed at Asher's back. "He's Mikey, Bella, and Alec's uncle. Did you know their parents are in heaven now too? Like Tamara's daddy?"

"Honey, it's not polite to point," I reminded him.

"Didn't Dad tell you not to talk about it?" Jordan cautioned his baby brother. His in-charge expression was so much like Niles's when we were kids, I nearly snorted.

"I didn't say anything," Jaxson protested. He crossed his arms over his chest and glared up at his brother. His lip pout could win him an Academy Award.

"Go get your stuff packed up and I'll sign you

guys out," I said.

I watched them head over to the table where Bella was now having a complete meltdown. She pushed Asher away with both hands. "I want my daddy. Where's my daddy? He picks us up from camp."

"Mom and Dad aren't coming back." Alec was red-faced and pointed his finger at Bella's tear-streaked cheeks. "Stupid baby cry." He was tough for a six-year-old.

"Alec. Don't...don't talk to your sister like that." Asher had lost that authoritative voice he'd used at the church.

Asher's bitter tone from earlier was gone and replaced with this heartbroken shell of a man. His normally sun-kissed complexion was white as a ghost, and his red-rimmed eyes glossy with tears.

"Bella, sweetheart, come on, let's go to Nana's house." He tried to hug her, but she pushed him away and this time ran for it. Poor Asher wavered on his feet. He called after her, but her black ponytail swayed behind her while her little legs rushed to the other side of the room and crashed into her eldest brother, Mikey. A very defeated Asher sat on the bench and rubbed his face.

CHAPTER 7

My stomach twisted in knots and my eyes stung at the sight of that sweet boy wrapping his arms around his sister. He was only eight, and that big-boy gesture made my waterworks start right up.

"Why do you have to be mean to your sister?" Asher asked Alec.

"Tamara's daddy died, and he didn't come back. Mommy and Daddy are not coming back too," Alec stated in a matter-of-fact tone and ran off.

Asher covered his face with both hands and bowed his head. His shoulders slumped—so broken and defeated. My heart cracked a bit more.

"Ama, Bella is crying." Jaxson tugged at my skirt.

"I know honey. Why don't you try to cheer her up. I'm going to talk to her uncle," I said.

"Good idea." Jaxson beamed and rushed over to Mikey and Bella. I noticed that Jordan, my beautiful, sweet nephew was already over by Alec, and they were playing with his tablet.

"Need some help?" I wasn't sure my company was welcome, but I had to try anyway. If not for the friendship we once shared, for the kids and their gone-too-quickly parents.

His shoulders drooped further, but his eyes wouldn't meet mine.

"I have no idea what I'm doing." His voice hoarse and slightly trembling, he ran his hand over his buzzed head. "I don't know how to help them."

"There's no rulebook." I sat beside him, making sure to keep my hands firmly in my lap even though every inch of me yearned to wrap this wrecked man in my arms. "Everyone must heal and adjust. It won't happen overnight."

"Bella cries all day for her parents, Mikey only speaks when spoken to, and Alec is angry. So angry."

The familiar helpless feeling of Tamara's grief flashed in my mind's eye. "Tamara was older when my husband died, but she acted out too. It took time, but she started to heal. We both did."

"I just feel so helpless."

I glanced up and noticed that by some miracle Jaxson had gotten Bella to stop crying. An idea came to me, but I worried about overstepping and pissing him off. Yet, I was a fixer. I couldn't see a problem without wanting to help find the resolution.

CHAPTER 7

I steeled my spine for the rejection. "I have an idea...if you're game."

He stopped pacing and his red-rimmed eyes stared directly into my own. He shrugged. "I'm open to anything at this point. I just want to take away some of their pain."

Translation: he would tolerate me if it helped the kids. Memo received. This was about the children, not him and not me. Not us. It was about three grieving kids.

I lifted my chin. "I'm taking Niles's boys to my parents' house. My sisters and the kids are all going to be there, and my daughter has a full day of activities planned to entertain them. Why don't you bring them? They love hanging out with the boys."

"Will they want to come?"

"One way to find out."

I stood and made my way over to where the kids sat, and he followed. Jaxson and Mikey sat on either side of Bella at the long cafeteria-style table and were entertaining her with a game of Connect Four.

"Hey guys, Jordan and Jaxson are going to their nana's house for a beach party, and once it's dark, we are going to have a movie night. You guys want to join us?"

Bella's head popped up. "Will you have popcorn?"

"Of course I'll have popcorn."

"We have s'mores too," Jaxson said.

"Is Tamara going to be there?" Bella asked.

"She is and so is Scarlett."

Bella's face lit up with excitement, and the tension in her shoulders eased.

"Are you sure it's not too much trouble?" Asher asked.

"No, not at all."

And then he glanced at Mikey. "You guys want to?

Bella's little face was still blotchy from tears. "Can we, Mikey?"

He shrugged his shoulders. "Yeah."

"I want to go," Alec said. He and Jordan had migrated over to us.

"Okay," Asher said. "As long as you promise to be on your best behavior."

"We will," Jordan said.

"What should I bring?" Asher asked me.

"Just the kids' bathing suits and some warm clothes for nighttime. I have everything else."

As the children lined up, Asher and I signed them out of camp. A little of Asher's coloring returned to his cheeks, and he seemed to relax

CHAPTER 7

a bit since the little ones were excited about an afternoon on the lake. I, on the other hand, was becoming a big ball of nerves. Asher still made my heart race after all these years.

Chapter 8

Asher

B ella needed a bathing suit. After flipping through the neatly folded clothing in the white wooden chest, I lifted a black cottony thing and inspected it.

"This one?"

Bella watched me with concern in her big gray eyes. I swear she was evaluating me, and I was failing miserably. "No. That's not a bathing suit." She rolled her eyes as if she were a teenager.

CHAPTER 8

I took another look at the material in my hand and flipped it over. "Are you sure?"

"I wear that with my tutu, silly."

"Okay, what about this one?" I pulled out a blue-green suit with a pony on it.

"No, I want my pink one," Bella argued. "And my *Trolls* lifejacket."

"*Trolls?*"

"They're right here." Mikey had entered the bedroom in the middle of my turmoil and held up the little pink fabric and a tiny lifejacket with a hot pink cartoon character on it. "They were in the laundry room."

"You found it." Bella's smile could easily steal my soul. If only I could do something right to keep it there.

Mikey was the greatest kid in the world. Period. Not only was he patient with his siblings, but he was also helpful and really took care of them. I thanked God because I was perplexed by simply packing Bella's beach clothes.

Since my parents were at church with the mourners still paying their respects, I had to get the kids' stuff for the lake packed on my own and had no idea what I was doing. The sad truth was I was practically a stranger to these kids. They never saw me unless you counted the weekly video conference calls with Bass when the kids would pop up and say hey or the short visits on random holidays. We'd never really bonded. The weight of my guilt was drowning me deeper in my regret. All that time I wasted—assumed I had more time with my brother. I had pictured us as two gray-haired old men on the dock fishing, drinking beers, and talking football well into our eighties.

"I'm ready." Alec came into Bella's room with a backpack and superhero towel around his neck. He wore a matching pair of shorts and T-shirt.

"All right there, Superman."

"I'm Spiderman. Not Superman. See. The spider? He pointed to his little chest. "You don't even know the difference." The sarcasm in his tone was not lost on me, and I suppressed a chuckle.

"My bad, Spiderman. You'll have to teach me the ropes. I never really watched superheroes."

The look he gave me was pure dismay. "Then what did you watch?" Alec asked.

"I was more into karate."

"You know karate?" he asked with a skeptical tone.

CHAPTER 8

"I'm a black belt."

"Cool. Will you teach me?" Alec asked.

"Yeah, I can. But right now I must get changed out of my uniform. Mariam and the boys are waiting for us." I undid my tie that was surely going to suffocate me at any moment.

"Don't take too long," Bella said.

"Yes, ma'am." I held back a snicker at the authority in her tone.

I made it behind the closed bedroom door and nearly collapsed from exhaustion onto the bed. I'd been going nonstop from the moment I received the news of my brother and sister-in-law's accident. That was nearly four days ago, and I hadn't slept more than a few hours at a time since then. Four long days of funerals, burials, prayers, and people all wanting to help in some shape or form, but there wasn't anything anyone could do to bring them back. Bassam was gone. I still couldn't understand it. I'd never see or talk to my brother again.

My breathing shallow, I struggled for air. I prayed for the strength to just get everything settled for these kids and my parents before I had to get back on a plane in eleven days. The buzzing in my head and throbbing between my ears made it hard to think, much less plan. I pressed my thumb and fingers to my forehead to relieve some of the pressure against my skull. It worked for just a moment before the pounding in my head was awakened again by Bella's screams.

"Amoo Asher, Alec took my doll again." Bella's voice bellowed from the other side of the locked door.

"Liar, I didn't touch your stupid doll," Alec shouted.

"You did. You did." Bella's voice was near a shriek.

"I did not," Alec said.

I cringed from the throbbing in my temples.

"Enough." I rubbed my burning eyes. I could do this. I owed it to my brother to help his children adjust before it was time to return to San Diego. My stomach sank—the Captain's Mast was only thirteen days away, and we still didn't have any word that the girl would press assault charges on Lieutenant Dickhead or even testify on our behalf. I groaned and pushed my worries out of my mind for another day. I could use a shower, but Bella's screeching out in the hallway stopped me from trying it.

CHAPTER 8

With a shake of my head, I hustled to change out of my uniform into a pair of navy training shorts and a T-shirt from my gym bag before Bella and Alec started World War III. Luckily, I had left my gym bag in the car, or I would have had to go to my parents' house too for a change of clothes. I made it into the hallway just in time to catch Bella swinging her life jacket across Alec's shoulder.

"Bella, don't hit your brother."

"He started it." Tears streamed down her face, and her perfect little nose turned the color of a cherry-red apple.

"Crybaby cry." Alec sang then pushed her finger out of his face.

I stepped in between the two little monsters and bent to their level. "All right, you two. If you can't be good, we aren't going."

Bella's lower lip trembled, and my heart broke just a little bit more. "But I want to go..." she whimpered.

"And I want to take you guys there, but I will not allow you to ruin everyone else's fun with your fighting."

"I'll be good, I promise." Alec lifted both hands in the air in surrender.

"Me too." Bella mimicked Alec's movement.

"Promise."

I sighed. "Okay, let's go."

After loading up the kids in the car, nervous tension buzzed through me. I was spending the afternoon with Mariam. It had been ages since I'd seen her, and the old sentiments haunted me like a bad dream. But I didn't have time for those head-tripped feelings. I had to compartmentalize my deep-seated resentment of her because right now it wasn't about me, or my little-boy hurt feelings. It was about three kids who had their lives shattered by the loss of their parents.

Alec and Bella stormed out of the car before I even had my seatbelt off and raced to the front door. Mikey, God bless him, grabbed his siblings' bags and waited for me.

"Thanks, buddy. I can take these." I reached for the bags, and Mikey's hand trembled.

"Okay."

I hadn't spent as much time with Mikey as I'd done with the other two since I'd arrived, and it was the first time I noticed the pure fear in the eight-year-old's chocolate eyes. Bass's eyes. He looked the most like Bass out of the three kids. Bronzed skin, curly black hair, and the same slight hook in his nose.

CHAPTER 8

"Hey, hang on, what's up?"

"Nothing." He tried to walk away, but the dread in his eyes made me reach for him.

"Hang on a second," I said.

I heard the door open, and Mariam stood waving. I waved and pointed one finger in the air then heard Mariam's cheerful voice greet the other two monsters, but my focus stayed on Mikey.

"You know you don't have to do everything for your siblings. They can pick up their own stuff." I took the bags from his hands and set them on the ground.

"No, I have to…because…" His face scrunched up with tears, and he shoved his hands in the pockets of his dinosaur swim shorts.

"What is it, buddy? You can talk to me." I placed a hand on his shoulder. "I'm here for you, Mikey."

His watery stare found mine. "If my siblings or me are bad, you're not going to want to take care of us. Neither will Nana and Jidu. We'll end up living with strangers. My friend Billy in school, he moved away because his mom died, and he didn't have a dad."

If there were any sizable shards left of my shattered heart, they were surely smashed into a billion more pieces. This poor kid had been worried that he and his siblings would be sent away if they misbehaved. Tears burned in his eyes.

"Oh, buddy. That will never, ever happen."

Mikey's face fell, and I dropped to my knees to face him. "You are family. You are my brother's son, and that means your blood runs through my veins. And Nana and Jidu's too. We will always have your back. No matter what you do or don't do. We love you. Do you understand?"

Tears pooled in his eyes, and I wrapped the little man in my arms. "I love you, Mikey and Bella...even Alec."

Mikey chuckled in between sobs, and I just held the boy, my brother's eldest son, Bassam's boy, in my arms until my own tears had finally eased. "You good now?"

"Yeah." He wiped his face with the back of his hand.

"I like your shorts. Dinosaurs seem to be your thing."

His face lit up. "Dinosaurs are totally my thing. I collect them and, well, I study them. Do you know that there were more than seven hundred species of dinosaurs?"

"I didn't. That's super cool."

"Yup. My dad took me to the Detroit Science Center. It was so cool. There are other Dinosaur museums...on our list to visit." At the mention of his dad, the excitement he exuded only seconds ago disappeared, and he looked down at his feet.

"Maybe you and I can go one day. I don't know much about them. You can teach me."

His eyes met mine, and a tear rolled down his cheek.

"Yeah," he said. Probably more for my benefit than his own. I wasn't his father, and he knew as well as I did I was a sorry replacement for my brother.

"All right, let's go check on Thing One and Thing Two."

"That's a good name for them." He rewarded me with a wet grin.

"Right, we should get them T-shirts." I snickered.

I heard little energized kid voices echoing the moment we entered the charming house. It was a lot bigger on the inside than I remembered, with an open floor plan—a joint living and dining area and even a cozy sitting area in front of a massive fireplace. Everything had this warm but glamorous feel to it, with cherry wooden tables, chestnut wooden flooring that looked to be original, and sparkling crystal chandeliers all around the house.

"Hey, there." Mariam's dimpled smile was warm, kissable, and stirred emotions inside me that should have long ago faded yet seemed so fresh.

"Wow, your parents' house looks a lot different from the last time I was here."

"Yeah, Mary insisted my parents could no longer live in the retro-chic eighties furniture and they remodeled the house about ten years ago. Ever since, my mom has turned into a Home Shop packrat."

"Home Shop?"

"Yeah, it's like a discount store for home stuff. She's addicted." She looked around to make sure she wasn't overheard. "So am I."

"Well, she did a nice job. It looks great in here."

"There you guys are." An older vision of Mariam with wider hips and a raspier voice entered the room.

"Mary, thanks for having us," I said.

She kissed both my cheeks and took both my hands in her warm and tender grasp. "I was embarrassed to come over to the men's side today." She glanced at Mikey and switched to speaking in Chaldean. "May God rest their souls, they will both truly be missed."

"Thank you," I mumbled.

"Mom." Voices and footsteps came in from the kitchen. Bella followed four high school or maybe college-age girls closely into the living room.

"Tamara...girls...come meet Bella's uncle, Asher," Mariam said.

"These are mine." Mary waved at three ash-brown-haired, green-eyed girls. "Lena, Bianca, and Lauren."

"I remember the twins. Mariam and I would take them out for walks in the stroller with Rena, who insisted on pushing the stroller. Wow, I can't believe how big you girls are."

"Lauren is starting med school and Lena is starting law school in the fall." She pointed at the first two. "And the last one, my baby Bianca, starts college next year."

"Then she's going to try to arrange our marriages." Lena lifted Bella onto her hip. Bella beamed and played with the girl's hair, happier than I'd seen her in days.

"I wish." Mary snickered. "I don't think anyone will agree to take you off my hands."

"Whatever, Mom. We are the best daughters in the world." Lauren hummed in a lyrical tone.

"Nice try. *I'm* the best daughter in the world." The dark-haired one of the girls stepped forward, placed her arm around Mikey's shoulder, and beamed.

This girl had to be Mariam's daughter. She was a mirror image of Mariam at that age, except her coloring was completely different. Like Mariam, she had long, flowing hair, but instead of Mariam's silky mud-brown hair, hers was a mass of black ringlets. She had her dimples and the same mole on her cheek, but instead of green eyes, hers were dark as night, and her skin was a warm sun-kissed brown compared to Mariam's pale complexion.

"I'm Tamara. You're my cousin, right?"

"Yeah, I guess I am."

"Thank you for your service. The family always refers to you as our family hero."

I nodded. "Nice to meet you, Tamara. Thanks for helping the troops." I patted Mikey on the top of the head.

"Sure thing. You look like you need a break, so you can relax. Khala Rena is at the beach,

CHAPTER 8

and we are taking the kiddos down to meet her. Ready, Mikey?" Tamara said.

Mikey glanced up at me, a little unsure. "Can I go?"

"Go, have fun," I said.

Tamara took Mikey's hand, and the troops piled outside.

Mary, which was short for Maryanna, led Mariam and me out to the patio. Mikey and Alec sat on the dock with fishing poles, and memories poured through my mind like flashes of a foggy dream. I could see my parents' house from here, and I pictured Bassam and I fishing on the edge of the lake arguing about who would catch the biggest fish. Bass's infectious laugh echoed in my mind's eye, and I remembered him letting me tell Mariam that the bigger catch was mine. Bass teaching me how to swim, coaching me on how to talk to girls, and asking me not to join the Navy after Mariam got engaged. Him being my biggest supporter after I came home from training but asking me to try to come home more after he had children. But I was too prideful to tell him that seeing Nabil with Mariam would kill me a little each day. I let him down and I let so much time I could have spent with him waste away because of my pride. Fuck, I couldn't believe he was gone. How could someone so full of life and love disappear? In the blink of an eye, my only sibling was not here. I was an only child.

"Asher, are you all right?"

I blinked away the fog of my guilt, pain, and sorrow to find Mariam watching me.

"Yeah—it's just a little strange being out here after so long."

I noticed a boy—more like a college guy sitting beside Tamara on the dock. He was pretending to almost fall in and was getting a lot of laughter from her and Bella. I was a little envious of his ability to make Bella light up like that. "Who is that with Tamara and Bella?"

"That is Tamara's best friend, Cross. They have been inseparable since elementary school."

"The boy is what I call Tamara's Asher," Mary said. "They're always together, just like the two of you were. Baba would make Niles watch you because he didn't trust boys and girls to be alone."

"Baba didn't think girls should leave the house unless accompanied by parents or a brother." A different woman's voice had joined us. I looked up to see a curvy woman with

CHAPTER 8

chocolate-brown hair rolled up into a ball on the top of her head had come out onto the patio to join us.

"Sara?" She had the same plumped face and rounded frame, but now it was a little more on the curvaceous side. Big green eyes that were the trademark feature of the Shammas family shined bright when she looked at me.

"Little Asher, is that you?"

Sara always called me Little Asher, and even though it made me angry before, now it just made me laugh. "Am I really still Little Asher?"

Her eyes raked over me with a devilish grin. "Oh no, I don't believe there is anything little about you anymore."

All the tension of being back here eased. She came over, and I reached down to hug her. She squeezed me tightly and whispered her condolences in my ear, probably not wanting to ruin the lighthearted moment.

I muttered thanks before trying to let her go, but she held on to my neck a little tighter.

"And if I wasn't married or if I was a cheating kind of woman, I would love to be the girl to comfort you." She proceeded to slap my ass with her palm right before she released me.

"Sara," Mary scolded while everyone else laughed. I glanced at Mariam—her wide-eyed shock mirrored my own.

"I needed to lighten the mood. It was all kinds of morbid when I got here," Sara said. "Now, Shammas women to the kitchen. My boys are bringing in the groceries, and if we don't prep the dinner, they just might eat it raw."

"She's not kidding about her boys." Mariam smiled. "Will you be okay here? Or if you want to leave the kids with us and take a little time for you, we don't mind. Not that you are not welcome to stay, because of course you are, I just want you to know that you have choices," she rambled, twirling her hair around her fingertips like she did when she was nervous when we were kids.

"He's staying. What does he have to do all alone in that house?" Sara insisted.

I glanced out at the lake and watched Bella playing with Tamara's hair. "Yes. I'll stay."

"That settles it. You relax. We'll be right back," Sara said.

Chapter 9

TAMARA

"Who wants to participate in my school project?" Tamara asked.

All her cousins and aunts were together for the first time all week so she could gather their DNA for her genetics class. She still hadn't been in the mood to sort through her father's box for pictures, but she'd already completed her mother's family tree. Gathering her mom's side's pictures, memorabilia, memories, even names of great aunts and uncles was easy. She had known all of them her entire life, but her father's side was a mystery.

She'd never met her grandparents. Her father had four sisters who were each married and in a different country. Except for one sister, Ama Layla, who lived in California. Tamara had only met her once when she flew in for her father's funeral. She never heard from her again after the services. The only contact with blood relatives from her father's side was with Uncle George's family. Now, Bassam was gone. Her heart ached for him and his wife, Lydia. They had been a large part of her life and so were their three beautiful kids. Then there was Asher—he looked a lot like Bassam, but harder somehow. It was his whole dark and dangerous vibe—and he was a Navy man, to boot. He was checking out her mom, and her mom was enjoying the attention. That made Tamara smile. Her mom really needed a little happy in her life, and Asher would make a great stepdad.

The mounds of food were set out on the patio table, and everyone had just finished their plates of barbecue fixings.

"I do, I do!" Jordan and Mikey said at once.

"I'm not volunteering for nothing unless I

CHAPTER 9

know what you need," Khala Mary said. "The last time I agreed to help without knowing what you needed, I was roped into buying ten dozen boxes of Girl Scout cookies."

"No one forced you to buy that many," Tamara's mother accused. "Your greedy butt wanted them."

"Insults are not a good way to get my cooperation either." She glanced at Tamara. "Damn, now I want some Girl Scout cookies."

"Yes, Thin Mints." Aunt Sara chimed in. "And the s'mores ones."

"I will buy you the cookies." Tamara smirked. "I simply need"—she paused for dramatic effect—"a little spit from each of you."

Khala Sara shuddered. "What in the hell would you need spit for, and while we're eating?"

"It's for my genetics class," Tamara said. "It's a whole presentation with stats and percentages of biological relationships."

"So, we have to spit in a cup?" Khala Sara asked.

"Ew, Mom, no. We just swab our mouths." Lauren gagged. "I'm in. This will be fun. Maybe we'll find out that Bianca was switched at birth."

Bianca tossed her napkin at Lauren. "I have Mom's booty. If anyone was switched at birth it was you. Your behind looks like it's been ironed."

"You all have the same hair color, eye color, and features, so I doubt any of you have been switched at birth." Cross tossed his plate in the trash can and stood beside Tamara. "You want me to start passing out the cups and Q-tips for you?"

"Yeah, thanks." He always made her smile with his thoughtfulness.

"Did you want my DNA sample too?" Cross wiggled his eyebrows.

"Ew, no. I know we aren't related, but if the test showed were like fifth cousins once removed or something crazy—I just couldn't bear it."

He leaned in close to her ear. The scent of grass, sandalwood, and something so completely mouthwateringly him washed over her, and she ached to touch him. "The sex is just that good."

Her face burned. "Absolutely."

He laughed, and her soul swooned. Then she realized where they were and whom they were with, and she glanced around nervously, but

CHAPTER 9

everyone seemed to be engaged in a conversation about who resembled whom more, and no one was paying them any attention—except Asher. He had just stopped to toss out his plate when his gaze met hers, and he gave her a questioning stare. She made her way over to him in an attempt to cover up what he may have overheard.

"So, since you're really my only cousin from my father's side that I'm in contact with—besides your parents and the kiddos—would you mind me taking your DNA too? I was supposed to ask your parents, but it would be inappropriate to ask them right now."

"Yeah, that's fine. The kids too, I think they'll get a kick out of doing the swab." He pointed at Alec intensely watching Thomas swab his cheek with the Q-tip.

"So, you're not in touch with any of your amat?" Asher asked her.

"No, I don't know my dad's sisters at all. Some of their kids are my friends on social media, but I don't have any communication with them. To be honest, my dad's side, other than your family, is weird."

"I haven't seen most of them since we left Iraq in the early nineties—but even then, they were strange." He smirked. "It's a good thing you take after your mom."

"Did you know my dad well?" She didn't know why she asked, but for some reason, she wanted to know about her dad's family—just wanted to know more about her father. He always seemed too mysterious.

Asher hesitated for a moment before answering and she knew she was getting a washed-out version of the truth. "Yes, I guess so. As well as you can know someone as boys who didn't have the same interests. He wasn't really into sports, he hated swimming and being outside, he just loved music. He was good with the Arabic guitar."

Her chest squeezed. "When I was really little, he would sit me down and play for me...before he got sick."

Grief danced in his eyes. "I'm really sorry you lost him at such a young age."

He didn't realize she had lost her father way before he died. She had been grieving for him while he was still alive, but all she could muster was a small, "Thanks."

She should feel pain when someone mentioned her father but instead suffered nothing. All the places that should ache became still at the mention of his name. Something was truly broken inside her if she couldn't feel remorse at the mention of her father's death.

"Ready to get swabbed?" Cross handed Asher a cup with his name on it and then one to Tamara, pulling her out of thoughts of her dad.

"Absolutely." Asher took the cup and turned to Cross. "You're not testing?"

"Umm." Cross nervously glanced at her before answering. "No, since we aren't related, there's no point."

"And it would suck if she turned out to be your cousin." Asher winked.

"It would be weird, yes, you know because I'm, he's just been, you know, my friend for so long," she rambled.

"Don't worry, your secret is safe with me."

Chapter 10

ASHER

I never ended up relaxing and found myself playing soccer for most of the afternoon. Sara's boys, Thomas and Nicholas, and Tamara's "friend," Cross—was I the only one who saw that they were more than friends?—had me running all over the backyard with that ball. The little ones had a blast, which made the bone-tired exhaustion completely worth it.

The sunburst of red over the blue lake filled me with familiar warmth. I'd missed the sunsets on Bloom Lake, careless days in the sun and the long nights cuddled by a roaring fire toasting marshmallows. This sunset reminded me of so many nights when Bass and I would camp out on the beach and tell scary stories. The memories tugged at the hollow ache in my heart.

"Hey, Ash." Niles handed me a cold beer and plopped in the seat beside me.

"Thanks." I took the beer, and when we fist-bumped, I noticed the pristine white Virgin Mary statue glowing in a beam of solar lights. "Looks like your dad upped his landscaping game?" I gestured to the beacon of lights.

"If he isn't at the store rearranging my stock shelves, or my mother hasn't dragged him one place or another, the man is out here doing something to that statue. Either painting it or cleaning it or adding lights, flowers, or a new crown."

"Then nothing has changed." I chuckled. "How's work?"

Niles shrugged. "All right." He leaned back in the chair and opened the beer. "How are you?"

Heartbroken. Exhausted. Shocked. Overwhelmed. So many fucking emotions rolled through me. I didn't know if I was coming or going anymore.

"Okay." I took a long drag of the bitter golden liquid.

"I love it out here," Niles said. "Where are the kiddos? I haven't seen my boys all day."

"The monsters are looking for a movie to watch."

"Let me guess, *Spiderman*?" He sipped his beer.

"I wouldn't be surprised."

"How are the kids doing with all this?"

"Better today. Coming here helped," I said.

"I'm glad. You know we are always here for you."

"Thanks, I appreciate it. Mariam saved me today. Bella was having a complete meltdown and Alec was just fucking with her. I don't know how to deal with all of this. Shit, you know I haven't been around enough for the kids to really get to know me. In a lot of ways, I'm a stranger to them."

"I know, but you'll get used to it. After my ex left, I had to learn to be a single dad. It was a lot of trial and error, but my boys and I figured it out. I won't lie, my sisters and parents have helped every step of the way. We all can't do everything alone."

"I'm sorry about your ex."

"I'm not. She was a sorry excuse for a mother, and my boys are better off without her." Niles's tone was as cold as his words, and I thought I'd better change the subject. "I have to be on a plane in eleven days, but I'd like to get Bass's house emptied and ready for sale before I go."

"You're leaving?" Niles wasn't angry, but there was shock in his tone, and it surprised the hell out of me.

"I have twenty-six years in the Navy—I can't walk away from it." I didn't mention that I might just get kicked out for the fake charge of striking an officer. I took another sip of my beer.

"Sorry, Ash, it wasn't an accusation. I just thought you'd be staying, under the circumstances."

"So do my parents. But even if I don't sign on for another tour, I still have about eight months on my current tour that I can't get out of unless I'm discharged or go AWOL." The word *discharged* left a sore taste on my tongue—the idea of being dishonorably discharged after so many years was a huge blow to my pride.

What the hell was I supposed to do for work if I came back, anyway? Work as a photographer with my dad? Take Bass's place?

"So, you're on bereavement right now?"

"Yeah." I decided to omit the mandatory leave until the hearing. I didn't even have the energy to explain the whole clusterfuck.

"Dad. You're here. Come inside and watch the movie with us. You too, Amoo Asher." Jaxson leaped into Niles's arms. The picture of the two of them reminded me of all the times Bass would do that exact thing with his boys while on our weekly video chats. My brother's kids would never be able to jump in their father's arms again.

Niles laughed. "Are we watching *The Little Mermaid?*"

Jaxson made a priceless facial expression that was between disgust and shock. "No. *Spiderman.*"

We made our way into the living room where the floor was covered with blankets, pillows, and the largest vat of popcorn on the floor between all the kids. I checked on the children, but they seemed content. Holy hell, I was so fucking thankful to Mariam that I could almost forget all the heartache I suffered all those years ago.

The older kids sat on the floor with the younger kids, Niles claimed the recliner, and that left the sofa for Mariam and me to share. Apparently, Rena had left with her infant daughter, along with Sara and Mary who had to cook dinner for their husbands. Grief washed over me. Niles, Bassam, Mariam, and I had many memories together just like this—watching movies together while our parents socialized late into the night. Bass was the only one missing from our old gang.

Mariam placed another vat of popcorn between us, and Tamara turned on the movie.

"I made a large one since I remember you used to like to hog all the popcorn," Mariam said.

"I didn't. You used to always say you were on a diet. So I ate most of it to help you out."

"Well, I gave up on that diet crap a long time ago."

"You didn't need it then and you most certainly don't need it now."

Our eyes met in the dimly lit room, and that familiar pull of attraction sparkled between us. The slight catch of her breath and the heavy-lidded stare took me back to all the times we would manage to be alone and our fingers would touch in the popcorn bowl. As an inexperienced boy, I'd assumed the sexual tension that seemed to suck out all the fresh air around us was just a figment of my imagination, but now I recognized that pull of attraction between two people. It was the same if not even stronger now. But fuck that. I wasn't going down that path with her again.

"Amoo Asher." The sound of little Bella's voice awakened me from the spell. "I'm tired."

Without waiting for an invitation, Bella climbed up and curled in my lap. That was the first time since I'd returned home that she'd willingly come to me. I glanced at Mariam, who must have sensed that this was a huge moment for Bella and me.

She beamed and handed me a throw blanket, and I covered Bella, who relaxed even more against my chest to watch the TV screen. The weight and heat of her little body filled me with so much emotion, I didn't understand. Through the scars of the hurt and pain bloomed a little bubble of love, hope, and relief. *My niece and nephews are going to be okay* was my last thought before my eyelids grew heavy and I let sleep carry me away.

"*You have to, Ash. Ash. Ash.*" Bass's voice rang in my ears on repeat but changed to a sweet, feminine whisper.

"Ash." A gentle hand caressed my arm, and I jerked awake. Mariam. It wasn't Bass. Bass was gone. That dream, though. He was asking me, pleading with me. To do something, but what? I couldn't remember what he wanted from me.

"I think you might want to take the kids home. Your mom called three times worried about you guys."

I squinted my eyes to find Mariam watching me. I blinked away the blur of sleep. My left arm felt like I'd found the backside of a porcupine. Bella's sleeping form was still curled in the crook of my elbow. I groaned from the heavy ache and shifted her to my right side—flexing my fists to get the blood flowing to my fingertips. She didn't even stir.

"Shit. What time is it?"

"Ten."

"Why didn't you wake me?"

"I fell asleep myself. My mom just got home and woke me up."

I sat up, cradling Bella just to see the back of Niles's head as he led his boys up the stairs.

"I don't know how to thank you for everything today."

"You don't need to thank me. I had fun." She used that motherly gift she oozed and tucked a wild strand of Bella's hair behind her ear. "Why don't you get Bella in the car while I help the boys pack up their things?"

My brain wasn't firing on all cylinders yet, and I just stared at her like a lost puppy, Bass's voice still ringing in my ear. *"You have to."* *Have to* what? I knew it was a dream. Maybe it was exhaustion, but that dream had rattled me down to my very soul.

"You, okay?"

"I dreamed of Bass. He was telling me that I had to do something."

"What?"

"I don't know."

Chapter 11

MARIAM

Why did that man still make me aware of every inch of my skin? Just like before, when Asher George was around, something inside me awakened. Something inside me sang and danced to a joyful melody. I hadn't felt this alive or aware of my body since I was eighteen years old.

But he wasn't the same boy as before. He had strengthened in more than just build. His personality was tougher. Hard-edged and sometimes cold, but the kindness inside him still seemed to make an appearance despite himself. The pure joy in his eyes when Bella climbed into his lap was so heartwarming and sweet. The comment he made about me not needing a diet reminded me how different he was compared to my dead husband. Nabil never made me feel desirable.

Guilt and shame at comparing the two men washed over me. It was something I did often for the first few years of our marriage, and I hated myself for it. But in retrospect, I couldn't deny that my feelings for my husband never developed into anything but tolerance, much less the intensity of my teenage passion for Asher.

"You still care for him." My mother came up beside me at the window as I watched the black SUV pull out of the driveway. It wasn't an accusation, just a statement. She had always known how I felt about him. I think everyone knew. My sisters knew, and Niles had admitted to knowing this morning. But none of them had my back and stood up to my father. Not even me.

"My feelings for him were from a long time ago, Mom. But you knew back then. Looks like you all knew, yet you didn't fight for me," I retorted.

I turned to face my mother. The age and stress of the years were evident around her eyes. She'd endured a lot throughout her life. Besides being a homemaker and a mother of five children, she dealt with my father's addiction to scotch and gambling, and the different moods that went with addiction. She'd been a beauty once. Still a stunner when all dolled up for a party, but after a day of mourning, she just seemed like a broken woman.

"You know I had zero say when your father was dead set on something. He is a stubborn old man with ridiculous ideas of how women should be raised."

"I know." I started cleaning up the living room from the popcorn and blankets that scattered the floor. Too many thoughts jumbled up in my memories of those last few weeks before my father and I traveled to Iraq.

"You know, he admitted to me that he made a mistake with you."

"When?" I was shocked. My father was very prideful. I thought he would have never made that type of confession.

"It was shortly after your husband had gotten ill. He said that he damned you into a marriage with a man who couldn't properly provide for you. He also argued with George once for not telling your father that Nabil had a heart condition before you married him."

I was frozen from the admission—stunned, my words stolen. It was in this spot in the living room that my father had completely shattered my hopes and dreams. The memory was burned into my brain. We had just returned from Bloomington Manor in celebration of my high school graduation. Asher had given me the most beautiful earrings with a note that I just had to decode the moment I got to my room. Niles and Bassam had slipped me a couple shots of vodka that one of the older boys got them and I was feeling fantastic. I was heading to my bedroom when my father's voice called me over.

"Mariam, come here. I have something for you."

Despite the growing need to get upstairs to decode that letter from Asher, I made my way into the living room. My father sat on his throne-like recliner with my mother beside him and Niles stood across from them both with his back against the wall and his arms firmly crossed over his chest.

CHAPTER 11

My mother had beamed when she handed me a rectangular white box, but thinking back now, that smile hadn't reached her eyes. As an adult, I recognize it as her fake smile, her pretend *everything is okay* smile.

Acid roared in my stomach, and on wobbly legs, I stood before my father. The blood rushed to my ears. It was the same scene I'd witnessed four years earlier when Maryanna had graduated high school, and a few years prior when Sara got engaged. I prayed that the outcome wouldn't be the same for me as it was for them.

"This is from me and Baba," my mother said.

My hands trembled as I opened the box to find a diamond tennis bracelet inside. "It's beautiful," I said.

As my mother reached in to take out the bracelet and clasp it around my wrist, I glanced at Niles. His expression was undeniably unhappy, and the vodka inside my gut churned. My pulse raced. The big gift meant my life was about to change. Forever.

"We have some great news for you as well," my father said. "We do not have to worry about your future now. I have secured you a very good marriage match."

"Marriage?" My knees weakened. Could Asher have asked for my hand in marriage? Was that what the letter was about?"

"Yes, George asked me today."

I swallowed hard. Asher's father had asked for my hand. Oh my God. Asher wanted to marry me. My heart leaped, and my chest soared. Blood rushed to my ears, and I almost missed what my father said next. "For your hand in marriage to his nephew in Iraq."

"What?" The velvet box tumbled from my fingertips, and I swayed on my feet.

"I accepted the proposal for your hand in marriage to Nabil—George's brother's son."

I stumbled to pick up the box, but my knees gave out and I almost ass-planted onto the floor. Somehow, I was saved by Niles. He was beside me now, helping to steady me on my rubbery legs.

"I got you, sis," he whispered in my ear.

"Marriage?" I asked again.

"Yes. We will need to get visas for us, and you need a passport."

"But, Baba. I've never even met him. And what about college?"

"You will meet him when we get there. He has seen your picture and approves of your appearance. Though you might want to lose a few pounds before we go. As for school, you have your high school diploma, which is all you really need. If your husband will see it fitting, you can continue your education later."

"But Baba, I don't want to marry a stranger."

"He has sent you a picture," my mother chimed in cheerfully. "He is very handsome. And his family has lots of money. He will be able to support you comfortably."

My mom handed me the picture with earnest eyes. I read her message to accept my fate but shook my head. Everything inside me raged. I squeezed her hand with the picture of this stranger in it for help.

"What will looks do for me if I've never even talked to him? How will I know if we are even suited for one another?"

"I have decided that this is a good match for you, do you not trust me? I chose your sisters' husbands, and look—they are both happy in their homes. Secured with husbands to support them."

"But Baba, I can't..." Tears burned in my eyes, and my voice trembled.

"You will not embarrass me, Mariam. I have already given my word. A man is as good as his word. You will do as I say. I have allowed you too much freedom as of late and you believe yourself like an American girl."

"Baba please, don't make me do this," I pled.

The tears were now pouring down my face, and anger fueled by scotch radiated from my father. "This conversation is now over."

Chapter 12

ASHER

Children need stability and a routine. Alec's soccer summer camp coach had scolded me this morning because I'd been late dropping off Mikey and Alec at their pregame practices. His words had echoed in my brain all morning. I knew the children needed steadiness, some type of schedule, but I was completely new at this and failing hard. I had no true concept of anything going on. My parents had no clue how to manage three young kids for more than a couple hours on a weekend. I was a Navy man, I thrived on schedules and routines, but lately, I couldn't get my shit straight.

A loud cheer came from our side of the metal bleachers just as Mikey made a goal with a kick and head-bump combination in the final few minutes of his game. Camera-ready, I snapped the picture quickly.

"Mikey is a natural player." Ragheed sat beside me with Bella on his lap.

"Yeah, so was Bassam."

"You're into photography?"

I examined the camera equipment. Bassam was probably the last to use it. My heart stung with a pain so great, I was sure my body would collapse on itself. To make matters worse, I didn't really know what the hell I was doing, but I'd agreed to replace my father for tonight's communion party—just to keep him from going himself until we could find another photographer to take the photos for the already scheduled events on the calendar.

"I used to help them before, but it's been a long time."

"Probably when they used film and before digital pictures were a thing." Ragheed chuck-

CHAPTER 12

led.

Ragheed sat with Bella all smiles on his lap, and I focused on them with the digital screen and snapped a few pictures. "Probably not since high school."

"Oh, speaking of high school, isn't that your girl, Mariam?" He pointed at a newcomer climbing up the seats. She looked gorgeous, and my insides did that leaping thing they always did around her. Her brown hair was in a neat high ponytail, highlighting her high cheekbones, and she was dressed casually in white Chucks, a simple blue T-shirt, and jeans that hugged every inch of her lush, soft curves. My body responded the moment my gaze found her—it had always been like that with her. My mind never won against my heart and body.

"Again, she isn't my girl." I peeled my eyes off Mariam to find a smiling Bella, her arms wrapped around Ragheed's neck.

That little girl was a true traitor. It took four full days for her to even look at me, but Ragheed was her new BFF after only spending a few hours with her since we'd arrived in Michigan. But he didn't get the name Charming for nothing. Even six-year-old girls weren't immune to his charm.

A whistle blew out on the field, and I heard Alec's angry voice. My stomach sank. I was so enamored with Mariam, I hadn't noticed that Alec's team had taken over the soccer field.

"Foul," the rep called, but Alec continued to argue with him. Fuck, the kid was out of control. Two of his teammates stepped up to calm him down, but he wasn't hearing it. I handed the camera to Ragheed and made my way down the seats, but the coach beat me there. He nodded to tell me he would handle it and walked a sullen-faced Alec to the bench. I stood dumbstruck for a few moments until I heard my name.

Mariam was seated a bench away from where I stood, and her sincere gaze eased my worry.

"Let the coach manage it. He's okay."

My legs gave out beside her. I covered my face, and my groan was between a sigh and a growl.

"How are you doing?"

"I have no idea," I said.

"Amoo Asher," Bella called from above, looking for me. My heart fluttered just a little bit. It both scared and elated me that she wanted me around.

"I better get back to Bella before she runs off

with my buddy."

She looked over her shoulder and waved to Bella. "She does look happy with him."

"She adored him after ten minutes. Me? She only acts like she cares if I walk away."

Her laugh was like sunshine on a rainy day, and I wanted to bask in it. But Bella's persistent voice brought me back to my senses.

"I'll catch you later."

Ragheed winked at me when I returned to my seat. "Mariam is gorgeous. Now I know why you never got over her."

"I like Mariam. She's nice and very pretty," Bella said.

"I think you are pretty too." Ragheed pinched the bridge of Bella's nose.

She gave Ragheed a dreamy smile and batted her eyelashes at him. If I didn't know any better, I'd think she was flirting with him. I rolled my eyes mostly out of pure jealousy.

I gritted my teeth. "Thanks to my father, she was never my girl."

"Well, the way you look at her says a different story." He shook his head. "I still can't believe your dad did that shit to you just for money. Did Nabil's dad ever give your dad the money he owed him?"

"No." Nausea rolled over me, and I remembered sitting in the kitchen and begging my father not to ruin my life. After finding out that Mariam's marriage was arranged to my cousin, I nearly lost my shit. I loved that girl with everything I had, and my own father had arranged to have her taken from me.

My legs had burned by the time I had reached my house. I had run home after seeing Mariam on that fucking beach. My father was to blame for me losing Mariam. My heart pounded in my ears with every step of my Nikes on the concrete. My knees gave out when I reached my house and spotted my dad's car in the driveway. I sent a quick thanks to God that he and Bassam hadn't left for work yet. I knew if I just told him that I loved Mariam and wanted to marry her myself he would put a stop to this madness. He would. I was sure of it.

The scent of cumin and spices that normally made me salivate turned my stomach. On shaky legs, I followed the clatter of dishes into the kitchen where my mother was in full swing, mixing a pot on the stove. The sounds of Arabic music played on the radio, and my father sat at the kitchen table with his camera while Bassam was packing the video equip-

CHAPTER 12

ment for tonight's event.

"Asher, where have you been?" My mother was the first to notice my arrival. She stormed over with a kitchen towel and tried to wipe my forehead, but I sidestepped her attempt. It wasn't hard—she barely reached my shoulders in height and was maybe a hundred and ten pounds. Her short, dark hair fell from the knot she placed on the top of her head when she swiped at me with her kitchen towel, and I ducked her second attempt.

"At the beach." I glanced nervously at my father. "With Mariam."

"Then you heard the good news?" My dad looked up at me from over his newspaper. "Your cousin Nabil is coming to America." The pride in his voice sliced at my chest, and memories of my father always taking Nabil's side over mine when we were children slapped into me.

"Nabil?" Bassam seemed to register what my father was saying and came over to the table to stand next to me. "Wasn't that the little shit who always wanted everything you had?"

"Baba, I love Mariam," I blurted. I hadn't intended to reveal my feelings like that but the panic in my chest and Bassam's words jumbled my brain. I'd forgotten how my cousin made my life a living hell back when we were children, and the memories heightened my fears because my father always tried to make me a better "man" by making things harder on me. If I wanted a toy, I had to earn it. If Nabil wanted something I had, he gave it to him because it "builds character."

"What are you talking about?" Baba dropped his paper onto the table, and his cheerful tone darkened. His round face turned that pink shade that always showed that his blood pressure was rising. He took off his black-framed readers and glared at me.

"What's happening?" Bassam looked from me to my father with a puzzled expression.

"Mariam is engaged to Nabil. Her father is taking her to Iraq to marry him and bring him here," Baba said.

"Mariam?" Bassam's expression turned to pure disgust. "That little shit can't marry Mariam. She's so much better than him."

Fire and an explosive rage shot through me. "Baba, I love Mariam. I have always loved her. I want her to be my wife, and I think…I think she loves me too."

"Love?" Baba tossed his glasses on top of the

paper and stood. "You silly children with your idealism of marriage and love." He shook his head. "Marriage is about more than love."

"But why would you arrange his marriage?"

"He's going to turn of age, and he needs to leave Iraq before he is forced to join the Iraqi army."

"So, arrange his marriage to someone else. Why her?" I spat. "Why do you have to always give him everything I've wanted? Everything I considered mine?"

"I made a deal with my brother that I would arrange a good match for him, and I will not go back on my word."

Then everything was made clear. "What deal did you make with Amoo Amir? What is he giving you?"

"What do you mean?" Baba scoffed.

"Deal? What kind of deal?" Bassam asked.

The pieces finally started to fit together in my head. When did my dad give two shits about his brother? Up until that very moment, my father had been angry with his brother for stealing his inheritance. What changed? Could he have been using it as leverage to get his piece-of-shit son married?

"Is Amoo Amir finally sending you your

share of your family holdings and land in Iraq?" I asked.

"Well, yes, but that's not the reason. Nabil is not strong enough to enter the Iraqi military. It is the only way to save the boy," Baba said.

"So, his happiness is more important to you than mine?" My voice trembled with each word.

"Don't be silly." He returned to his seat. "Where is lunch? We have to get ready to leave soon." That was my father's way of letting me know that the conversation was over.

"Baba, please." I kneeled before him. "Don't do this to me. I can't imagine him with her. I don't think I could live the rest of my life seeing him with her."

"Baba, find Nabil some other girl. There are plenty that will go back home to get married." My big brother—always coming to my rescue.

"Absolutely not," my father barked. "How would I look to Manni if I took it back? He has already agreed to give Mariam's hand in marriage to Nabil."

"So, Nabil's future, money, and your pride are more important than your own son's well-being?" My body quivered from head to toe, and white-hot fury sizzled beneath my skin.

"That's not what your father is saying." My mother regularly smoothed out my father's harsh words.

"That is exactly what I'm saying," Baba said.

"Then, you don't care what happens to me?" I spat. "That's good to know." I stormed out of the kitchen and out the back door. Two things were made clear. I needed to leave as soon as possible and find the means to support myself. I remembered the Navy recruiter who spoke to me during the last week of school. He had said that I could join the Navy and get my degree in engineering at the same time. Wouldn't it be ironic if by trying to save my cousin from fighting in the Iraqi military, my father pushed me to join the Navy?

Chapter 13

Mariam

"Do you need anything before I leave?" Noor, my boss asked while touching up her cherry-red lipstick after another busy day. The color looked amazing with her dark chestnut hair and fair skin.

"Nope, I'm getting ready to head out too. I'm just cleaning up."

"Are you sure you don't want to meet up for a drink? Farrah and her boo, Kal, are already down the street. I think one of his buddies is

CHAPTER 13

joining us." She winked.

"Mom, you should totally go." Tamara had her cross-body purse around her torso and a pile of books in her arms.

"Where are you headed?"

"Home. I'm tired and need to finish my homework."

I surveyed her face. Dark circles were under her eyes, and her naturally tanned complexion seemed pale. "Are you feeling, okay?" I dropped the brushes that were in my hand and touched her cheeks.

She pulled away and hurried toward the door. "I'm fine, Mom, just really tired today. Go out with your friends." She zoomed out the door before I could do anything else.

"Your smart daughter knows you should get out and hang with us. So, are you coming?"

Before I could answer, the door chimed, and little Bella's very distinct bellow echoed through the salon.

"Auntie Mariam." She pushed away from a very distraught-looking Asher and ran straight to me. Her little arms wrapped around my thigh, and I bent down to her level. Tears streamed down her cheeks, and her cheeks were the color of bright red apples.

"Bella, honey, what's wrong?" I wiped her tear-streaked face with my fingers and looked between Asher and her.

"Alec put gum in my hair, see." She turned to show me a clump of gum embedded into the bottom of her pretty, silky-smooth curls. "He is such a meanie."

"Oh no, it's okay. I can fix it."

"Are you going to cut my hair?" Bella hiccupped.

"I'm only going to cut a little, I promise."

"I want my hair long like Tamara."

"You do have the same hair. It was just like yours when she was your age." I tapped the bridge of her nose with my finger. "It will be just like hers when you're big like her." There was a lot of resemblance between them. Same dark curly hair and pretty features, but while Bella's eyes were gray like her mother's, Tamara's were a dark black, like sparkly black diamonds.

"Are you sure it's okay? My mom said to call you, but I didn't know your number, so I just decided to drive over." Asher was in pure panic mode.

"Yeah, it's fine. The gum is only at the bottom, so I'll just need to give her a little trim. It won't take long."

"Okay, thanks, I really appreciate this. You've been a godsend for me." He weaved on his feet like he needed to sit down, and I felt bad for him. He seemed so overwhelmed.

"You look like you could use a break. Why don't you head next door for a coffee, maybe a snack, and I'll bring her over there when we're done."

"Yeah, coffee sounds good right now." He scrubbed his face with both hands, and I couldn't help staring at his forearms in his very form-fitting white T-shirt. My gaze slid down to his hard, muscled chest and lingered a little too long down his frame right to his crotch. I mentally slapped myself for checking out his sizable package through his gray sweatpants. It was a dirty little habit ever since Farrah and the other girls talked about being able to see the outline of a man's penis in gray joggers. I'd sworn off relationships, but that didn't mean I couldn't look or daydream.

When I finally forced myself to glance at his face again, his heated gaze was on me, and a smirk was plastered across his face. *Busted.*

Heat rose to my cheeks, and I turned my attention to Bella. "Ready to get that gum out of your hair?"

"Yes." She snuffled.

"I'll meet you next door in about twenty minutes." I couldn't meet his eyes.

"Is that okay, Bella?" he asked.

"Are you going to buy me ice cream like you promised?" she bargained.

"Yes, right after you're done. Promise."

Her eyes lit up. "Okay, you can go."

He nodded and thanked me once again before glancing over at Bella. She gave him a little wave, and he beamed. That little girl had him wrapped around her pinky finger, and he didn't even know it.

"Holy Mary, mother of God. That's Asher?" Noor stammered the moment he stepped out of the salon. "He looks like a Greek god."

"Shhh." I tilted my head in Bella's direction, but she was too busy playing with my rollers to pay any attention to us. "Yeah, he is something, right?"

"He totally caught you checking him out too and didn't seem to mind one bit," she whispered.

"That was mortifying." I covered my face.

"You need to take that on a test run or I might have to try." She winked. "Looks like you're

CHAPTER 13

going to be busy, so I won't look for you at Liquid Lantern." Her heels clanked out the door.

Before long, Bella's hair was gum-free and styled with bouncy curls. While I finished closing, she admired her reflection.

"My hair looks like Tamara's now."

"You could be her twin." I smiled. My heart tugged at the memories of when Tamara would come to the salon with me when Nabil was hospitalized. Like Bella, she loved all the girly things, and everyone here would spoil and pamper her with makeup, fun hairstyles, and manicures. Noor would interlace strands of pink and purple hair into hers and style them into the coolest French braids.

After locking up, we headed to A Taste of Iraq, but Asher was already outside shaking hands with someone I didn't recognize. He was tall and average-looking but was in a nice, tailored suit.

"Amoo Asher, do you like my hair?" Bella did a little twirl, and her hair spun along with her pink summer dress.

His face lit up at the sight of Bella. "You look beautiful." He lifted her off the ground. "Thank you, Mariam, but I didn't get a chance to pay you. I was coming back and bumped into Bassam's lawyer."

"Don't worry about that—it's on me. Lawyer? Is he working on the…" I glanced at Bella. "The estate?"

"He asked me to come in to see him tomorrow. Apparently, it has to do with the will."

"What's a will?" Bella asked.

Asher's eyes widened, and he looked at me for help.

"It's just a paper adults use for the things they own," I said.

Bella seemed to take that as a good answer. "Auntie Mariam is coming for ice cream too, right?"

"Yes. If she won't let us pay for a haircut, she must let us buy her ice cream."

Every fiber of my being warned me this was a bad idea, but I couldn't pull myself away from either of them. Something about the two of them together tugged at my heartstrings. If I was honest with myself, it was all those times I contemplated a moment just like this—if our families hadn't arranged my marriage to his cousin instead. What could one ice cream cone hurt, anyway?

"You know I love ice cream."

"I know." He smirked. "Chocolate with

CHAPTER 13

brownie bites."

"You remembered."

"I remember everything." At his words, my face flushed hot.

The Beauty Squad salon was on Main Bloom Street and only a short distance from an adorable ice cream parlor. I liked to call our city a town since everything we could ever want or need was a stroll or a short car ride away, but Bloomington Hills was a chic, charming city with a vibrant downtown area with fancy shops, trendy restaurants, and it was walking distance from a private beach on Bloom Lake. It had a population of about twenty thousand.

It was a beautiful summer evening. The freshwater scent of Bloom Lake danced in the air. The summer sun was still high and warm on my skin, and I basked in the heat. Bella and I found a table outside while Asher ordered our sweet treats. After I set her up with the kids' cartoon app on my phone, a memory slammed into me like a runaway train.

Tamara was about six years old, and I'd convinced Nabil to take us for ice cream, despite his persistence to stay home. He was a homebody and his illness made him even more so.

Getting him to go anywhere with us was like pulling teeth. But on this particular day, the gods were mocking me. Because the moment we were all seated with our ice cream cones and enjoying the perfect summer day, three men in Navy attire parked a few feet from us. Nabil's back was to them, so he didn't notice, but I immediately saw Asher. I couldn't help looking for him anytime I saw a man in any military apparel.

He wasn't the same Asher I remembered. He was bigger, broader, and when his eyes bored into mine, anger burned back at me.

"What are you thinking about?" Asher had placed my ice cream in front of me, and I hadn't even noticed. Bella was excited for her sprinkles and dove in while she watched a cartoon on my phone.

"I was remembering something. It's nothing."

"When I saw you sitting in this same spot with your husband and daughter?" There was a little edge in his voice that I hadn't heard in a few days.

"Actually yes, I was thinking how your hatred for me has changed since then. Your eyes don't shoot daggers at me anymore."

CHAPTER 13

He laughed. "Daggers?"

"Yes, daggers."

"In truth, I still wanted to hate you, but I just couldn't find the strength, not after everything you've done for me since I've been back."

"Asher, you meant so much to me—you still do. You don't know how badly I wish things had been different. If I'd had the voice or backbone to stand up to my father..."

"Do you think we would have ended up together if our families had not interfered?" His voice was barely a whisper.

I glanced in Bella's direction before answering. She was still busy with her ice cream and the cartoon she watched on my phone. "I don't know. The only absolute was my feelings for you."

He watched me for a long moment, and I couldn't quite discern his thoughts. "Do you think about that night?"

At the mention of our one and only night together, my face flushed hot. Only if he knew how often I'd thought about his hands on my body, his lips on my skin, and him consuming my mind, body, and soul.

"Yes."

"Me too." He cleared his throat and gestured

to the ice cream. "You're going to let that just sit there?"

I lifted the spoon and nearly swooned at the first bite of the heavenly concoction.

"I've always loved how happy you get around your favorite foods."

I looked up to find him watching me with amusement. "What can I say? Food is to be enjoyed."

Chapter 14

TAMARA

When Tamara was a little girl, her mother used to claim that if she lied, God would write "liar" on her forehead, and only she would be able to read it. Sometimes, she was still self-conscious about lying to her mother. It wasn't the fear that God would rat her out anymore, but guilt about deliberately deceiving her mom plagued her. The same unease of a thirteen-year-old crept up her chest and twisted her insides when she opened the front door for Cross.

That worry didn't stop her from falling into his arms and crushing her lips against his mouth. It didn't stop her from locking the door and leading him to her bedroom. Her body seemed to be extra sensitive, and every stroke of his hand was like a beacon to her core. Her breasts ached from the lightest touches of his fingertips, and her lips quivered from his slightest kiss.

Sated and naked in her bed, his warm body snuggling her own, his fingers entwined in her hair, Cross chuckled. "I think your mom knows."

"Knows what, exactly?" She sat up on her elbow and turned to face him.

"About us. She was looking at us weirdly at your grandma's house the other day, and I'm not going to lie—she scares me."

"I think she's always suspected we liked each other, but she doesn't know about us."

"Why are you hiding us? You always talked about dates with her before."

"Because we are having sex, and she'll know."

"Don't tell her."

"She'll see right through my lie and make me

CHAPTER 14

have the sex talk with her. She's got a superpower or something."

One of the many things her mom prided herself on was their friendship. As she'd gotten older, Tamara told her about crushes and her first kiss. When she started college, she talked about dating experiences, good and bad. They even talked about sex. But she'd always told her mom that she wanted to wait for marriage. She knew in her soul it made her mom extremely happy.

And that was the plan—until one night, everything changed with Cross. Now she had two secrets from the person with whom she shared everything. She knew if her mother learned about Cross, she was going to warn her about sex and birth control, and Tamara wouldn't be able to lie. She wouldn't read it on her forehead from God, but her expression would be a dead giveaway because the woman saw right through her.

Cross reached for his phone and looked at the time. "I better get dressed." His warm weight lifted off her, leaving her cold. "I rather not have her hold something over my head when I ask for your hand in marriage."

His words pulled her out of the dream-like

euphoric state and doused her with cold water. She gathered her clothes and headed for the shower. "I'll be right back."

Her muscles were achy, but it was a delicious kind of ache. Every throb and twang were another reminder of how he drove her body wild, but it wasn't only with lust, it was an all-consuming sensation. He took over her senses, mind, soul, and the entirety of her being. So why did she freeze at the word *marriage*?

Because love wasn't forever, and she wasn't fooling herself into believing otherwise. Yes, she loved Cross—he was her best friend and lover. Two of the absolute best parts of her life all wrapped up in a gorgeous package. But that didn't mean that it would stay like that for him. What if they got married, had children, and one day, he decided that he didn't love her anymore? She couldn't handle that kind of rejection again.

She returned to the bedroom, her body drained and completely depleted to find Cross sitting cross-legged on her bed and looking through the box of her father's things. Anger rumbled through her—she hadn't gone through those things. She couldn't bear to look at them. She just wasn't ready, and finding

Cross in her personal space going through the one thing that made her want to jump out of her skin was a violation of the highest kind.

"What are you doing?" Tamara's voice trembled from the attempt to keep her tone level.

"I just pulled out the pictures for you, I know you're not ready to go through everything else yet, but you really need to get started on that PowerPoint. Isn't the first draft of the presentation due next week?"

Her anger deflated. He knew her hesitation and had done this to help her. He picked up the box and placed it back in the corner of the bedroom. "Here are all the pictures I could find."

The one on the very top was of her dad and her at her Holy Communion party, and probably one of the very last happy memories she had with him. Her right thumb promptly touched the ring on her right ring finger for reassurance. It was the last gift from her father, a white gold ring with a diamond cross in the center. Despite her confused sentiment toward him, she hadn't taken off the ring for more than a few minutes since the moment he'd given it to her.

"Thanks. Can you just put them on my desk?" She returned to bed, exhaustion seeping deep into her bones. "I think I'm going to get some sleep. Wanna tuck me in before you go?"

His beautiful face glowed at her words, and he nodded. She climbed into bed and watched him place the pictures on the desk before he returned to her side.

"Can you stay with me until I fall asleep?"

"Of course." He wrapped her inside the covers and climbed in behind. Pulling her close to him, he kissed her forehead. The last thing she remembered was his strong arms and his whispered, "Sweet dreams."

Chapter 15

Asher

My limbs numb, I crossed the threshold of DK Law Firm. I hadn't told my parents about the appointment with Davison Kaji, Bassam's longtime friend and lawyer. They'd dealt with so much already with loss, grief, and the three children, the very least I could do was get my brother's finances in order on my own.

Davison's administrative assistant, Sandy, was a cute brunette with big brown eyes and a curvy frame that could entice a monk. She smiled brightly. Her witty charm would have piqued my curiosity a week ago, but now I couldn't seem to muster the energy or the interest. I blamed my lack of attention on Mariam. The woman had invaded my mind just as she had back in high school and despite my best efforts, I just couldn't shake the attraction I had for her.

Sandy led me to an empty conference room. "Please have a seat." She gestured to one of the many plush leather chairs surrounding a large wooden table in the center of the room. "Can I get you something? Coffee, tea…"

"No, thank you."

Before she could offer anything else, Davison entered, and she eased out of the room.

"It's really good to see you, I just wish it were under better circumstances," Davison said. He was a beefy man, particularly around the middle, but had surprisingly broad, muscular shoulders. Standing at six-foot-three, he was eye-to-eye with me, and his brilliant blue eyes shone with sadness when he greeted me. We shook hands from across the table and he unbuttoned the jacket of his tailored blue suit before taking his seat. I appeared underdressed in my black polo shirt and dark denim jeans, but I quickly dismissed the thought.

"I didn't bring my parents. I figured it would be better for me to arrange everything and just bring them when everything was settled for the kids."

"I can't even imagine what they're going through, but their presence isn't necessary at these meetings." He opened the file he had brought in with him. "Since you are the sole beneficiary of your brother's estate."

"Right, so I can just help out with the sale of the house and maybe be the signer to the kids' trusts after they are created?"

"Bassam and Lydia have you listed as the sole guardian to their three children and the sole beneficiary of their estate. House, cars, life insurance policy."

My pulse pounded in my ears, and a cold sweat broke out over my skin. "What?"

"Bassam left this for you, and it should explain his reasons. I had suggested he speak to you about this when he updated the paperwork after Bella was born, but I'm guessing he did not."

"No." I wiped my palms on the legs of my jeans.

Davison shook his head and sighed before he

handed me a white sealed envelope. It shook between my damp fingers.

"Why don't I get you some water while you look over the letter."

I couldn't quite decipher the different sensations surging through me. On the one hand, I would be reading a letter written by my brother, the last words he would ever say to me. His last words. His last request, and I stared at the envelope as if it were a bomb about to detonate.

Taking a deep breath, I unsealed the envelope and took out the letter with unsteady hands. Bassam's familiar script greeted me like an old friend. When I'd first enlisted in the Navy, he would write to me weekly and send treats from home. I didn't realize how much I missed getting his letters until now. I would be reading the very last letter from him. My stomach tightened.

Asher,
What can I say, brother? If you are reading this letter, the worst possible scenario has happened—leaving our three beautiful children orphaned. This is something that terrifies me to my very soul. Leaving our children while they are still small and defenseless with-

CHAPTER 15

out someone we trust wholeheartedly to raise them in the same loving and safe environment keeps me up at night. Lydia and I have thought long and hard about whom we wanted to raise our children if we couldn't, and we both agreed we would like it to be you.

Asher, I know Mom and Dad would do their very best, and I think they might be a little offended that I didn't ask them. Tell them it's nothing personal. They are excellent grandparents. In truth, they cannot offer the same security and well-being as I know you can. You are their uncle, my baby brother, and the closest thing to them being raised by me if I'm gone. Please be my children's guardian, and adopt Mikey, Alec, and Bella. They need stability and a family—at the very least a father very much like the one they already knew. I know you're reading this right now and freaking out, but don't.

I trust you. Lydia trusts you. And I'm going to need you to trust you too. I recognize that this is a huge ask and a major adjustment to your life, but there isn't anyone else we would trust with our children. Take them as your own. Love, teach, and protect them in the same way I looked out for you. Take them fishing, swimming, and camping—like we used to do. Tell them stories from our childhood. Make sure you let the kids know how much their mother and I loved them. Besides, you owe me a life's debt from when I saved your life all those years ago, and I'm cashing it in, baby brother.

Davison has all the information about our estate. Please know I wouldn't have asked if I didn't know deep in my heart you are the best person for my children. They are precious to me. As you have always been, brother.

Love always,
Bassam

I sat staring at Bass's words and tears streamed down my cheeks. My chest ached. My ribcage tightened. I inhaled deeply but I couldn't get enough air in my lungs. He wanted me to adopt his children, raise them as my own. Me? What did I know about kids? How could I possibly be a father—or live up to him? I reread the words in his ridiculously neat handwriting again. *Take them as your own. Love, teach, and protect them in the same way I looked out for you.*

"Bass, you have to be kidding," I whispered. Yes, he looked out for me way more than our father did, but I wasn't him. Bassam was kind, compassionate, and loving. I was selfish, irrational, prideful, and a moody prick. I had never been able to see past my own wants and desires, despite the cost. For heaven's sake, I couldn't even keep a goldfish alive, and he wanted me to be the sole caretaker for three grieving children?

My eyes slid down the page and his words about a life debt flashed like neon lights in a dark room. The memory of that day slammed into me like a runaway train. It had been a perfect day for the Fourth of July. The sun beamed brightly, and I let the little raft drift deeper into the center of Bloom Lake. The warmth of the sun washed over my face but didn't stop me from squinting my eyes and watching Mariam helping her mother and sisters prepare for their annual Fourth of July barbecue. She wore a pretty little green bikini top and jean cutoffs that hugged her ass perfectly while she sauntered around the patio. I caught her watching me a few times and that time when she looked my way, I waved her over.

I laughed when she pointed at her mother and then at her neck as if slitting her throat. Then her face changed, and she seemed to be trying to tell me something. But I couldn't understand her sign language. She started running toward the lake, and for some reason, there was shouting, but I didn't register what was happening until I looked up and saw a speedboat coming right at me. Then I was in the lake. Bassam had knocked me off my raft and dragged me deep under the water. We stayed as deep as possible, and I followed him toward shore.

When the water became shallow, we finally emerged out of the lake breathless. Bassam grabbed me in a big bear hug and squeezed the ever-loving life out of me when I pushed back.

"What the fuck, Asher?" Bassam punched my arm. "You must pay attention to your surroundings. I thought we were going to lose you."

"It's not my fault. That dumbass wasn't even paying attention to where he was going," I panted back.

"Luke. I'll deal with him."

"You saved my life," I said.

"Yeah, I guess you owe me a life debt."

"You name it and it's yours, brother."

"I think I'll hold on to that debt and claim it when I really need it." We fist-bumped and climbed out of the lake and onto the dock where Mariam, her mom, and her sisters were waiting for us with worried faces.

"Wait until your mother hears what happened," Auntie Nuha scolded.

"Oh Auntie, please don't tell her."

She tilted her head and surveyed me. "This will probably give her a heart attack, so I won't tell her for her sake, not yours. You better have learned your lesson.

"Thank you, Auntie."

"Ash." Mariam's voice quivered, and like a selfish asshole, I swelled with pride. This beautiful girl cared about me.

"I'm okay," I assured her.

"See," Mary said. "This girl almost jumped in after you guys fell into the water. She's lost all common sense. Mariam can barely swim."

"Whatever, I can swim." Mariam's face flushed the cutest shade of pink.

I had almost died. My big brother had saved my life, and now I owed him a life's debt.

Chapter 16

Mariam

The manila envelope trembled in my hand, and I glanced up at Zaynab. "My heart's beating so loud."

She laughed. "It's so exciting." She placed her mug on the coffee table. "I feel like getting on this table and belly dancing, but I'll wait until you sign the contract. You are still interested in becoming my partner, right? I mean, if you want to change your mind, it's not too late. Not that I want you to change your mind. It's just that I don't want you to feel pressure."

She tugged on the hem of her jean shorts and babbled like she always did when she was nervous. The partnership was a big step for her too. She'd started the bookstore all on her own and poured her soul into making it a profitable business. This venture wasn't just a risk for me, it was a risk to her livelihood.

"Zaynab, I'm not changing my mind. The more I've thought about this adventure with you, the more excited I've become."

"Okay, good." She picked up her cup and took a sip, a relieved look on her face. "My lawyer drew up the contract, but I want you to give it a read and take it to your lawyer. If there is anything you want to add or change, I'm totally open."

"Okay, when do you need this by?"

"I've already contacted the realtor and had them put me in contact with the owner. They are excited that we want it and are drafting a new lease for us to include the new property. They said they'll have the agreement next week."

"All right, I'll call my lawyer." I really didn't have a lawyer, but my cousin would be able to point me in the right direction.

"Have you told anyone yet?"

"Just Tamara, and she was ecstatic."

"That girl loves books almost as much as we do." She chuckled. "That reminds me, the book she ordered for her genetics class finally came in this morning." She reached down and pulled out a massive book from her tote bag.

"She's halfway through her semester. I thought she had all her books."

"This was for her extra reading," Zaynab said.

"I should have known." In high school, Tamara used to add books to her required reading list, and I wouldn't realize it until she'd spent an extra three hundred dollars on books. But I never truly minded. I loved how much she enjoyed learning.

"I have to get going. My"—she flashed me a big grin—"*our* employee needs to get off work early today."

"Our employee." I fist-bumped the air. "I'm going to be a boss."

"You are." She threw her arms open and enveloped me in a warm embrace. "Remember, any questions you have you can call me. Or better yet, I'll send you my lawyer's number, and you can provide your lawyer with the information."

"Yeah, they can handle the small details," I agreed.

After walking her to the door, my mind tripped over questions about whether I was doing the right thing. Was I really going through with this? Starting a whole new business—possibly putting my security and my daughter's in jeopardy?

Buying into the business would cost nearly my entire savings, but since I had Nabil's life insurance money in a separate account, I was in a fair position. I'd just left the money sitting in the bank collecting interest after I paid off Tamara's college tuition and the mortgage. Worst-case scenario, I still had seventy percent left for my retirement and Tamara's future wedding. For all those reasons, financially I could make it work. I picked up my phone and called my cousin Natalie. Before long, I had a meeting for Monday at noon with her partner to review the contract.

Satisfied and a little emotionally drained, I picked up my book and fell back into my novel to celebrate my success with my current book boyfriend.

"Mom, have you seen my cross ring?" Tamara entered the living room in a panic with her hot pink rolling suitcase in tow. "I thought I left it in the kitchen when I was doing the dishes, but I can't find it."

I shut the book and placed it on the couch beside me. I smiled brightly and raised my pinky finger to flash her the diamond dainty white-gold ring. It was a gift from her dad, and I knew how much it meant to her. Even though he had often been withdrawn because of his illness, he had bought her this ring, and she'd worn it ever since.

"Oh, good. I freaked when I thought I lost it." She pushed her thick, curly hair behind her ears and sat beside me.

"No, you left it on the windowsill, and I thought I'd keep it safe for you." I took off the ring and slipped it on her finger.

"Thanks." She lifted the book I'd been reading and skimmed the back cover. "This looks interesting. I'm adding it to my TBR list."

I swelled with pride. "My treasure trove is all yours."

"Great, because I've already swiped a few to read at the beach."

I cherished that I had this to share with my daughter. The love of not only books, but ro-

CHAPTER 16

mance novels. Since she was a child, we had read together. We journeyed through the Harry Potter series to young adult romances like *Twilight* together, but I always kept a stash of steamy love stories for myself hidden in my bedside table until I realized the little minx was stealing them in high school.

There was something so beautiful and gratifying about reading a romance. Maybe it was the promise that love conquered all or the physical and emotional connection the book provided every time I finished a story. The comfort of it wrapped around me like a warm and cozy blanket. This book had hit a chord with me, maybe because I related to their second-chance romance and I'd been facing reuniting with my childhood love, but I'd been consumed with this story.

"I'll be done with it by the time you come back from Traverse City."

"You know, I love the chance to curl up with a great book, but I think you should meet Farrah and Noor at the bar tonight."

"And why would I do that?" I looked blankly at her. The idea of changing and doing my hair and makeup didn't seem appealing at all. Not while I was perfectly comfortable in my shorts and T-shirt.

"So maybe you can experience some of the stuff we read about." The little stinker waggled her eyebrows at me. "Maybe with Asher? I mean you did have that ice cream date."

"It wasn't a date." My face flushed hot, and I twisted my hair into a ponytail. "It was a thank-you for getting the gum out of Bella's hair."

"But it could have been." She smiled again.

"You look better today. Do you feel better?" I searched her face. Her skin still had a slight paleness to it.

"I'm fine. I think the tacos I had for lunch yesterday didn't agree with me."

"Are you sick now? Maybe you should stay home with Mommy. We can have a movie night. Maybe watch *Sabrina* and I'll make you my magic soup?"

She made a face like she was really debating taking me up on my offer. "Which *Sabrina*?"

"Harrison Ford."

"If you had said Humphrey Bogart, I would have changed my mind."

"Dang it. I'll remember that for next time." I snapped my fingers. "Anyway, you just missed Zaynab." I handed her the ginormous book she'd brought for Tamara.

"Oh, my book. Finally. I'll read this on the drive up."

"It's a road trip. You should be listening to music and flashing truck drivers."

"That will only take like five minutes, I'll read for the other three hours and fifty-five minutes to the hotel."

"You are such a great multitasker."

"I learned from the best."

"That's me." I flashed her my "I'm charming" smile and held out the envelope with the contract.

"What's that?"

"This is my business contract with Zaynab."

"Really?" She grabbed the envelope. "Are you taking it to Natalie?"

"I am. I have a meeting on Monday."

"I'm so happy for you, Mom." Her eyes gleamed. "This is so amazing. You are going to be an owner of a bookstore."

"I'm so nervous." I covered my face. "Am I crazy to spend my savings on this?"

"No. It's a lucrative business. You have seen its success and have already been there for all the store's milestones. You're ready for this next step."

"Yeah, you're right."

"Aren't I always?" She kissed my cheek. "I'm so proud of you, Mom."

Outside, a car horn sounded, and Tamara stood. "That's my ride."

I walked her out and said hello to my nieces. I was so happy Tamara had them. They were like sisters more than cousins, and since she was an only child, I was always thankful for their relationship.

Tamara pulled me into a tight embrace. "At least consider going for drinks with Farrah and Noor. You need to get out and have a little fun, Mom."

"Khala, live it up a little." Bianca blew me a red-stained kiss coupled with a mischievous laugh.

"You girls be careful. Don't take anything from a stranger, don't drink too much and..."

"Mom, relax...we'll call 911 if we see any weirdoes around our hotel," Tamara said.

"Are any boys coming?" I asked.

The girls glanced at each other nervously. "Just a few of Thomas and Nick's friends," Lauren said.

"What about Cross?" I gave my daughter a pointed stare. My gut told me something had

CHAPTER 16

shifted in their relationship. She just hadn't copped to it yet. I knew it was only a matter of time before things would develop between them. I think I realized she crushed on him way before she did.

"He has to work but might come up on Saturday." Tamara again averted her eyes.

"Maybe I'll tag along with him and come up too."

The horror on their faces let me know what they thought of my idea.

"Oh yeah, bring the Navy dude, Asher. The two of you looked really cozy on the couch together at Nana's house." Lena wiggled her brows.

"Funny girl, point taken. Call me when you get there so I know you made it safely."

With a few more byes, hugs, and kisses, I stood in my driveway and watched the black Jeep drive away, with a whispered prayer for their safety on my lips.

Instead of getting back on the couch, I grabbed my keys and purse and got in my car. Unease rippled through me as I parked my car at my parents' house. It was the easiest route to my favorite spot on the beach.

I noticed my dad in the backyard tinkering

with the Virgin Mary statue. I hadn't planned on stopping, but at the sound of my name being called, I paused.

"Mariam, are you not even going to stop and say hello to your father?"

I wasn't in the mood for idle chatter, much less questions and judgment from my father. With a sigh, I turned around and made my way to where he stood. He was a thin man with frail shoulders and a balding head of hair. He was in his routine attire for the summer, white short-sleeved button-down, khaki shorts, and flip-flops. The sight of him now made me wonder why I'd feared him so much as a child. Sure, he'd been strict, ill-tempered and worse when he was overly intoxicated, but now there wasn't any fear left. Instead, here stood a relic of a bygone era.

"Hi Baba, what are you up to out here?"

"I'm cleaning the Virgin Mary, what does it look like I'm doing?"

I muffled a giggle. "Baba, it looks spotless."

"Spotless? Look, right here." He pointed at a pristine spot on the shoulder of the statue. "I think the squirrels are doing it." He made the sign of the cross and returned to his scrubbing. "Where is Tamara?"

"She's just left for up north with the rest of the grandchildren."

"Girls on a trip without parents?" He shook his head in disbelief. "You and your sisters are letting your daughters grow up without any restrictions. You don't want to arrange marriages, you let them go and come as they wish. You are not raising Chaldean girls. They do not have the values or respect I instilled in you."

A flash of heat and resentment from so long ago washed over me. "My daughter is not being raised without values or respect. The difference between my daughter and the way you raised me is I'm not going to control my daughter's future. She's a beautiful, smart, kind girl, with respect for herself and her family. But her life and her choices are her own."

"If you believe this, you are even more naive than I thought."

He returned to his statue, and I had to fight the urge to throw something at him. I balled my fists at my sides, then turned away in a huff. "Tell Mom I had to go."

I had to walk away before I said something I couldn't take back. There were many things I wanted to tell my father, so many accusations and feelings that I'd held inside my entire adult life. But what would that get me? Only excuses and outrage, never an apology for the way he ruined my life, despite my mother's claim he was aware he'd "messed up" with me.

I took the ten-minute walk from the beach at the back of my parents' house to my favorite hideaway spot on Bloom Lake. The freshwater scent filled me, and the breeze welcomed me. I hadn't found myself at the alcove in a very long time. After I married Nabil and returned home while we waited for him to come to the US, I camped beneath the arch on the lake every day.

It was the one refuge that filled me with joy and comfort. Even after all these years, it was still the place that brought me the most inner peace. The lake was the place where I'd grieved my adolescence and childhood dreams. It was where I fell in love with Asher and mourned the loss of his love. This hideaway was the only link to the hopeful young girl I used to be—the young woman with romantic notions and stars in her eyes. In the roaring tides and grainy sand, I found traces of that sparkling youth I'd locked away in the protective spaces of my soul. I pressed my body in the hot sand and allowed the waves to lap over my toes.

I pulled out my journal from my bag and contemplated why I allowed that lively girl to go away. I shouldn't have lost my sense of self, or let my dreams or aspirations go because I'd had an arranged marriage. I could've been the librarian I sought to be, but in its place, I worked the reception desk at the salon and trained under Noor to become a hairdresser for the money. I needed the income because I had to be the breadwinner due to my husband's illness. Did I really forgo all my hopes and dreams because he got sick? Partly, but my ambitions started being chiseled away slowly the moment my father insisted I marry Nabil. It was my wedding night that I discovered the art of disengagement. There's power in the ability to unplug and reconnect emotions. It was the only thing I had any control over from the moment I boarded the flight to Iraq.

My mom had packed my belongings for that entire trip, refusing to let me take any cotton panties or T-shirts and shorts—my favorite nightwear. Instead, she only allowed me long silk negligee sets with matching silk panties and bras. Everything had to fucking match. Tea-length summer dresses with matching cardigans and not one pair of jeans or slacks. I hadn't realized I'd hated dresses so much until that moment. She'd packed multiple ensembles for every day and night for the three weeks we were to be away. Then there was the dreadful wedding dress that encased my entire body in pure white satin, just in case anyone had any doubt of my virtue—the dress would remind them of my purity. If only they'd known my purity had been tainted before my wedding night.

Fresh tears streamed down my cheeks at the memory of Nabil's harsh drunken words and ill treatment of me. In retrospect, he was just as inexperienced and scared as me. He used whiskey for liquid courage but his being drunk only made matters worse.

My father and I stayed at Nabil's grandparents' home in Baghdad. I had been given my own room and I was pleased with the privacy. The bedroom had been nice, with comfortable European-style furniture and a balcony that led onto a beautiful rooftop garden. Unfortunately, for the wedding night, the in-laws had prepared a wedding night suite for Nabil and me to share. All my belongings were transferred into it, and I had no other choice but to change in the bathroom while Nabil waited right behind the closed door.

CHAPTER 16

I eased out of the satin ballgown and dressed in a white modest negligee. I surveyed my reflection in the mirror and a stranger stared back at me. My brown hair pooled around my shoulders in ringlets from hot rollers, my lips stained in a shade of pink I would have never chosen for myself. I was covered with so much satin and lace between the nightgown and robe that I barely could see the outline of my own frame. My mouth was dry, and tears shone in my red-rimmed eyes.

Taking a deep breath, I counted to three and exhaled. Resigned to my fate, I unlocked the bathroom door. Nabil sat on the gold-edged chair near the sliding door, still dressed in his white dress shirt, black slacks, and loafers from our wedding. He hadn't looked up when I'd entered but took a long pull of the amber drink, then tangled a hand in his black, unkempt hair. With a sullen face, he studied the contents of his glass. I took a moment to analyze his features—he was my husband, yet I hadn't had a moment to observe him without feeling like everyone was watching me. He had a narrow, long nose, a strong jawline, and large brown eyes. I wanted my body to respond to something about him—his eyes, lips, the way he tousled his hair, but nothing. Not a single reaction registered within me. I wasn't expecting the strong emotions I felt for Asher, but I hoped I'd feel a little flutter inside, at the very least. I slowly made my way to the bench at the foot of the bed and sat on my hands to hide my trembling fingers. I was chilled to the bone, as though my blood had turned to solid ice in my veins.

I didn't know Nabil at all. We'd barely spoken in the last week—family had always been around and anytime we found ourselves alone, he found hundreds of reasons to run for the hills.

His gaze finally found mine and traveled over my frame, deepening his scowl. "What are you wearing?"

His words jolted me from my observations and a whisper of caution trembled down my spine.

"My mom said I was supposed to wear this tonight." I knew how naive that sounded, but I was young.

He took another gulp of his drink before he stood and walked over to me. The aroma of liquor made my stomach turn sour. His sturdy hand gripped my arm and pulled me to my feet. My knees weakened. My ears rang, and my chest constricted. His mouth collided with mine. I nearly retched from the bitter taste of alcohol and smoke on his breath. His hands clumsily roamed my body, and something happened in my brain. A mental switch was extinguished. All cerebral circuits that had run rampant and flashed red throughout my heart and mind were immobilized. My desire to flee was suppressed. It wasn't gone. Somehow, I pressed pause on my emotions, and the tears that pooled in my eyes just moments ago evaporated. And when he mounted me, my body and mind were frozen.

Chapter 17

ASHER

"You were at the lawyer's office all this time?" Mama was seated in her normal spot on the couch, wearing head-to-toe black and holding a crystal rosary. The sorrow would have been clear in her sullen eyes and hollow cheeks even if she hadn't been dressed in customary mourning attire.

"Yes," I lied.

After the meeting with Davison, I'd been too rattled to go home and somehow found myself sitting between the two mounds of dirt that covered Bassam and Lydia's graves, his letter still clutched between my fingertips. A howl had torn from my lips and rattled me from the depths of my soul. It was the first time I just let go and let the grief flow free, unencumbered by bravado.

I was angry with God for taking my brother, livid for three helpless children who needed their parents. I hadn't known Lydia very well, but the few moments I'd spent with her, I truly adored her. She had this lightness in her eyes, the kind that came from deep down a person's soul. It was a shame that someone so loving wouldn't be able to share that light with her children and future grandchildren.

"What did he say?" Baba, who was merely a shell of the man he once was, handed my mother a cup of Turkish coffee and sat beside her. It was the first time I'd actually taken a good look at him in a long time. His once round belly had diminished, his hair all white and nearly completely gone, his extensive shoulders now frail, but it was his expression that was the most jarring difference. Before, he had an air of arrogance in his expression, but now, all that sat before me was a brokenhearted father.

I sat in the chair adjacent to my parents and tried to get comfortable, but my limbs were numb. The house was quiet because I'd taken the kids to camp on the way to my appointment. It was the perfect opportunity to talk without being overheard. The last thing I wanted was to damage them more than they already had been.

"Bassam and Lydia left everything to the children and assigned me as their trustee."

My father nodded and took a sip of his steaming mug. "That is to be expected."

"He left me a letter," I said.

My parents both sat up a little straighter, but it was Mama's unsteady voice that spoke first. "Just for you?"

"Yes." I swallowed hard. "He asked me to adopt the kids and raise them as my own."

"Can I read it?" Tears welled in Mama's eyes.

I nodded and handed her the letter. "He mentioned you and Baba in there."

"That is the best for them." Baba's hand shook as he placed his cup on the coffee table. "Your mother and I..." His speech wavered. "We are too old to chase the kids—and in case anything happens to us, they will be more secure with you."

CHAPTER 17

"I honestly hadn't considered staying. What do I know about raising children? I didn't realize until this past week what it really meant to have children. I assumed I'd get everything settled with the house and finances and return to work." My voice was uneven.

For the first time in my life, I found understanding in Baba's eyes when he looked at me. He understood my position, the frustration, the fear, the insurmountable grief. For once, we were on the same side. Same page of the same story, and it was comforting somehow.

"But this is your brother's dying wish," Mama said.

"I know." I covered my face with my hands. "I still have eight months left on my current contract." Unless I was dishonorably discharged for the incident, but I kept that last little nugget to myself. The last thing my parents needed to worry about was me being dishonorably discharged or something more drastic.

"When do you have to leave?" Baba asked.

"I'm on leave for eight more days, and I'm not sure when I can return to Michigan. I'm going to retire at the end of my enlistment in eight months." Again, all this was pending a hearing, but I was trying to hold on to the fleeting scraps of faith I had left.

"We will figure it out. Your mother and I can do our best to care for them while you are away."

It was still astonishing to me that my father was for once the voice of reason, and I had just over a week to figure it all out. How was I going to get my life together to essentially become a single dad of three unruly, heartbroken kids?

"The kids' things need to be moved here before you leave, and the house should also be cleared out..." My father's voice was a near whisper. "This way, you could settle other matters virtually."

"Yes, it might be easier on the kids to have all their things here. They wouldn't feel so displaced," I agreed.

"I can help you," Baba said.

I looked over at the shattered man. It was like he'd been taken over by some parasite, an invasion of the body snatchers. My father was so agreeable and understanding. I wasn't used to it. "No, Baba, I have it. I will get Khalid and Ragheed to help me."

My father nodded. "They are good men."

"Abni, why don't you go lie down for a while before you have to pick up the kids." Mama's voice brought me back from my distracted thoughts. "You look tired."

"Yeah, I think I might." I stood and kissed her forehead, but before I even got the chance to place my head on the fluffy pillow, my cell rang in my pocket.

I fetched out my phone and my pulse raced when Landover Elementary appeared on my screen. My hand trembled as I hit the green button to answer.

"Hello."

"Can I speak to Mr. Asher George?" The voice on the other end was calm and controlled, but it didn't ease the growing turmoil in me.

"Speaking."

"Hi, this is Miss Thorn from Landover Elementary. How are you?"

"Are the kids okay?" I cut her off because my emotional state couldn't take any more pleasantries.

"Yes, they are all fine but..." She hesitated, and I heard an audible sigh on the other end before she continued, "There has been some concern regarding Alec's behavior."

I exhaled. "You do know that he just lost his parents."

"I do and I'm so sorry. I didn't want to call,

but..." She hesitated again. "I don't have a problem working with him on his anger issues, and I have been, but today he hit another boy in the face with a closed fist and there have to be consequences for his actions."

Fuck, this kid was tougher to deal with than my naval training. "Is the other kid okay?"

"He's got a shiner and really angry parents, but he's fine."

"Please don't tell me you're kicking him out of the program?" I pleaded.

"Not exactly. He will be suspended for three days, and the principal advised that he should be picked up from camp as soon as possible."

"I understand. Any advice for a struggling uncle on how to manage this?"

"He's normally a sweet kid. This behavior is all new and it's because he's hurting. The only advice I have is to help him find new ways to channel his anger and get him to talk about his feelings. I think he's just bottling it all inside and that's why he's lashing out."

"Thanks, I'll try that." It sounded like great advice, but where the hell did I start? After assuring her that I'd be picking him up in a few, I returned to the living room.

"Why didn't you nap?" Mama was still in the

CHAPTER 17

same spot I'd left her, but Baba had left.

"Alec got in a fight today at school and is suspended for three days."

"Mother Mary, give us strength." She made the sign of the cross. "What are we going to do with this boy?"

I sighed. "I'm not sure, but I'm going to spend time with him alone for a couple hours. Maybe I'll get him to talk to me."

"What about his siblings? Will you leave them there until their usual time? Do you want Baba to pick them up for you?"

"No." I glanced at the time, and it was just after noon. "I'll get them and maybe take them all to dinner."

If this was going to be my life, I'd better pull up my socks and see if it was even something I could possibly do on my own.

"Good idea. I have people coming to pay their respects around five and that would be really helpful."

Then the panic set in and continued with me until I reached the school. I called the only single dad I knew.

"Hey, Ash." Niles's voice was both comforting and painful all at once. He had been Bass's best friend.

"Hey, I need advice, and you're the only person I know who can help me." I spoke quickly, not stopping until all the words were out, everything from Alec's anger issues, the teacher calling, the upcoming hearing, and finally my concerns over how to handle it all.

"Shit, he gave the kid a shiner?"

"Yeah, it's bad and I have no clue how to deal with it."

"It's tough, but I think the teacher is right about finding something to help channel the anger into something positive. You were a pissed-off teenager, what helped you?"

"Boot camp...think it's too early to sign him up for the Navy?"

He laughed. "Just a little. Today, make him do physical work and get him to talk to you. We can think of something else later."

"The kid is six. What kind of physical work?"

"The church has a cleanup crew every day between twelve and three—you can start there. He can wipe down pews, but he is a kid so no longer than an hour. Then take him fishing."

"Yeah, that might just work, but I have no idea where all the fishing gear is right now."

"Use mine and just go out on our dock," Niles

said. "It's all in my parents' garage."

"You're a lifesaver, Niles."

"Anything you need, I'm here."

Armed with a battle plan, I picked up a very brooding and angry Alec from the principal's office and headed to church. He had my temper and unruly attitude when things didn't go his way. He was playing the part of the victim very well, and I was still trying to figure out how I was going to have this discussion with him.

"Why are we at church?" Alec's tone was bitter, almost too acidic to be coming from a six-year-old boy.

"Because today we are going to volunteer."

"What does that mean?"

"You'll see."

We parked the car and headed toward the door. I could feel the resentment radiating from his little body. The kid had taut shoulders, a stiff upper lip, and his strides were strong and wide like he was walking onto a battlefield. He was just a child. How could he physically carry that much aggression?

It wasn't long before I found someone to give me the supplies. I led him to the front pew and handed him a rag and spray bottle.

"What am I supposed to do with that?" He

eyed the rag like it was a snake ready to bite.

"Clean the seats."

"What are you going to do?" He looked at me with suspicion in his dark eyes.

"Help." I moved to the other end of the same pew, sprayed a little of the disinfectant, and wiped. He rolled his eyes and mimicked me. I observed him from the corner of my eye. At first, there was pure irritation in his face while we worked, but the longer we cleaned, the tension in his shoulders eased, and his features relaxed. It was as though with every wipe of the cloth, a little more annoyance would evaporate from him. We worked together, and within the space of an hour, we were done cleaning every single pew.

"Look at that. These benches have never looked so good." Father James's blue eyes sparkled with amusement. He was a little guy with naturally blond hair and a kind face. And if I remembered correctly, a funny personality.

"Thanks, Father. We really enjoyed the quiet time working."

"I think you guys make a great team." He bent down to Alec's level. "How are you doing, Alec?"

Alec shrugged. "Okay."

CHAPTER 17

"You did an impressive job, buddy. Jesus is very proud of you. Why don't you head over to the fridge in the kitchen and get you and your uncle a drink for your hard work."

Alec nodded, but before he left, he glanced at me. "You're waiting for me, right?"

This kid. Where the hell, I mean heck, would I go? I really had to watch my swear words—even mental ones in church. "Yes, sir." I bit back a laugh.

"That one is something," Father James said. "He always gave the Sunday school teachers a run for their money."

"Father, I can only imagine. He is truly going to be the one to break me."

It was still strange calling him Father, considering we went to high school together, but after the wise and kind eulogy he gave Bass and Lydia, I couldn't help the mad respect I had for him. He was truly what our church and community needed. Unlike the priest of my parents' generation, he understood the struggles of growing up in the modern age. He made it cool to come to church.

"How are you doing, Asher?"

"Hanging in there, I guess. It's just a lot to deal with, and I don't know if I'm the right man to do it."

He clasped my shoulder. "God doesn't give us anything we can't handle—pray to him, and he will guide you."

How would I tell Father James, a priest, that I was angry with God right now? That I found it hard to turn to him because he was the one who took my brother away from his kids and from me.

"It's all right to be angry. God knows your heart." It was as though he read my mind. "Just know that despite your anger, he is with you every step of the way."

Tears threatened to appear, and I inhaled a jagged breath.

"Anyhoo, if you need anything, the church and our entire community is behind you." He released my shoulder and walked away just as Alec returned with two juice boxes.

"Now what?" The edge in his tone had calmed as he handed me a drink.

"Let's go wash up. I have something else planned."

"More cleaning?"

"No, something else."

"What?"

"You'll see."

CHAPTER 17

The little demon spawn rolled his eyes to the back of his head but didn't say a word the whole way to the beach. When we reached Niles's house, all the questions started again, but I refused to answer until Auntie Nuha opened the garage for me. I picked up the gear and waved to Amoo Manni, who was rearranging the solar lights around the Virgin Mary statue.

"We're going fishing?" Alec's little face lit up, and in his excited expression, Lydia's face appeared. The light I loved in her eyes shone in his, but he'd been scowling so much, I'd nearly missed it.

"Yeah."

After settling on the dock with our fishing lines in the lake and the poles firmly in the nifty holds, I asked quietly, "Do you know why I had to pick you up early today?"

"Because I hit Jake in the face."

"Why did you hit him?" Though hitting wasn't appropriate no matter the circumstance, I wanted to know the reasoning behind his action.

"He wouldn't pass me the ball."

"You know it was wrong to hit him?" I did my best to keep my voice even and emotionless.

Though the bluntness in his words made me want to laugh.

"Yes." His voice broke.

"Then why did you do it?"

"I don't know. I got mad and it happened." Tears started to stream down his cheeks, and my muscles tightened.

"You get mad a lot lately. Do you know why?"

He sniffed and wiped his eyes with the back of his hand. "I miss my mom and dad and I don't know what I did to make them go away."

Well, shit. He thought they hadn't come back because of something he did. So much of his behavior was explained in just that one realization. He blamed himself.

"Oh, buddy no." I reached over and pulled him onto my lap. He buried his little face in my shoulder, and sobs escaped on choked breaths. And I'm man enough to say I wept along with him. I don't think my soul could tolerate any more pain.

"It wasn't your fault." I said the words over and over until he finally stilled in my arms. "Listen to me. You didn't do anything wrong. Do you understand me?"

"But why didn't they come home?"

"Because your parents are such special people that God wanted them with him in Heaven."

"It's not fair."

Truer words were never spoken. Death and the accompanying sorrow absolutely weren't fair, but for a child to experience it was truly unjust. The bell on the fishing pole jiggled, signaling a catch and pulling us from our lowest point of the day. Alec jumped from my lap, and excitement danced in his tear-streaked face at the prospect of catching the fish. I wanted to bask in his delight, and for the rest of the afternoon, I got to know my nephew a little better.

Chapter 18

MARIAM

The stench of tobacco, whiskey, and desperation lingered in the air of the Riverfront Casino in Detroit. Slot machines clinked, beeped, and flashed with the allure of easy money. Unease filled me. I'd much rather be at home with my book, a bottle of my favorite rosé from my wine subscription, and my comfy cotton T-shirt, shorts, and fluffy socks. No bra, and for damn sure, no heels. Instead, my feet ached from the four-inch red-bottomed stilettos Farrah had insisted I wear tonight.

"My baby's free." Farrah hustled over to an empty slot machine and slid into the stool.

I inspected the screen filled with baby pandas, a tic-tac-toe board, and a colorful assortment of flowers.

"This is your baby?" I laughed.

"Yes, it's my lucky machine." She inserted her membership card and a hundred-dollar bill into the machine. The screen sang to life with a cartoonish tune, and baby pandas danced with moves that mimicked the 80s.

"What makes it lucky, the cute little pandas?" I teased.

Noor walked over and handed me a chilled tall glass of Tito's and tonic. "Don't laugh. This bitch won nine hundred and fifty dollars on that game last week while we were waiting for our table." She sat in the seat beside Farrah and placed a fifty in the machine. Her machine was one of those old-school ones with the sevens.

"How did I get here again?" I plopped into the seat on the other side of Farrah and flexed my tender pinky toe in my shoe.

"Because we had an intervention and

dragged you out." Farrah's fingers were swiftly pressing the SPIN button, and her big gray eyes were peeled to the screen.

"I didn't need an intervention." I rolled my eyes and surveyed the slot machine at my seat. Fairies and jewels twinkled on repeat on the screen and the words *big jackpot $15,454* flashed in hot pink neon lights to entice players.

"You for sure needed one," Farrah said.

"I agree. Even your daughter thinks you need to live it up some. Now, put some money in the slot and drink your liquor. The party is just beginning," Noor said.

"When are our reservations?" The digital clock on my Apple Watch read 9:34 p.m.

"Nine forty-five," Noor said.

I sipped on the straw from my drink and fished out a fifty-dollar bill from my purse. "Can't beat 'em, join 'em."

I had to admit, I was having an enjoyable time. There was something very exciting about the chirping game, the twenty-five cents to two-dollar gains coupled with the R&B music playing in the background. Not to mention the relaxed feeling I was getting from the Tito's and the laugh-out-loud stories courtesy of Farrah's sexy-time adventures with her new guy, Kal.

"Wait." Noor put her drink on the little side table. "Are you telling me you actually came eight times in one night?"

"Yes, ma'am." Farrah's cheeks flashed red, and she fanned her face with her hands. "Damn, I can't wait to do it again."

"Do what again?" The sexy, smoky male voice caught me off guard, and my fingers fumbled the keys on the mechanism. I twisted in my seat and observed the tall, bronzed, and gorgeous man hugging Farrah from behind. Must have been Kal, based on the description she'd shared.

"I'll tell you later, babe." She kissed him on the lips. His smile was mischievous but his dark gaze was loving.

He greeted Noor like an old friend before his brown stare landed on me in what seemed to be a double take, but he covered it with a generous smile before he glanced behind him.

"This beauty is Mariam," Farrah said.

Kal's strong grip clasped my own. "It's nice to finally meet you."

"Likewise." I smiled and glimpsed two men behind him. My eyes traveled to one of the men. He was attractive—buzzed brown hair and bright blue eyes. He was built in the same massive form as Kal, but slightly taller. There was something so oddly familiar about him, like I'd seen him somewhere. He glanced at the man behind him who looked at something on his phone and wasn't paying any attention to us. My body reacted before my mind even registered Asher. Awareness weaved down my chest and spooled in my belly.

"These are my Navy buddies, Ragheed and Asher."

Ragheed stepped closer and shook my hand in his robust grip. I realized this one was the man who'd been with Asher at the kids' soccer game. "Nice to meet you."

My breath caught when Asher's onyx stare found my own. Heat burned my cheeks, and my mouth went dry. What was it about this man that awakened my entire body with one glance? My hormones raged around him. Everything finally came together in my head. Farrah's Navy hottie *was* friends with Asher.

I said *hi* quickly, then turned my attention to my drink. Taking a bigger slurp than I intended, I hit the SPIN button on my slot machine. The glass nearly tumbled from my fingers when my whole slot machine flashed with red lights. An alarm bell chimed and wouldn't stop blaring from the damn thing. Everyone around me started to clap and cheer, but I had no idea what the hell was going on.

"I think you hit the jackpot." Asher had moved beside me in a protective stance, and I shivered from the closeness.

"I was just playing the minimum bet." The credits on the corner of the screen soared higher, and I watched in disbelief. The number escalated. $6000, $8000, $10000, $12000, and just kept growing.

"You played max bet and 200 lines." Farrah chimed in.

"What? No." Then I remembered I hadn't actually paid attention to which button I'd hit, and a laugh escaped me. "Shit."

Finally, the machine stopped making sounds but the lights still flashed around the words *WINNER $15,454.* "What now?" I looked at the device, afraid to screw anything up.

"Girl, cash out." Farrah high-fived me. "Now that's what you call beginner's luck."

An attendant, a burly bald-headed man with a serious expression and dressed in all black came over to validate the machine. While he fiddled with the slot machine, my body tingled with adrenaline, and after a few moments, he gave me the "all clear" to claim my winnings.

"Okay, you can cash out," the attendant said.

"How?" My insides vibrated from the adrenaline rush. I'd never won anything before, and the excitement of having this extra money after making plans to put my savings into a new business seemed like kismet. The truth was, I felt guilty for not leaving any extra money for Tamara, and now this was going to get deposited into her account for emergencies.

"Let me." Asher reached over me, his hard chest pressed against my arm, and a current licked from the heat of his frame right to the center of me. I nearly sighed from the contact but did everything I could to disguise the longing that raked over my body.

He pressed a button on the panel, and the machine spit out a gray ticket. "Congratulations." He beamed at me and handed me the slip.

"Dinner and drinks are on me tonight." I laughed.

"Let's get this cashed in. I'll come with you," Asher said.

"Our reservation is ready, just meet us at the

restaurant." Farrah grinned and clasped Kal by his outstretched hand.

I sat shell-shocked for a moment watching them walk away. "Did that really just happen?"

He gripped my hand and pulled me from the chair. "Sure did. Now put that ticket in your purse so you don't drop it," Asher said.

I did as he said and zipped up my crossbody. I was astonished by all the congratulations from strangers as we walked to the cashier. People cheered and high-fived as we walked through the rows of players that must have seen my win. It was like a whole community of people was supportive and fascinated by my luck. One older gentleman asked me to touch his machine for a little of my good fortune.

"Did you know our friends were dating?" Asher asked.

"I wondered if Kal and you were friends when Farrah wanted to introduce me to one of his good-looking Chaldean Navy buddies from Michigan."

"You think I'm good-looking, huh?" He puffed out his chest.

"Please, like you don't know you're hotter than fire and brimstone."

Asher's hand gently grasped my arm and stalled me. His firm and intense gaze burned into my own. "And you are still the most extraordinary woman I've ever met."

A sense of overall weightlessness whirled around me. "Thanks."

His eyes softened and his hand slid from the hold on my arm to the small of my back and we continued the walk through the casino.

"Taking a break from the kiddos tonight?"

"Yeah, I needed it—Alec was suspended from camp for three days."

"Oh no. What did he do?"

"Gave a kid a black eye."

"That boy is so angry."

"Yeah, but I'm going to have some one-on-one time with him while the other two are at camp for the next two days. I need to find something to keep him channeling his emotions in a more positive way and burn off that aggression."

"You control your temper better these days. How do you do it?"

"Niles asked me the same question." His unguarded laugh was rich, raspy, and it sent signals to my core like a mating call. "Was I really that aggressive?"

"No, you just were stubborn and bullheaded if you didn't get what you wanted."

"Stubborn, huh?" He flashed me the same mischievous grin from long ago, and I lost my footing. I stumbled with those horrible shoes and nearly toppled over. I clutched his wide forearm to steady my feet, and heat licked up my spine when his other arm clasped my waist to help keep me upright.

"Look at God reminding you to be humble." His lips were so close to my own that I nearly moaned from the much-needed contact. *No, no, no.* That couldn't happen. I released his arm like it was on fire and took a large step backward.

I gathered my wits and did my best to hide my attraction. He was the match to my flame and even after nearly twenty-six years, I still burned for him, body, mind, and soul.

I cleared my throat. "Where is the cashier?"

"Right behind you." His all-knowing stare searched my face. "Let's get this cashed in and you can buy me a drink."

"Yes, drinks all around." I needed one. Something in my hands to keep me from climbing him like a big tree.

We made our way back to the restaurant and

found our group in full party swing. The table was covered with empty shot glasses and a server was making her way back to the table with another tray filled when we arrived.

"Yella, bitch...take a shot." Farrah slid a glass over to me and then another one toward Ash. "You look like you could use one too, my man."

"You have no idea." He glanced at me, and I nodded.

He lifted the glass, and I took mine. "Bottoms-up." The bitter burn of the tequila warmed me from throat to belly and I nearly coughed before I had finished the entire shot.

Balminess traveled through my body, and I eased into my chair. "It's been a long time since I've had tequila."

"Was the last time when you..." Noor looked around the table and then back at me. "Were you with us?"

I thanked the heavens she had the sense not to disclose the most embarrassing moment of my life in front of the guys.

"Yes," I mumbled.

"Oh..." Farrah covered her red-stained lips with her hand. Her "I remember" was followed by a loud "Ha-ha."

I gave her my death stare and demanded

with my expression to not share.

"I'm not saying anything, promise," Farrah said.

What I didn't need was these guys and especially Asher hearing the horrors of my first attempt at a one-night stand after my husband died. It was a complete disaster, and the thought of that night made me want to hide under the table.

"Sounds like an interesting story." Kal leaned in closer to Farrah. "Tell us, what did Mariam do?"

"Oh no." I waved my hands madly. "That's vaulted information."

Farrah nodded in agreement. "Yeah, you have to be part of the club to get that info."

"I used to be your best friend. You're not going to tell even me?" Asher leaned in closer, and his warm breath tickled my earlobe and teased my senses.

"You're the last person I would tell." Heat pooled between my legs.

"Oh, it's got to be bad," Asher said.

"You have no idea." Noor made a retching expression and covered her mouth.

I yelped and hopped off my stool. "Stop that." But I couldn't help the laugh that escaped my lips.

"I'm not doing anything." Noor looked down at her finger. "I just have a bit of dirt under my fingernail."

Ragheed looked at Noor and back at me. "You threw up, big deal—not like you threw up on a dude or something."

"Oh my God. I need another shot." I waved my hand in the air.

"Come on, don't leave us hanging," Ragheed pressed.

"Yeah, I feel like you girls are leaving us men out in the cold." Kal's gaze wasn't looking at me but directly at Asher.

"Yeah, how do we get into that vault group of yours if you're not open and honest with us?" Asher asked.

"Well, we have initiation questions. If you answer them open and honestly, we will allow you entry into our club," I said.

"And you will tell us all the details of the last time you drank tequila?" Asher asked. "His eyes sparkled with amusement. He turned to Ragheed and Kal. "Fellas, I'm game. You?"

"Hell, yeah, I have nothing to hide or be embarrassed about." Ragheed wiggled his eyebrows at Noor and turned to me.

"Yeah, me too. I'm an open book." Kal pulled Farrah into his arms. "This girl has me spilling all my deepest shit anyway."

My stomach knotted. I hadn't thought they would agree to share dirt of their own. I glanced nervously at Farrah and Noor. "I don't know which question to choose."

"Oh, I do." Farrah pulled away from Kal's embrace. "First let me flag over the waitress."

After she'd shown we needed another round to our server, she rolled up the sleeves of her fitted black top and rubbed her hands together like she had a master plan brewing.

"First time you had sex—how old were you, with whom did you have sex, and where did the act occur?"

My pulse raced. I knew Asher's answer already, had replayed it in my mind a million times. "Maybe a different question?" I glanced at Asher and his stare bored into mine.

"Oh, I have more, but this is the starter round." Farrah didn't get my subtle hint to change the line of inquiry, and I stewed in my seat.

"Are you ladies telling us your stories too?" Kal asked.

"Absolutely not. This is your admission to

the vault group, not ours." Noor's tone was matter-of-fact, and I nodded my head in agreement.

"I see, okay, well, I'll go first," Kal said. "Sixteen. My friend's sister and me in the basement of their house while my buddy was in the shower."

"Younger sister?" Ragheed asked.

"Nope, older, by like two years." Kal shrugged. "She sure as hell taught me a few things."

"Damn, well, mine isn't too wild. It was my high school girlfriend, I was eighteen and it was prom night in the hotel room—Stay Inn," Ragheed said.

All eyes turned to Asher. My mouth went dry, and the blood rushed to my ears.

"Your turn, Asher," Farrah pestered, not knowing how badly I didn't want to hear what he had to say. How the words uttered aloud would just open another gash into the past neither of us had time to explore.

He leaned back in his chair and crossed his arms, but his eyes were still on me. "Eighteen, home visiting after boot camp. On the beach…" He paused and if it was even possible, his stare intensified. My legs quivered. "With my high school crush."

"Oh shit…" Ragheed's voice broke the spell of Asher's gaze, and I glanced away. My body trembled from the force of Asher's full attention on me. Was it getting hotter? Had all the air been suctioned out of the bar, or was it just me who was having trouble breathing?

I glanced up to see Ragheed watching us. He knew. I suspected they'd all figured it out, but no one else alluded to knowing anything.

"Okay, next round." Farrah smacked her hands together. "Name the most romantic thing you've done for someone and also, the naughtiest thing someone has done for you?"

"Hot air balloon ride, and a blowjob while I drove a convertible. In traffic," Ragheed said.

"Nice." Kal turned toward Farrah. "Baby, you know I'm not the romantic type, but I guess rose petals and a candlelight dinner. For the naughty thing, I can't stop thinking about that dance you gave me the other night when…"

"Okay, we can finish that answer in private." Farrah clasped her hand over his lips before he shared all their sexual exploits with the group.

"Asher," Noor said. "Tell us your most naughty and romantic."

Asher cleared his throat. "A foursome and a

love letter."

"Now that juicy intel. Spill about the love letter," Noor said.

"I want to hear about the foursome," Ragheed said.

Noor rolled her eyes. "Typical."

Asher bit his lip. "A woman I dated in my twenties was into group activities, and I was a willing participant."

"Nice," Ragheed said.

Kal gave him a high five.

"And the love letter?" Noor, a romantic much like me, persisted.

His eyes darkened. "I don't know, she lost the letter."

My love letter. I averted my gaze and shifted in my seat.

"Oh, that's horrible." Noor put her hand over her chest.

Asher let out a heavy sigh and I felt his arm wrap around the back of my chair. "It's cool. It was a long time ago."

The tension in my shoulders eased at his sweet gesture, and I relaxed into my seat.

"Okay, we shared. It's your turn, Mariam. What happened that night with the tequila?" Kal broke the tension that still surrounded us.

CHAPTER 18

I didn't even chance a glance at Asher.

During the intensity of Asher's admission, the server had returned to our table and a double shot was sitting in front of me. I held out my finger for him to wait and downed the drink. If I was going to spill all tonight, I needed to be heavily intoxicated.

"It was two years after my husband's death, and one thing was for sure—I didn't want a relationship. But these two convinced me I should have a one-night stand while we were in Vegas for a hair show."

"The girl hadn't had sex for like years, since her husband was sick for a long time before he died," Farrah explained.

I turned to see Asher watching me, but I ignored his stare and picked up his shot glass. "I'll order you another one."

He nodded. I swallowed the rest of the drink in one large gulp, and this time there wasn't a burn, but sweet soothing warmth circled me from head to toe.

"Okay, so I met a guy, he was cute and had game, but it might have been the tequila that gave the illusion of all this charm. Anyway, we go back to his room and start kissing, and my stomach started to burn. Acid started to move up my throat and I tried to push him off, but I was too late and..." I giggled, the tequila doing its job of calming and concealing the mortification of this story. "And..." I shuddered. "I threw up all over him."

The guys roared with laughter. Well, Ragheed and Kal did. I didn't chance a glance at Asher. I didn't think I could bear any eye contact with him now.

"Wait, that's not even the worst of it." Farrah waved her arms eagerly. "She had alcohol poisoning obviously, from all the tequila. This one"—she pointed at me—"runs into his bathroom and locks herself in for an hour. The poor guy used a sheet to get the puke off him because she wouldn't open the bathroom door."

"So, you just left the guy hanging?" Kal said.

"Yeah, after I finished getting sick, I called these knuckleheads, and they came and got me. I was mortified. It was literally the most embarrassed I've ever been in my life."

"He was a dick anyway. You were visibly drunk, and he took you back to his room." Asher's voice startled me.

"True that, brother," Ragheed said.

"It wasn't his fault. I was using it as liquid

CHAPTER 18

courage, and that was stupid on my end."

My eyes found Asher's and black ice stared back at me. "You don't need a drink for bravery. You just need the backbone to go after what it is you want."

I flinched. His words were as sharp as glass and sliced down to my very soul. His comment was a jab at the fact I'd never had the courage to go after what I wanted, too scared to fight for my own wants and desires. Too frightened to go against my father when he arranged my marriage and too afraid to admit that I was in love with another man—not just another man, but Asher George, the beautiful, brooding man who always had my heart.

"It's easier said than done." My voice trembled on my words.

"Nothing is standing in your way anymore."

"This conversation is getting a little deep for my mood tonight." Farrah's voice broke the spell of Asher's words.

"I need carbs," I mumbled. "Lots of carbs."

But my mind remembered all too well the moment I had courage twenty-six years ago, and if I closed my eyes, I could still feel his mouth on mine. He had been right, there was a moment in time that I had just taken what

I wanted, and as I glanced at him from below my lashes, I wondered if I had the courage to do it again.

Chapter 19

TAMARA

"Tampon. Tampon. Tampon," Lauren chanted, each 'tampon' hitting an octave higher as she fumbled inside her duffle bag. "I think I forgot..." She continued to sing in her best imitation of an R&B artist. "...them in the car. Bianca. Can you? You. Get them for me?" Even though Lauren had an amazing singing voice, the singing random phrases could get old real fast.

"Absolutely not." Bianca sat on the edge of the

bed and kicked off her sneakers.

"Oh, please. Oh, please. Bianca," Lauren sang.

"Use mine." Lena tossed her a hot pink package. "For the love of all things holy, please stop singing every syllable."

"Thanks. These will work for now, but I like the unscented ones better." Lauren caught the package and hustled to the bathroom. "I'll give you a break from my musical renditions."

"You guys already have your periods. Aren't you early?" Tamara's heartbeat raced.

"I started this morning." Bianca fell back on the bed curled in a fetal position.

"Day two for me." Lena cradled her belly. "Why did we decide to vacation on our periods again?"

"That's because we booked this hotel last year, and I'm on day four—it's not heavy for me at all," Lauren called from the bathroom.

"I haven't gotten mine yet..." Tamara's stomach sank. They were all on the same cycle, normally. Tamara spent so much time with her cousins that their periods had synchronized in their teens and stayed that way. She quickly searched for her cycle application on her phone. The blood rushed to her ears and her finger trembled on the pink and red icon before clicking it open. Her gut twisted in knots when the number seven appeared with the words LATE in all caps beside it.

"I'm late seven days." The blood rushed to Tamara's ears.

"It's okay, you've been late before," Bianca said.

"You have been using protection with Cross, right?" Lena sat beside her.

"Yes, of course." Her mind ventured to the second week of their relationship over a month ago, and a vivid memory of an unplanned coupling in the shower came to mind. "But..."

"You use protection every time, right? My mom swears the Shammas women could get pregnant if a man breathes on us." Lena shook her head. "She talks about pregnancy like it's something you can catch."

"Once, in the shower, no...but he pulled out."

"It's going to be fine. I'm sure your period will be here any minute." Lena held Tamara's hand and squeezed.

"Yeah, you're right, I've been late plenty of times." Tamara's tone wasn't as convincing as her words.

"Let's get our swimsuits on and focus on our

summer tans and maybe one of you can get me a drink," Bianca said.

"The girl is young but wise," Lauren said.

"You'll get me a frozen daiquiri?" Bianca's eyes lit up.

"Yes, a virgin frozen daiquiri. One for you and one for the possible prego," Laura said.

"Oh my God, no. I'm not pregnant." Tamara covered her face.

"Yella, let's just enjoy our trip and pray that Tamara's period remembers to show up today." Lena started to change into her bikini.

Tamara did the same and noticed the bathing suit top was a bit snugger than it had been the last time she'd worn it, but it was Lena's "Holy crap, your boobs have gotten big" that made her want to hide under the pillows. God, please. She couldn't be pregnant.

Chapter 20

Mariam

I was shocked when Asher decided to drive me home. I'd been about to call an Uber. He insisted he needed to leave as well since the kids were early risers. Of course, Farrah and Noor—along with Ragheed and Kal—had no intention of keeping the night short.

Even though I'd eaten a good dinner, I was still intoxicated when I got in his car, and I fell asleep on the ride home. Asher's warm hand rubbed my arm.

"Mariam, you're home." His voice was a soft whisper on my skin.

"My eyes fluttered open to see Asher had already gotten out of the driver's side and moved over to mine. The door was open, and he had a gentle hand on my shoulder.

"I'm sorry," I said. "I feel like a jerk for falling asleep."

"You looked like you needed it."

"I think I did, but now I feel completely refreshed."

He reached for my hand and helped me out of the car. His touch set my flesh ablaze, and it ran throughout my entire body. My legs were somewhat still asleep, and I staggered out of the car, but his firm grip on the small of my back kept me upright all the way to my front door. His strong arms eased away from me, and my stomach sank. I didn't want this time with him to end, but he had already started to move away from the front step and toward the car.

"You have a really nice house."

"Thanks..." I fumbled with my keys, desperately trying to find a reason for him to stay. "I think I'll make some chai. Would you like some?"

"Maybe another time."

"Okay." My eyes dropped as I inspected my shoes. "I better get inside."

"Mariam…" My name was raw on his tongue.

I looked up to see he had moved inches away from me and his eyes burned with hunger. "If I come inside, we wouldn't just have chai. We would pick up where we left off twenty-six years ago, and I just can't allow that to happen while you're intoxicated."

I felt my pulse in my throat. My whole body yearned for his touch. I reached out and caressed his cheek. "I want that."

He closed his eyes and pressed his face into my palm. "Mariam, what exactly do you want?"

"I want you…" The thirst in my tone surprised me. I'd never been able to voice my longing for him out loud.

His lips teased my inner palm with a lingering kiss, and his dark eyes stared into mine. "I've wanted to hear those words from you for a very long time, despite trying really hard to forget you."

His words were a sharp blade to my pride. He'd tried to forget me, and I'd held on to the memories of us like a security blanket. They were the memories that warmed my soul on the darkest days of my life.

I averted my gaze away from his. "I'm so sorry."

His warm hands cradled my cheeks. "Look at me."

I hesitated for a moment before locking eyes with him. "I've always understood why you didn't fight for us, I just hated it, hated..." He shook his head and looked up at the sky.

"You hated me for not fighting, I get it." I tried to pull away, but his arms locked around my waist, holding me against him.

"I never hated you. I fucking loved you."

"And now?"

He licked his lips and closed the space between us. "I think I'm still in love with you."

"Kiss me." I wanted his lips on me like my next breath depended on it. The need to have his mouth over mine was as though my life force would wither up and die if he didn't.

He pressed his forehead against mine. "No."

Embarrassment washed over me, and I stumbled away from him, fumbling with my keys to open the door. My hands trembled too much to get the key in the hole.

"Goddammit." Asher's arms wrapped around my waist and pulled me flush against him. My back and ass pressed against his body, and I melted into his touch.

"Do you know how hard it is for me to walk away?" His hand slid over the curve of my hip, and his warm breath tickled my ear.

"Seems like it's easy for you," I panted. My entire body was burning for him.

He spun me around, and before I knew it, his lips were on mine. Kissing me with a passion I had only read about in books. His hands in my hair, his body against mine, caging me between him and my front door. My fingers greedily slipped under his shirt and caressed warm, solid muscle. I wasn't sure how long we stood there, but it wasn't long enough. He placed his forehead against mine again, his breath as shallow as my own.

"So does that mean you want to come in?" I asked.

"Nope... You had your liquid courage tonight."

He picked up the keys that had somehow landed on the ground, unlocked my door, and ushered me inside. I stumbled through my front door in a dreamlike state... I was still drunk off the tequila and the mind-blowing kiss we'd just shared. I had fantasized about this moment for so long that my body was floating from pure adrenaline.

"Meet me at our spot tomorrow at one p.m. if you really want to give us a fair chance."

"Ash."

He turned on the middle step of my porch, and I nearly staggered from the emotions I found in his eyes.

"I'll see you tomorrow at one at our spot."

His face lit up, and traces of the boy I loved appeared. "Our spot."

I watched him get in the car and pull away before I closed the door. Memories of our last encounter at "our spot" came to me as easily as if it were yesterday. That memory had been my source of both comfort and pain for so many years.

It was the night before my father and I had flown to Iraq. I was climbing out of my skin—crying and grieving for my lost freedom. My father had taken my choices and was forcing me to not only get married to a stranger, but in my eyes, he had taken away any chance of a happy life. That was when I saw Asher walking past my house. It had been weeks, eight long

CHAPTER 20

weeks since I'd laid eyes on him, and the betrayal I had felt when he left for the Navy without saying goodbye flooded my common sense. I climbed out of my window and followed him all the way to our spot on the beach. The little stretch of sand and water hidden below a slight hill had been Asher's hideaway, and mine, for many years.

"Why did you follow me, Mariam?" I was surprised when he spoke.

"Why did you leave without saying goodbye?" My own words were bitter on my lips.

He whirled on me and then closed the distance between us. "Are you kidding me? You really don't know?"

"I...no, I don't." I stuttered on my words. I'd never seen him so angry before.

"Well, if you hadn't lost"—he made air quotes with his fingers at the word "lost"—"the letter, you would know." He rubbed his freshly buzzed head.

"I would know what?" My pulse raced.

"Nothing, forget it. Go home."

My feet started moving of their own accord. I wrapped my arms around his neck and placed my lips over his, kissing him with every ounce of love I held inside. For once, I didn't care. I was bold and went after what I wanted for the first time in my life. I wanted him.

He quickly responded to my touch, and we were a tangled mess of fumbled caresses and strokes. On the ground, he kissed and tasted every inch of me—my mouth, my breasts, and between my legs until he shattered me into a million pieces. My body thrived with every stroke of his hands, each nibble of his teeth, and pleasure rocked me.

I watched in fascination when he opened the foil package and slipped it over his arousal. He seemed nervous and unsure, and I took comfort in the fact that he was as inexperienced as me. His entire form was illuminated by the moonlight, and I marveled at the change in his body in such a short time. He'd left eight weeks earlier a boy, but right now, a strong man inched over my body.

"Are you sure?" He pinned me beneath him, his hard eyes questioning.

"Yes. I want nothing more than to share my first time with you."

"Me too."

"Am I...your first?" A little hope flourished in my soul. Sharing this together meant something really big to me. We would always have

CHAPTER 20

this moment. They say you never forget your first.

"Yeah." He glanced shyly away.

"I'm glad."

His lips quivered against mine, and when he entered me, it was exactly what I'd expected it to be—an act of pure love. His eyes burned into mine with every inch he took of me, and soon my body adjusted to him. When he released inside of me, the moment would be locked away in a very special place in my heart, and I'd only be able to relive it in the privacy of my dreams.

"Where did you learn to do that?"

He beamed. "I stole some porn from Bassam's collection and studied." His hand traced the curve of my breasts.

"All you did is study. You didn't practice on anyone? I'm sure girls would line up to practice with you."

He closed his eyes. "No, no one else."

I wrapped my arms around his neck and pulled his body over mine. "After tonight, this can never happen again."

"Stand up to your dad, Mariam. Fight for your freedom of choice."

"I can't..."

"Why?"

"Because I'm a coward." Tears pooled in my eyes.

He looked at his watch and sighed. "I have to go."

"I'm sorry."

He stood up and looked down at me. His dark stare pierced into mine. "How am I going to not see you or touch you again?"

"I was asking myself the same thing," I said.

"The difference is I'll always fight for what I want, but you pick the easy way out." He got dressed, and I slid on my T-shirt and shorts. Somehow, I'd lost my panties.

"Let me walk you home." He took my hand in his and we walked home together for the very last time.

"Asher, please don't leave angry." I clasped him around the waist. He wrapped me in a big bear hug—molding me against his frame. His face pressed against my neck, and he trembled in my arms. He kissed me once more, hard and fast, before he left me standing at the tree below my bedroom window, taking my happiness along with him.

Chapter 21

ASHER

I took the long path around the beach, and my feet carried me on pure muscle memory to the sandy beach and alcove of my youth. What if she didn't show up? Was I fooling myself to believe that we could have something even after all these years? Was I a fool to want her after she wouldn't stand up for me...for us?

Mariam was seated cross-legged at the edge of the shore in nothing but a bikini. Her luscious thighs and her ample breasts in her bikini top were still the most beautiful sights I'd ever seen. Her long brown hair swayed in the breeze, and her eyes were focused on a point in the distance. Her muffled sobs echoed over the deserted beach, and a familiar ache burned in my chest. The need to comfort her was overwhelming. I quietly took a seat beside her on the sand, and she flinched.

"Ash, you scared me." She placed her hand over her chest and scolded me with her red-rimmed stare. Her eyes, blueish green today, had always and would forever be my kryptonite. I melted every time she turned her gaze on me.

I caressed her cheek. "Why were you crying?"

"I was just remembering the past, I guess." She sniffed.

"What are you thinking about?"

She pushed a strand of hair behind her ear. "Just stuff I can't change." Her expression was open, and kindness oozed from her expression despite the red nose and wet cheeks.

"Open up to me, Mariam."

She sighed. "I was thinking about how my need to be the dutiful daughter robbed me of my hopes, dreams, and time with you."

CHAPTER 21

Her lashes lowered, and another tear escaped her lid. "I'm just being dramatic."

"We can't change the past, but maybe we can look toward the future." I brushed her tear away with my fingertip and cradled her cheek with my hand.

She closed her eyes. "I'd like that."

"No more tears."

A small smile curved her lips. "No more tears."

"No liquid courage today and you're still here, or have you been day-drinking?"

The soft sound of her laugh was music to my ears and medicine for my soul. "Nope, not one drop of liquid courage. I meant what I said yesterday, I've always loved you, Ash."

I placed my hand over hers. For years, I'd suppressed my emotions. My admission to her was like setting myself free for the first time. I was tired of lying about my feelings for her. She was the one who got away, the girl who held me within her grasp when I was a young man, and it had only taken a few days with her again for all those feelings to come back full force. "I haven't been able to stop thinking about kissing you again."

"Me too." She bit her lower lip.

"So, what now?"

"Maybe we should date?"

"Date?" The word "date" was bitter on my tongue. Movies and dinners were for strangers to get to know one another. But we had history, memories, and a connection that would take strangers years to form. Unless she wanted to keep things casual. I recoiled. Did she want to date other men while she *dated* me?

"It's been a long time since we were last on this beach. Maybe we should get to know each other as adults."

"I don't share, Mariam."

Her stare burned into my own. "I don't either." Her delicate fingers tightened around mine. "I don't want anyone else, Asher. Just you. I just meant we should take it slow."

At her confirmation, the tension in my shoulders eased and my playful mood returned. "So...this is our third date?"

"How do you figure?" She laughed.

"Ice cream with Bella, date one. Last night, date two, and this is date three."

I caressed her cheek, and she leaned into my touch. I traced the curve of her jawline and the lovely slope of her neck. Her breath hitched, but her gaze stayed locked with mine. My finger teased her plush lips, and her lower lip quivered.

"Dating, huh?" The idea bounced around in my head. Me and Mariam dating? I liked the sound of that a little too much. The truth was my life was a complete clusterfuck at the moment, and taking it slow was a good idea. I hadn't told her about the shit show back at the Navy base and the hearing that awaited me, nor had I mentioned Bassam's request for me to adopt the kids. If she were to become a permanent person in my life, all of that would affect her too.

"Bassam left me a letter asking me to adopt his children." I kissed the bridge of her nose and turned to face the lake.

Her small hand touched my shoulder, and I fought the urge to crumple in her arms.

"Is this the first you're hearing about this?"

"I assumed my parents would take them, and I'd help out, make Michigan my home base whenever I could." I grabbed a handful of sand and let the grains fall between my fingertips. "But be the guardian of three children? Adopt them? What in the world was Bassam thinking?"

"He was thinking from a place of love. If

anything had happened to me when Tamara was a child, I would have wanted one of my sisters to raise her."

"What about your husband?" The word "husband" was sour on my lips.

"He was sick and couldn't care for her properly. He would've let my family raise her."

"What was wrong with him? I heard he had heart problems after he arrived in the States, but I didn't know the extent of it."

"He had a heart murmur, but it wasn't a true issue until he caught pneumonia. He never fully recovered. He also grew more antisocial the sicker he became and fell into clinical depression."

"That must have been really hard for you." I touched her cheek again.

Her expression faltered. The strong-woman facade seemed to flicker, and the scared girl I once knew stared back at me.

"It wasn't easy. Sometimes it was a little much to carry all on my own," she whispered.

"Do you wonder what life would have been like if you had run away with me?"

"All the time...but then I wouldn't have had Tamara, so for that, I don't regret my decision."

"She reminds me a lot of you," I said. "Smart,

CHAPTER 21

witty, funny. She looks like you too, but her coloring is different."

"She's my everything, but even she is bugging me about getting a life." She shook her head. "Enough about me. So if you adopt the kids, how will that work while you are on active duty?"

"I still have eight months left on my four years of reenlistment, and my parents said they would keep them until I return home, but I don't know if they can look after them on their own for that long…" I hesitated, not sure how much to share yet. "There is something in the air right now back at the base, and I might be home earlier than expected."

"When do you go back to base?"

The permanent knot in my stomach twisted every time I remembered my twenty-six years in the Navy going down in a heap of smoke because of a douchebag. "I must be back on the base in six days. But if all goes well, I'm planning on returning on leave as often as possible."

"I can help them with the kids while you are gone. You know my family and I are here for you guys."

"We are really grateful for all of you." I

kissed her palm. "So...we're dating?" I moved a little closer, desperate for the comfort only Mariam could provide.

"Yes." She licked her lips.

"Mariam, I'm going to kiss you," I whispered.

"Please." She leaned into my touch, and I lowered my lips to hers.

My body trembled as our mouths fused. Ever so slowly I savored her. I relished the taste of strawberries, mint, and something that was pure Mariam. Her scent of ocean breeze and coconut had been imprinted in my mind for twenty-six years. Nothing I'd done had eased the attraction I had for her or the love that clung to the memory of one scandalous night all those years ago.

Her arms wrapped around my neck and drew me closer. Our sweet kisses spun into red-hot desire, and I pulled her onto my lap, exploring the lush curve of her hips with my hands. My lips traveled down the slant of her neck to her bounteous cleavage. I pressed my mouth between the beautiful swells of her breasts, and her nails scored my scalp. A sweet moan escaped, and she tossed her head back to give me more access.

"You're so hard, everywhere."

CHAPTER 21

"I sure am." I gripped tighter and pressed her against the swell in my pants.

She yelped. "What are you doing to me?"

"I will do any and everything you want." I caressed her stomach just inches above the delicate trim of her bathing suit bottom. Her eyes closed and she bit her lower lip.

"I want you."

"Are you sure?" I used my tongue to trace the outline of her nipple over the frail cups of her swimsuit.

Her finger traced my abs and happy trail beneath my shirt, and she placed a playful kiss on my lips. "Come over tonight."

"What about your daughter?" I trailed little kisses down the smooth column of her neck, relishing the taste of her skin.

"Tamara left for a girls' weekend yesterday morning. I have the house to myself for two more nights." She arched her back, and I groaned to the feel of her warmth moving over me.

I gripped her hips and stilled her movements. "Mariam, you're going to make me come in my shorts."

She slid her palm against the growing swell of my pants. "Would that be so bad?"

"Not at all."

She bit down on her lower lip, and greed gripped me. I groaned and arched into her hand.

"Asher. I've dreamed about this so many times. I never thought I had the guts to go there with you again. But I can't fight my feelings for you. I..." Her words trailed off.

I clasped her face. "Look at me."

Her eyes glowed in the sunlight. All the colors of the rainbow danced behind the lust and desire.

"You what? Tell me." I waited with bated breath.

"I want you." Her core eased over the swell in my pants, and her hips rhythmically moved over my erection. Her warmth heated me from the inside out. I clasped her hips and pressed her deeper against my lap, her moans of pleasure making me even hungrier to be inside her warmth.

"Do you know how many times I visualized this exact moment when we were teens?"

"Show me." A playful smile lit up her face.

"What if someone sees?" I whispered.

"This spot is still all ours."

"You've never shown this place to anyone

else?" I teased her center over the fabric.

"Never." She licked her lips. "Tell me your fantasy."

I was mentally checking off possible role-playing sexual acts in my memory like a rolodex, and I remembered the perfect one.

"Okay, I have one. Do you remember that pool party at Matt Mitchel's house two days before graduation?"

"Yeah."

"That was the first time you sat on my lap. Do you remember that?"

"Yeah, I do."

I tugged at her hips and cradled her behind in my hands.

"Everyone was sitting around the fire that night. There weren't any more seats, so I just sat on your lap," she said.

"Did you realize how hard you made me?"

"Yes."

"But you didn't get up. Why?"

"Because I loved the way you felt against my sensitive places." Her voice trembled. "I hadn't felt anything like that before."

"Do you remember what happened next?"

Her face flashed red, and she bit down on her lower lip. "Everyone went inside, but we stayed behind by ourselves."

"And you made a move on me." I stilled my movements, and her eyes fluttered open.

"I wanted you to kiss me," she said.

"I was a chicken shit..." I shook my head at the memory. "But I had finally gained the nerve to do it when you wrapped your arms around my neck and straddled my lap."

"That was our first kiss."

"I was so scared of taking things further because I thought I'd lose you."

"I think we were meant to lose each other and find our way back."

I wanted to lay her on the sand and make love to her, right here, right now. But we weren't kids anymore. I wasn't hiding away from the world trying to steal moments with the girl I loved. We were adults and had nothing to hide.

Her phone rang, pulling us from the magical world we'd created. She grabbed my wrist and checked my watch for the time. "Shit, I'm late for lunch at my mom's house."

"I need to pick up Mikey and Bella from camp." I sighed. "And Alec is with my parents."

"Oh yeah, what did you do with Alec today while he was suspended?"

"He helped me wash the cars this morning, and I let him watch *Spiderman* with my parents while I came to meet you."

"How is he taking doing all that manual labor?" Her eyes widened.

"He enjoyed it. I think it helps him focus his rage into something positive. So today, I'm taking all three of them to a karate class."

The idea had come to me in the middle of the night. The routines, the discipline, and the active movements would help teach Alec how to cope with his emotions—hopefully. It had worked for me, and I saw a lot of myself in him.

"I think they'll enjoy that."

"Alec was really interested in karate when I mentioned it the other day, so I think I'll give it a try."

"See, you're better at this than you thought." She placed a soft kiss on my lips before standing up and putting on a white and green summer dress that covered all the delicious bare skin and every mouthwatering curve.

"Yeah, maybe."

She reached out for my hand and tugged me to my feet. "You got this, and I'll be here to remind you."

With her beside me, I felt like I could do anything, even be the sole guardian of three grieving children.

"See you tonight? At around nine?" I basked in the yearning in her eyes.

"Yes."

With one more delicious kiss, we held hands and walked back up the trail to our families—only the possibility of later that night allowing me to let her go.

"Hey." She tugged me back to her when I stepped away to open her car door. I thought it was an invitation to kiss her again, and I pressed her against her car. Tasting her one more time for the road.

She snickered halfway through the kiss and tugged at the hem of my shirt. "So, can I get your number?"

"Libby," he began, and my heart tightened at him calling me my heart in Chaldean, "you can have anything."

Chapter 22

MARIAM

"Sorry. Sorry I'm late."

I hustled through my parents' front door to find the living room empty except for Rena rocking Scarlett for a nap. In between the choruses of "Loy, Loy Lou We Ya"—a surefire Arabic lullaby to put the crankiest of babies to sleep along with rhythmically timed back pats, Rena's green eyes peered up at me. "Shh."

"Sorry," I whispered and sat in the seat beside her. Scarlett's flushed cheek pressed against Rena's shoulder, her rosy lips pouted, and her long blonde eyelashes fluttered asleep. The sight of her gave me that old maternal ache for those precious moments of cuddling a child. I'd always wanted more than just one child, but God had other plans for me, and I had accepted that Tamara was my one and only blessing.

Rena eased Scarlett from her shoulder and placed her in the playpen. She wrinkled her nose. "You smell like outside."

"I was at the beach, didn't shower, and figured we were having lunch outside anyway."

"What were you doing at the beach?" She arched her brows. "Your face, your lips are puffy and..." She moved in closer. "You've been making out."

"No." My "no" wasn't even convincing to myself. My pulse raced. Should I come clean with my baby sister? I remembered the feel of Asher's arms around me, the taste of his mouth, and heat rose in my face.

"You're blushing." She grabbed the baby monitor and ushered me into the kitchen. "It's Asher, isn't it?"

The heat in my face doubled, and I turned away and busied myself with getting a bottle of water from the fridge.

"Oh my God, I'm right."

I turned to face her. "Yes, but I'm not ready to tell anyone else. I'm not sure how the rest of the family will react."

"Considering he is your late husband's cousin."

"Yes, that too, but Sara and Mary always teased me about him. I'm not ready to come clean about my feelings for him just yet."

"Promise. Now spill. I want all the details." She propped herself on the kitchen island, and I spilled every detail about the two days and our plans for later.

"So, are you telling me that he's loved you this whole time?"

"Yeah, and honestly...I'm embarrassed to admit it, but I've always loved him. Even married to Nabil, I longed for Ash."

"Well, arranged marriages aren't always great." Rena fiddled with the hem of her yellow summer dress.

"I thought you and Jon were happy. I thought you guys actually fell in love during the whole getting-to-know-each-other stage."

Her arrangement was different from mine and my other sisters'. Rena's husband wasn't overseas—he was actually from just a couple towns over. Their arrangement wasn't as traditional as mine either—they were introduced at a wedding, liked each other, and then the parents got involved so that Rena and Jon could get to know each other over the phone. She didn't just get off a plane and marry him the following week.

"I'm more than in love with Jon—I freaking adore him—but I feel like something is going on. That woman we saw at the funeral." She placed her hand on her stomach. "I feel it, deep down in my gut, that it has something to do with her."

"Did you ask him?"

"Yes." She sighed. "He said he didn't know who I was talking about, but I got the sense he was hiding something from me."

"You could just be reading something into nothing."

"Maybe." She shrugged. "Anyway, what are you making Ash for dinner tonight?"

The butterflies in my stomach were in full swing, and the thought of food made me queasy. "I think I'm going to make a lasagna. He always loved Italian food."

"Good, that's one of your best dishes. What are you wearing?"

CHAPTER 22

"Does it matter? I'll be home—probably leggings and a T-shirt."

"You better not..." She rolled her eyes. "You wear a summer dress—the red one with the pretty white flowers."

"I can't wear a bra with that dress—it's open back."

"Even better." Rena winked. "Now let's get outside...I'm starving. Breastfeeding always makes me hungry."

I smelled the barbecue before I even made it outside, and my stomach growled. Evidently, even the butterflies in my belly wouldn't say no to delicious foods. There was nothing like the scent of kabob. My feet carried me toward the yummy goodness.

My mother was toiling away at the grill, the fat from the meat causing a little flame to mix with the smoke. But she was a complete natural.

"Hi, Mom." I made my way over and kissed her cheek.

"Mariam, you're here. I was getting worried."

"Sorry, I lost track of time."

"She came late so she didn't have to prepare anything." Sara stepped closer. "What's with your face?"

Jesus, I might as well have placed a scarlet letter on my chest. Did I really look that disheveled? I needed to get to a mirror quickly.

"Nothing." I twirled the ends of my hair, trying desperately to act casual. Rena, I could tell anything to. Despite the age difference, she was more like me than Sara or Mary.

"You're doing that hair thing... That means you're nervous about something," Mary said.

I quickly twirled my hair into a messy bun and tied it up with the rubber band on my wrist.

"What hair thing? I was just picking it up. It's hot out here."

Sara's eyes, so much like my own, searched my face. "Okay."

"Less talking, more preparing. Bring out the salads and rice. Food is ready," Mom said.

"Where is Dad?" I looked at the yard, expecting to see my father fixing something in his garden.

"He went to Home Depot for white paint." Mom shook her head.

I was relieved he wasn't home. I wasn't up for round two with him. "He's not painting the Virgin Mary again?" I asked.

"No, just a touch-up—there is a scratch on it." My mother chuckled. "I think the squirrels are starting to purposely sabotage his work."

"You're lucky you missed him," Mary said. "You just missed the scene he made about how we are raising our daughters."

"Like American girls." I rolled my eyes.

"Yeah, I got an earful yesterday."

"Just ignore him. That's what I do now." Mom set the aluminum pan filled to the rim with barbecue on the patio table. "I've learned a long time ago it's best to not engage with him when he's acting like that."

Lunch on the patio with my mom and sisters was good but different without all our kids. Since they were all up north, it was a much quieter meal without all the cousins' babble. There was more room for gossip without any interruptions.

"Juliette said Bassam left everything in Asher's name and asked him to raise the children as his own." Mom took a sip from her chai. "And he's going to do it."

"What about the Navy?" Mary asked.

"Juliette and George will keep them until he can retire, and he'll be coming back home for good." My mother's gaze burned into my own, and I wasn't sure if it was a warning or something else. But at the sound of his name, my mind instantly went to this afternoon at the beach, and heat slid down my spine.

"Wow, I didn't think he'd do it," Sara chimed in. "He never seemed to hold family close as Bassam did, but I guess I misjudged him."

"I think he and George had a falling out, and it took a tragedy for him to be able to put the past behind him." My mother's stare found mine again, and I nervously played with the hem of my dress.

"So, he's going to need a mama for those children. Regrettably, I'm still married." Sara fanned her face with a paper plate. "Because I would have freely volunteered."

"Girl, yes, I agree. I would too, but I feel like my husband wouldn't be happy. He did grow up to be a real manly man, didn't he?" Mary wiggled her brows.

"Yup, I remember him as a boy, following Mariam around. The Navy really did his body good," Sara said.

"Mariam is single, and they used to be best friends." Rena grinned at me. "You would get that second chance for the big family you always wanted."

CHAPTER 22

"Mariam and Asher, sitting in a tree," Sara started to sing, and I tossed my napkin at her.

"Shut up, you know we're just friends," I lied.

"Don't be silly. Mariam can't marry her dead husband's cousin, can she, Mom?" Rena asked.

I glared at Rena. She knew she was opening a can of worms I wasn't ready for—I at least wanted one special night with Asher before they blew up my happy bubble.

I didn't want to wait for my mother's answer, but I held my breath and continued pulling on the threading at the hem of my dress. If this conversation didn't end soon, my dress would be in pieces.

"I don't believe there is anything in the Catholic Church teachings that says she can't, but your sister had a hard marriage, and if she chooses to marry again, it will have to be her choice, and I would hope she would choose wisely for herself." I glanced at my mom from beneath my lashes, and she smiled. "Despite how handsome the man is now."

"Okay, enough talking about me like I'm not here."

I started bringing in the dishes, and soon everyone followed me into the kitchen. Luckily, the gossip had moved on to someone else, and I made quick work of washing the dishes while my sisters and mom chatted away.

"You need to get out of here if you want to be ready," Rena said.

"I'm going to kill you for what you did outside."

"You should be thanking me. Now you know there isn't anyone standing in the way between you guys." She tossed the dishtowel at me. "Tell them you have a client to take at seven p.m. and go home."

If Asher and I went down that path, the knowledge that I wouldn't be fighting my family was a huge relief—because as much as I wanted him, I wasn't sure I had the strength to go against their wishes even now. I didn't know if it was something in my chemical makeup, fear of disappointing my parents, or my obsessive need to please people—I would need my parents' blessing, and that made me pathetic.

"Thanks, little sister."

"Repay me with babysitting so I can get a little action too," she said.

"Anytime."

Chapter 23

николай

The great big house emitted an air of loneliness that seeped into Nuha's bones and wrapped around her weary heart. Once upon a time, her home was crowded with her children and grandchildren every day. Now, she was lucky if they all appeared for Sunday dinner. The solitude threatened to swallow her whole. The children and grandchildren were always on the go, and Manni compulsively puttered all the time—either toying with a new project or at the Nadi playing cards. She was left alone with too much time to reflect on all the mistakes she'd made while raising her children. As a mom, Nuha knew her children had been provided with the required provisions like food, water, clothes, and shelter. She nurtured, loved, and supported them, but the nagging sense of failure tugged at her gut.

She believed that arranged marriages were the best way to protect daughters from being mistreated, but she should have known better after her own experience. Her whole life changed in the blink of an eye after her arranged marriage. She was just shy of eighteen when Manni had come to Iraq from America to find a mate and set his sights on her. Eight years older than her, Manni had lived in the States for nearly ten years and had returned home to find a suitable wife. He believed American-raised Iraqi woman had converted to American ways, leaving their culture and customs behind.

Nuha could remember the evening she met her husband clearly. All the women in attendance at the party were excited about the prospect of being the one the rich and handsome American would choose to be his wife, but he had taken a liking to Nuha. They were introduced by a family friend and shared only bashful smiles and discreet looks before Manni's father asked for Nuha's hand in marriage. In the blink of an eye, she was married and moving to a new world. It took six long months to get her visa while Manni had needed to return home to the US and work. She was pregnant, and everyone—including his family—made horrible comments about Manni's lifestyle in America. Their proclamations forced horrible images in her mind, making her imagine he had mistresses to keep his bed warm while she waddled around swollen with his child in another country, a different continent, even. Those accusations were, of course, lies, but at the time she didn't know her husband's true character. They were, after all, mere strangers.

Finally, she kissed her parents and siblings goodbye and made the long journey to her new home. She only had Manni and her in-laws. Her mother-in-law, may she rest in peace, was a vindictive woman who had made the first ten years of Nuha's married life miserable. She was the kind of woman to criticize everything from Nuha's cooking to her big fanny—not a damn thing about Nuha was good enough for Mama Souad's son.

She should have learned from her own lived experience, but she followed suit by raising her children in the same close-minded and ridiculous manner. She allowed Manni to put their daughters and son into the same cycle of control. But thank God her children were smarter and stronger than she had ever been. Her grandchildren wouldn't be burdened with arranged marriages and were all getting an education. The cycle could have been broken with her own children if only she had a backbone back when Manni had arranged marriages for Maryanna, Sara, Mariam, and Niles.

Luckily for Maryanna and Sara, it worked out. Rena too—hers was an Americanized version of an arranged marriage. It was Mariam and Niles she'd truly failed. Mariam lived with the sorrow of that failure every day for twenty-six years and Niles put on a brave face, but a mother knew when her son was heartbroken. Nuha could never understand how Rula abandoned her sons without a backward glance.

The doorbell chimed and startled her from her reflections. Who would be at her door at this hour? Biting back the throbbing in her knees, she dashed to the door and peeked through the window. Juliette stood trembling in tears at her doorstep.

Distraught at the sight of her, Nuha swung the door open and threw her arms around her best friend. An earth-shattering wail ripped from Juliette's lips, and she collapsed in Nuha's arms in a pool of thunderous tears.

"Habibi, come. Let's get you inside." Nuha gripped her by the waist and led her to the living room. Juliette fell onto the couch in a heap of cries.

"I...can't...breathe," Juliette wheezed. "It...hurts. Too...much."

"I know." Nuha stroked her friend's hair, her own tears blurring her vision. "Let it all out."

"My Bassam. My firstborn," she sobbed. "Gone."

Nuha swallowed hard, and her own sniffles mirrored Juliette's moans. "I'm so sorry."

"What am I going to do?" Juliette continued in between sobs. "How am I going to live without my son? What will become of his children?"

"They have you and George. Asher. Us. You know me, my girls, and Niles will do whatever you need."

"Asher." Juliette pulled away from Nuha's arms and her tears seemed to still. "He is so overwhelmed. My son is drowning with the weight of the responsibility."

"He is a good man. He will make this right for the kids," Nuha said.

"He is broken. And it's all our fault." Juliette fixed Nuha with a stare. "We. You. Me and our foolish, bull-headed husbands. Ruined his life. Mariam's too."

"I know." Nuha patted her hand. "I was just reflecting on the mess we allowed to happen. I knew my daughter was in love with Asher. She had hearts in her eyes every time she said his name for years."

"Him too. He begged George to stop the arrangement when he found out."

"I should have stopped Manni. I should have given Mariam the letter Asher wrote confessing his love for her all those years ago."

"Letter? What letter?" Juliette gave her a questioning stare.

"Something I've held on to since the day they graduated high school."

"You still have it?" Juliette gripped my hand.

"Follow me." Nuha led Juliette to her bedroom and reached for the jewelry box, a wedding gift from her mother.

She ran her fingers over the delicate gold engraved heart in the center and lifted the latch to reveal the hidden compartment. Her fingertip traced the old paper folded into a neat little square. "If I had let Mariam read this letter twenty-six years ago, would her life be different today? Would she have gone against Manni and refused to marry Nabil? Or was she too wholesome to stand up to her father?" The parchment quaked in Nuha's hand as she placed it into Juliette's outreached fingers.

Juliette gently unfolded the letter and read. Renewed tears pooled in her red-rimmed eyes. Nuha waited for the scolding that never came from her friend. "My misunderstood son. He is a poet."

"The insightful words. And the love he expressed rivals Nazar Qabbini," Nuha said.

"Asher. Habibi, Mama." Juliette clasped the letter to her chest. "Do you think they still feel the same way?"

"I do. Earlier, Rena was fishing to see if it was against our culture for a widow to marry her husband's cousin. I know those two. Thick as thieves." Nuha's spirit lightened at the thought of this afternoon with her daughters. "Mariam and Asher still care for one another—I feel it in my bones."

"Maybe we can help bring them together. We owe them at least that much for not supporting them when they needed us most." Juliette smacked Nuha's arm. "I can't believe you never told me about this letter."

"Honestly, I can't either." Nuha chuckled and noticed Juliette's timid smile. The first she'd seen on her face in days. "Maybe it's time to give her the letter. Maybe Mariam and Asher can finally have a happy ending after all these years. Maybe all they need is to know we are sorry and that we support them if they want to be together."

"Asher... Even after he returns home from the Navy, he has three children to consider. Mariam is done raising her daughter."

"Yes, well, Mariam always wanted a large family of her own. She was crestfallen Nabil couldn't give her any more children."

"What are you waiting for—give her the letter." Juliette pushed the letter into Nuha's hand. "I couldn't think of a better woman to raise my grandchildren besides their...mom." Juliette choked at the mention of her daughter-in law, fresh tears pooling in her eyes.

"I'll have to translate it, there's no way she'd be able to read Arabic all by herself. Not since she hasn't had any interest in learning to read the language."

"Since Asher wasn't here to teach her anymore." Juliette shook her head. "We were such fools." She hugged Nuha. "Thank you for...everything."

Chapter 24

Asher

My palms were sweaty, and my stomach roared like a fighter jet during takeoff. I sat in the driver's side of my car with a bunch of flowers on the passenger seat, staring at Mariam's front door. We were actually going for it. Finally, we were a thing. I'd wanted to be a thing with her my entire adult life, and when it was finally happening, I was having a full-blown panic attack.

My phone vibrated in my hands, and Mariam's name appeared on the screen. I pressed the blue bubble and read.

Mariam: Are you sitting outside my house like a stalker?

The laugh that came out of me echoed through the car and loosened the tension in my shoulders. I typed back my reply.

Asher: Maybe.

Her response was instantaneous.

Mariam: Get your sexy ass inside. I'm hungry.

Asher: I should know better than to stand between you and food.

Mariam: No one stands between me and dinner.

With another chuckle, I turned off the ignition, grabbed the flowers, and walked toward the front door. Apprehension returned like an old friend, but that was when Mariam opened the door. I took one look at her smile, and my heart swelled.

"Hi." Her voice was a little breathy, and her stare darted from my face down to her bare feet. She was nervous too, and somehow, I took comfort in that thought.

"Hey." I handed her the flowers. "These are for you."

"Thank you, they're beautiful." Her fingers grazed mine when she grasped the flowers, and a shiver ran up my spine. "And they match my dress."

She held the bundle of white orchids against her dress and smiled. I hadn't noticed until she mentioned it, but they were the same flowers scattered over her silky red dress.

"They're almost as beautiful as you in that dress." Her lovely face was even more radiant than I remembered. Her long, dark hair was pulled into a ponytail, exposing her delicate neck. My gaze trailed the length of her body, and my mouth watered. What a fucking dress. The floor-length number hugged every curve of her delicious hips and thick waist and flowed around her legs to her feet. But it was the two red silk straps that tied around her neck and barely held her sizable breasts that made all the blood rush to the lower half of my body.

"We can't have dinner unless you come inside." She stepped aside, and I followed, closing the door behind me.

Just as I gathered my wits, I noticed something else—her back was completely bare. Those two little straps were the only things holding that entire dress up, and my fingers itched to pull them free.

"Make yourself comfortable. I'm going to put these in water." I followed her into the kitchen and watched as she struggled to get a vase from the top shelf of the cabinet.

"Let me help." I reached over her head and brought down the glass vase.

The crystal vessel slipped from her obviously shaky fingers and I caught it just before it crashed to the floor. "Thanks. Sorry. All of a sudden I'm nervous."

"Yeah, me too," I said.

"Why don't you pour us some wine while I put these in water." She pointed at the table set for two with candles and an ice bucket with a bottle of wine inside. I hadn't really paid attention to anything but her when I got there, but looking around, I realized she'd gone all out on this dinner for us. The delicious scents of garlic and herbs radiated through the kitchen.

"It smells amazing."

"Thanks, I made lasagna."

"My favorite." I poured two long-stemmed glasses and brought her a cup filled with red, rich cabernet.

"I know." She flashed me a shy smile. "It was

one of the first things I learned how to cook..." She bit down on her lower lip. "Because every time I made it, I thought of you."

Her confession was like a bandage to the broken pieces of me. For so many years I wanted to blame her for not fighting her parents, but the girl I knew was a lover, not a fighter, and I finally understood that.

"You have a lovely home." I handed her the wine glass and beheld the all-white kitchen decorated with vibrant colors from kitchen canisters with colorful flowers to brightly decorated sweets in glass-jeweled jars you'd find in a vintage candy shop. The entire space was happy and cheery.

"Thanks, I've been renovating one room at a time, but it's finally coming together. Come into the living room, and I'll show you my favorite space."

She reached for my free hand, and I clasped hers in mine. Something about this action seemed to tilt the world back into place, and pure joy replaced all the tension in her face.

"I'm all yours," I said.

"I'm counting on that, Mr. George." Mariam squeezed my fingers and pulled me into the living room.

CHAPTER 24

The room had more of the same airiness as the kitchen. Fresh, white walls, distressed whitewashed coffee table, but the wall-to-wall distressed bookshelves were the most impressive. "This is my treasure cave."

"I see reading is still your thing." I laughed. "Are you still reading those books with the shirtless dudes on them?"

"Absolutely." She smiled. "Please sit." She placed her drink on the coffee table and gestured to the plush green couch. I placed my glass beside hers and pulled her onto my lap as I sat down.

"I'm going to own a bookstore in the near future…God willing."

"Wow. That's great. You're going to buy a business?"

"Well, I'm going to partner with Zaynab. She is expanding her business, and I'm buying in."

"You know, owning a bookstore will really suit you. I can see you there, shelving books and talking to customers about all the new releases. Teaching them how to hide the covers from their families."

"I get caught hiding one cover, and I'll never live it down."

"You literally made a cover from newspaper

clippings."

"It worked, didn't it?" She nudged me with her elbow.

"It would have if you hadn't used the first page with a local crime and a classmate's brother's picture plastered on it."

"I didn't even look at the article. I just wanted to hide the romance cover."

"Right, you had to hide your little naughty obsession."

She wrapped her arms around my neck. "You're being really forward for someone who didn't even kiss me hello."

"Well, that's your fault." I caressed the smooth skin of her bare back. "This dress—I couldn't think straight after seeing you in it."

"You like it?" She peered down at the swell of her breasts and then brought her eyes back to mine. Her gaze was both daring and provocative.

I toyed with the strings that held the dress together at the back of her neck and brought my lips close to hers. "All I can think about is tugging at this little tie."

She leaned in to meet me, and we crashed together, mouths fusing. Our lips and tongues tasted and teased. Nipped and sucked. Our bodies melded together, each of us wanting to touch, stroke, feel, and caress every inch of the other.

I pulled away, panting, trying to control my breathing. "Wait. I don't want you to think that's all it is…that this is all I want from you."

Lips swollen, ponytail unfastened, and chest heaving, she stared up at me with lust-filled eyes. "I have one question."

"What's that?" I traced the swell of her lips with my fingertip.

"Will you eat microwave-reheated lasagna?"

"Yeah."

She pulled away from me and stood. I hated letting go of her, but I didn't want to force her into anything sexual if she wasn't ready. "One second."

With a wicked grin on her lips, she stood in between my parted legs and toyed with the two strings that held her dress together.

"You said something about tugging on these two strings?"

I leaned toward her and met her gorgeous green-eyed stare. "I thought nothing could keep you from dinner?"

"There is only one thing I want more than lasagna."

"What's that?"

"You."

Fuck. This woman was driving me crazy. She leaned forward and placed her hands on my knees. The straps fell over her creamy shoulders and hung between my thighs.

"All you have to do is pull."

I sat up and slid my hand over the soft, smooth skin of her arm, making my way over the swell of her breasts. Her breath hitched, and she closed her eyes as I teased the hard peaks.

"Look at me while I undress you, Mariam."

She peered at me from below her lashes. "Quit teasing me, Asher."

I chuckled. "Oh, I'm going to tease you, and you're going to enjoy every second of it."

She licked her lips. "All talk and no action."

I tugged at the strings, and the dress started to unravel. She stepped back and let it fall to her feet. To say her body was perfection was an understatement. She was all woman. I couldn't get enough of the full hips, the dip of her waist, and round, bountiful breasts. All that was left was a little red patch of fabric between her parted legs. But it was her eyes and the substance in them that set my soul on fire. I stood and sauntered toward her, taking off my shirt as I did.

She turned and walked to the staircase and looked at me from over her shoulder, inviting me to follow. I watched her climb the stairs, and the view from where I stood was spectacular. I was never the kind of man who liked those boy shorts women wear as underwear, but the way the little red silk hugged her backside and exposed the apples of her cheeks was enough to make me lose all self-control. I took the stairs two at a time and followed her into her bedroom.

"Don't follow me if you have pants on." Her giggle echoed throughout the expanse of the hallway. I undid my belt and pants and stepped out of them at the doorway of her bedroom. Her eyes roamed mine with hunger.

"These too?" I tugged on the waistband of my boxers.

She bit her lip. "Yes."

I slid them down my hips, revealing my cock at full attention. "Better?"

Her confidence wavered when I reached her, and apprehension replaced the blaze that had been looking back at me earlier. "Don't chicken out now," I said.

I was towering over her, and her stare slid down to her feet. "It's just been a while for me."

I lifted her chin with my finger. "You're perfect. And if you want to stop right now, just say so."

"No, I don't want to stop. I want this, I want you." Her warm hands caressed my chest and slid down to my erection, holding my girth in her hand. "I want this inside me."

I pressed my lips to hers, and just like the flick of a light switch, heat and passion from moments ago reignited. We moved in a desperate need to be closer, frantic hands, mouths, and body parts collided, hers pressed against the bedroom wall. My need to feel her and taste her overpowering, I made my way down to the vee between her legs and tore the little red fabric from her body. I watched the anticipation in her eyes as I lifted her left leg over my shoulder and the delicious center of her pressed against my lips.

I licked the supple skin between her thighs, and I held her bottom with my hands. Her back pressed against the wall. Her fingers clutched at my ears, and she cried out when I found that special part of a woman.

Mariam gasped. "What are you…"

"I'm going to make up for twenty-six years of fantasies." I placed my mouth over the smooth, soft skin and made up for all the lost time between us. I was like a savage, hungry and needy, completely starved for what only she could give me. I couldn't get enough of the feel of her, the little sounds she made while I devoured her.

She tugged at my ears and pressed my face deeper into her core. And when she came undone with my name on her lips, I nearly lost control.

I lifted her in my arms, and she wrapped her legs around my waist. We fell into her bed in a heap of tangled arms and hands. Kissing and touching. Exploring.

"Asher. Condom. Bedside. Table."

Well, someone was prepared. How could I have forgotten condoms?

I reached for the box she had on the bedside, and she watched eagerly as I shielded myself. "I remember watching you our first time. You're much better at it now."

"I was a nervous mess that first time." I covered her with my body and our gazes locked. "Ready?" I whispered.

She slipped her hand between her legs, caressed her delicate folds, and moaned. "Oh yes, I'm ready."

I covered her lips with mine and entered her warmth. Her body revived beneath mine. Her moans were erotic and right from my fantasies. Her teeth clasped my shoulder, her nails scratched down my back, and I was nearing coming undone.

Her core tightened around me, and when she came, I let go, allowing her to bring me with her. I fell onto her breasts, panting, but I wasn't ready for it to end. I pulled out of her warmth and got to my knees between her legs.

"What?" Her breath was labored and sated.

"I'm not done with you yet."

She gasped as my finger entered her, and when my lips teased her sensitive core, she bucked against my mouth. "Asher."

"Hold on tight. You have a very long night ahead of you."

Chapter 25

TAMARA

"I think I want to go get a pregnancy test." Tamara jumped up from her seat as though she'd been stung. She had been stewing in her fear for a day and a half.

"What about Cross?" Lena asked.

"No. This stays between us until I take a test and know for sure," she said.

"Let's go." Bianca grabbed the keys. "At least we are up north and won't bump into anyone we know out here."

"I actually picked up a few tests yesterday for you when I ran in to get us burgers," Lena said.

"Why didn't you say anything?" Tamara said.

"I wanted you to have them when you were ready, but I didn't want to rush you," Lena said.

"Thanks." Tamara took a deep breath and exhaled. "I'm ready."

Lena opened her bag and retrieved three pregnancy tests. "I got three to be sure, either way."

"Tam." Lauren placed her warm hand on Tamara's bare shoulder.

"I'm scared." Tamara's lips trembled.

"I know babe, but whatever happens, we've got your back."

Warm tears streamed down her cheeks. "Thanks."

With her cousins on either side, she finally had the courage to move her feet and head toward the bathroom door with the weight of the world on her shoulders. In a few minutes, she'd know if she was going to be a mom. Holy shit.

Lena opened all three boxes and prepared the sticks for Tamara. "Okay, pee on all three of them and then place them on this bag afterward."

CHAPTER 25

Tamara focused on the task itself and not the fact that her entire life could change after these results. "Got it."

After she ushered her cousins out of the bathroom, she did as she was told, washed her hands, and opened the bathroom door.

"You peed on all three sticks, right?" Lauren stared at the pregnancy sticks on the bathroom counter.

Tamara nodded and stepped out of the bathroom to find Bianca pacing the hotel room holding her phone. "The timer is set." She waved her screen to show the open timer application.

Lena sat beside the window on her knees in prayer.

Tamara splintered. Her legs buckled, and she slid down to the floor right outside the bathroom. *God, please. Don't let me be pregnant.*

That request to God was on repeat in her head. Her mind raced with more angst than a coming-of-age novel, her throat dry and legs quivering.

"How much longer, Bianca?" Lauren came out of the bathroom, and her reassuring arms encircled Tamara. "It's going to be okay."

"One minute and twenty-two seconds,"

Bianca said.

This was the longest three minutes of Tamara's life. She kept picturing her mom's disappointed face and the horror in her grandparents' eyes. Jidu would yell about her ruining the family name. Her entire life would change. Cross's life would change. She would be labeled a whore in the community.

"I've ruined the reputation of all the Shammas women." Tamara covered her face. "You'll never be able to get married to a Chaldean guy because their mother will say your cousin is a whore."

Lauren laughed. "You have lost your senses. If anyone even mentions you in a negative way, I'll cut them behind the knees."

"Great, then I'll be responsible for your jail time." She rolled onto her back to ease the panic in her chest. *God, please. Don't let me be pregnant.*

The watch timer buzzed, and Tamara's head shot up. "Do you want me to look?" Lauren whispered.

Tamara shook her head. This was something she had to do for herself. She found the strength to stand and shuffled to the bathroom. Now the results were in, and she froze at the door.

"You can do this." Lauren gave her a little shove and followed her inside.

"I'm still praying." Lena made the sign of the cross.

Tamara blinked rapidly to relieve the sting of tears and squeezed her eyes shut. With one more prayer to the heavens, her eyes fluttered open, and she tried to focus on the first test. Two pink lines. Her stomach sank. Her gaze shifted to the bold blue plus sign on the applicator beside it. Her legs weakened. If there was any doubt, the third spelled out her condition clearly with eight bold capital letters. PREGNANT.

"Oh, holy fuck," Lauren said.

Tamara glanced from the pregnancy tests to Lauren. Her chest constricted. Each breath stabbed like a blade of a knife in the center cavity of her chest. She bent over wheezing. "I...can't...breathe."

"It's going to be okay."

No, it's not. I can't be pregnant. I can't. "Air." Tamara fell to her knees clutching her neck. "Need."

"Water. Someone bring me water." Lauren slid to the floor beside her. "It's going to be okay.

You need to breathe. Breathe with me." She held Tamara's face and made her look into her big green eyes. Lauren inhaled and Tamara attempted to, but each inhalation burned.

"Breathe in." Lauren inhaled and exhaled. "*Hee hee hee*, and concentrate on my breath," she continued.

Tamara focused on her. The rhythmic sound of her breath. Slowly, the pressure eased the tiniest bit.

"Again." Lauren breathed in, and Tamara followed, and again when she exhaled, she made that noise. Whatever they were doing, it abated the tension in Tamara's chest. The knife slicing into her lungs dulled and was replaced by tingles.

"You're doing great. *Hee. Hee. Hee.*"

"Why are you breathing like she's in labor?" Bianca entered clutching a bottle of water, watching them curiously.

"Labor?" Tamara whispered in between her next set of breaths. *"Hee. Hee. Hee."*

"The *hee hee hee*." Bianca laughed. "That's Lamaze. I think we have at least eight and a half months before that's necessary."

The tension in Tamara's chest was gone. "You were doing Lamaze with me."

CHAPTER 25

"It worked, didn't it?" Lauren stood. "Ugh, and I sat on a hotel room bathroom floor with you. Eww. I need to shower."

A mixture of laughter and tears took hold of Tamara. Until her stomach turned, and acid burned her throat. If the test didn't prove her pregnancy, the stupid morning sickness was validation enough.

Chapter 26

ASHER

Wiping the fog of sleep from my eyes, it took a few moments for me to realize I was sleeping in Mariam's bed, and it was her warm body wrapped around mine. My phone rang from somewhere on the floor of the bedroom, but I was enjoying the feel of her body against mine too much to try to retrieve it.

"What is that sound?" Mariam stirred against me.

"That's my phone." I groaned.

"You should get that. Might be your mom." She rolled off me before I had the chance to tighten my hold on her.

"Come back..." I followed her to the other side of the bed, but she swung away and pointed at the digital clock on the bedside table.

"Ash, it's three a.m. Something might be wrong."

"It's probably nothing." I took her hand and kissed her fingertips. But before I could make my way to her lips the phone rang again. This time unease twisted in my stomach. With a sigh, I dropped her hand and rolled out of bed looking for my pants. I found them crumpled on the floor where I'd left them. The phone that had fallen out of my pants pocket blared louder, and the dark bedroom was illuminated by the glow of the phone screen, HOME flashing across the screen.

"Shit, it's my house." I quickly hit the ACCEPT button and slammed the phone to my ear. "Hello, Mom. What's wrong?"

"Asher. Abni, I've been calling you."

"I left my phone in the car. What's wrong?"

"Bella has a temperature. It's at 104, and it's not going down with Tylenol."

"Temperature of 104?" I repeated and

glanced blankly at Mariam. This wasn't in my wheelhouse. Mariam got out of bed and stood beside me. "Who?" she mouthed.

"Bella," I mouthed back and then placed the phone on speaker.

"Yes, and she is having trouble breathing. I think it's her asthma."

"Mama, what should we do?"

"You need to take her to the emergency. Your father and I will stay with the boys."

I glanced at Mariam, verifying if my mother was right.

She nodded and squeezed my hand.

"Okay, I'll be home in five minutes."

"Okay, Abni. Drive careful."

I ended the call and stood rooted to the spot. My stomach was completely twisted. Fever, asthma, emergency room. I didn't have a clue what to do about any of it.

"Do you know where to take her?"

"Bloom Lake Hospital on Tulip Ave?"

"Yes, I know Bassam and Lydia used to take the kids there when they were sick. They should have all her current health information already."

I went ahead to put on my briefs, pants, and shirt, looking frantically for my socks and shoes. Mariam followed suit by putting on joggers and an oversized T-shirt. When I was finally fully dressed, I turned to her, my heart in my throat.

"I'd better go."

"Let me know if you need anything."

I turned away before I begged her to come with me. My family wasn't her responsibility. And she had already helped so much, I didn't feel right asking her to leave her warm bed and hold my hand at three in the morning.

I made it home in what felt like the blink of an eye. My mind raced a million miles an hour. What would happen if one of the kids got sick while I was away? What if something happened and I was somewhere I couldn't be reached? The panic in my mother's voice still echoed in my ears.

When I made it inside the house, my mother cradled a sick Bella while my father was pacing the room.

"Where have you been?" my father barked.

"Out." I walked past him and knelt beside my mother and Bella's sick little frame. Her eyes were closed and her breath was shallow. Tears streamed down her cheeks.

"Do you know where to take her?" Mama

whispered.

"Yeah," I said.

"You can't be out all hours of the night when you are responsible for little ones," Baba said. "They need stability and a watchful eye."

"Not now, George." Mom placed Bella in my arms, and her little body snuggled against my chest.

"Daddy." Her little hand held on to the collar of my shirt. "Amoo Asher, I want my daddy."

Instead of crying for her father, this time Bella moaned for him. It was more a longing to be held in the arms of her dad instead of the tantrum cries she'd had all week.

"I know, baby, me too."

Her chest sounded like a Hemi engine, and her skin burned hot. "I'll call you once I know something."

"I will come with you." My father started following me out the door, and I shot my mother a panicked stare. I needed to focus on Bella. My father, though he meant well, would only be an unwelcome distraction right now.

"George, I would rather you stay with me and the boys, just in case."

He nodded. "I'll just help him to the car."

Once he opened the back door of my car, I gen-

CHAPTER 26

tly placed Bella in her car seat. She wasn't even stirring. The panic must have been showing in my face because my father placed a hand on my shoulder. "She's going to be fine. She just needs a little medicine."

"How do you know?" I brushed a strand of hair from her sweaty face. Bella seemed so very small and fragile.

"Because I know you will make sure she's fine."

I got in the driver's seat and prayed to God that my father was right.

It seemed to be a quiet night at the ER, and after one look at Bella, they took us inside a white sterile room. It smelled of antiseptic and was as cold as an ice box.

I didn't have much personal health information and even tripped up on her date of birth until I did a little math for birth year while the nurse looked up her information. She finally took pity on me and stopped making me verify information. Bella looked so small on that bed with an IV and oxygen mask with a treatment flowing to help her breathe.

"I didn't even know you have asthma." I was a crappy uncle. What else didn't I know about my only niece and her brothers? I clasped her tiny hand between my fingers, and my chest tightened. The medicine they had given her seemed to have helped her rattled breathing, and she slept soundly.

"How am I going to protect you if I don't know how?" I brushed a strand of hair from her face with my unsteady fingers. Bassam and Lydia should be at her bedside. Her parents were the ones who knew what she needed. If they were still alive, she wouldn't have been admitted to the hospital. My eyes stung, and my vision blurred. I dropped my head atop our clasped fingers and my body quaked with the tears I'd been holding in from the minute my mom placed Bella's sick little frame in my arms.

"Asher." A warm, familiar touch caressed my back.

It was Mariam, and I needed her comfort like I needed air. I turned my face into her abdomen and let her hold me until my sobbing subsided. She didn't say anything. Just held me and allowed me to release all my sadness, fears, and grief. After a long while, I was able to gather my wits and wiped my eyes with the back of my hand.

"I'm sorry," I said.

"Don't be. Let's step out in the hall so we don't disturb Bella." She turned toward the door and grabbed two traveling coffee cups she had apparently brought with her.

I opened the way out, but glanced behind me at Bella, not willing to leave her alone.

"Keep the door open so we can hear if she wakes up."

Reluctantly, I walked out of the room and peered in on Bella from the room window.

"Here." Mariam handed me a black travel mug. "I brewed coffee at home. I hate hospital stale coffee."

"Thanks." The bittersweet scent was welcoming, and I needed caffeine in an IV now. Bringing the cup to my lips, I wasn't expecting it to still be so hot, but I welcomed the burn.

"How is Bella doing?"

I glanced back at her little form in the giant bed, and panic seized me. "They're giving her steroids and oxygen, and they did this thing with a machine and mist that's supposed to help."

"A breathing treatment." Mariam nodded.

"Yeah, apparently, she is supposed to be taking these treatments at home. But I didn't know anything about them. I didn't know my niece even had asthma. What kind of uncle am I? I'll tell you. I'm a sorry excuse for a relative, and a worse uncle."

"Don't say that." She placed her hand on my arm, and it helped to steady me. "You're a good man trying your best to take care of everyone in your family."

"And I'm doing an excellent job." Sarcasm laced my tone.

"You are taking care of your family. Sure, it's a learning curve. But you got this. Bassam believed you were the right person to raise his children. He trusted you."

"I bet you knew she had asthma. I bet you know so much more about my niece and nephews than I do because you were here. You didn't turn your back because you aren't a selfish asshole like me. Why would he trust me? I've proven time and time again that my self-interests are what I've always put first before everyone."

"This is different. Look at that little girl in there. Is there anything more important to you than her safety and well-being?"

An animalistic protectiveness washed over me. I knew beyond a shadow of a doubt I would give my life for hers. I would stand before a bus, take a bullet, or give an organ from my body to save her. I would trade my life for hers. The same for Mikey and Alec. I would protect them with my dying breath. "She is everything."

"And that's why Bassam picked you. He knew no one would love them and protect them better than his baby brother."

A single tear slid down my left cheek, and I brushed it away. "Thank you."

She hugged me around my midsection and we both stood there watching Bella sleep from the doorway.

"Amoo Asher." Bella stirred in her bed, and we quickly made our way to her bedside.

"Hi sweetheart, I'm right here." She had pulled the oxygen mask off her face and the look of fear was clear on her expression.

"Don't leave me, okay?" Her voice was just barely over a whisper.

"I'm not going anywhere."

"Good." She lay back against the pillow, and her eyes drifted closed. The color in her cheeks was returning, but the exhaustion showed in her eyes.

"Bella honey, you need to keep your mask on." I helped her raise it over her nose, and her hand reached for mine, clasping it tightly between her fingertips. I glanced at Mariam, who was smiling. "Looks like Bella knows you got her back too."

Chapter 27

Tamara

Cross arrived Saturday afternoon, and Tamara avoided him like the plague. Every time he found her, she escaped into the sea of college kids partying and blowing off steam. It was easy to hide from him since the beach was lit. It had the spring break vibe with everyone partying and drinking. Girls in tiny bikinis, boys with kegs, music blaring through large speakers. By dusk, she'd retreated to the firepit, cuddled under her hoodie and nursing a peppermint tea Bianca had brought her from the hotel café.

Lake Michigan was enchanting at sunset. The sky was an array of colors. Hues of reds, blues, and oranges shimmered against the waves. The rhythmic sound of the lake clanked and splashed. She closed her eyes and let the melody of the waves ease the tension in her bones. Her world was crashing around her just like these waves. The reality of being a mother terrified Tamara. She wasn't ready. She didn't know how to be a mom. Couldn't fathom being responsible for another human at this point in her life. Wasn't financially capable of providing for a child—she was still in college.

But then an image of a little boy—a mixture of Cross and her—flourished in her mind and tugged at her insides.

"Hey, beautiful." Cross's quiet tone sent shivers up her spine. He had finally caught up to her, and the flight-or-fight response prickled beneath her skin.

"Hi." Tamara couldn't look him in the face. What she had to tell him would ruin his life and his perfect plans. Nausea rolled through her, and she sipped on her peppermint tea.

CHAPTER 27

"Peppermint schnapps?" Cross bumped her shoulder with his own, and heat crept up her neck.

"No, peppermint tea—no schnapps, that just sounds disgusting."

"Did I do something to piss you off?"

"What? No." Tamara found his gaze for the first time today.

"You have avoided me since I got here."

"I'm pregnant." The words were out of her mouth before she could stop them. That wasn't how she planned to tell him, but hiding things from Cross wasn't something she did well.

"What?" Cross had generally large almond-shaped eyes, but now they had tripled in size. He sat wide-eyed and with his mouth gaped open.

"I took three pregnancy tests this morning, and all three showed positive." The peppermint wasn't helping. Acid burned her throat, and she jumped to her feet. "I feel sick."

Tamara covered her mouth and ran for the hotel room but only made it a few feet before heaving on the sand. Cross was behind her, holding her hair as the contents of her stomach emptied—which was only a few sips of peppermint tea. The crowd around them cheered, believing it was alcohol that made her sick and not the fact that a little life was growing inside her body.

When Tamara finally finished heaving, without a word, she allowed Cross to steer her through the hotel and into the elevator. The cold from the air conditioner chilled her bone-deep.

"My head is pounding." She covered her face.

"It's okay. I got you." His warm and strong arms held her tight against his massive chest. "Always."

She closed her eyes and let Cross take over, basking in the warmth of his body. Leaned on his dependable strength. Her brain wasn't processing anymore. Her body was drained and depleted.

She realized he had taken her to his room and not the one she shared with her cousins. He pulled back the covers on the bed, sat her down, and took off her sneakers. "Lie down. I'm going to get you some water."

Tamara didn't argue. The throbbing in her head was getting louder. Her eyes watered, and it was difficult to stay upright. She curled up in a ball and closed her eyes. The warmth of blankets covered her, and she realized she

CHAPTER 27

had been trembling. The bed tilted, and Cross's warm body slid beside her before sleep carried her away.

Chapter 28

Mariam

Rena's red SUV blocked my normal spot in the driveway when I finally got home from the hospital. I glanced at the time—it was barely nine a.m. on a Monday morning. I pulled my car in behind hers and rubbed my eyes. My dreams of a nap before my meeting at noon with the lawyer were short-lived.

"Ren? What's wrong?"

"I'm here for the down and dirty." My little sister had gotten out of the car and wiggled her

CHAPTER 28

booty before she reached into the backseat for the little one. She was dressed in black leggings and a fitted matching tank top—giving the illusion she'd just stepped out of a fancy yoga class.

My smiling niece, Scarlett, wiggled her hands and feet in anticipation when I peered into the backseat.

"Hi, galab Khala." Scarlett waved and smiled wide for me. The moment she was out of that car seat contraption, I swooped her out of her mother's arms and inhaled the fresh scent of baby shampoo.

"Wait, where were you?" Rena eyed my ratty joggers and T-shirt. "Please tell me you didn't wear that out in public."

"I sure did," I sang, and Scarlett laughed.

"Where did you sport *that* fabulous attire?"

"To the hospital."

"What? Are you okay? Was the sex last night that wild? I mean, I know it's been a long time since you had some, but I didn't think you would send the poor guy to the hospital."

"That's where your mind went? Not whether Tamara, Mom, Dad, or basically anyone from our seriously large family was injured or in the hospital?"

"Um, no, I just talked to Mom on the way

here. If anyone was hurt or sick in the family, you know she would have told me."

"I was there with Asher."

"I knew it, you broke the man."

I rolled my eyes. "We were there because Bella's asthma flared in the middle of the night."

"Oh my God, is she okay?"

"Yeah, she is doing much better." I passed Scarlett back to Rena and fished out my house keys.

"He must've been terrified."

"He was pretty overwhelmed, but I think he's going to be a good father to them." The scene I walked in on at the hospital flashed in my mind. His body trembled from the force of his tears. His face pressed against Bella's hand. Fear and pain shaking him from the inside out.

I opened the door with Rena on my heels, a happy Scarlett cradled in her arms.

"Make us a pot of coffee, I need a quick shower." I placed my keys and purse on the table in the entryway and headed for the stairs.

"Wait." Rena stood with Scarlett on one hip and her hand on the other. I halted my step. "Did you at least get laid before Bella got sick?"

My heart smiled before I realized I had been

grinning like a schoolgirl.

"Never mind, continue. I will be right here waiting for all the dirty details." With that, Rena turned away and left me standing on the staircase.

My bed was still tangled and unmade. The sheets were a mess from our lovemaking. I stared at the imprint of where he'd laid his head on the pillow. The memory of the peaceful sleep in his arms, the comfort I found in our closeness was something I'd long forgotten was possible. He had turned me inside out with how he cherished my body, tasted every inch of me, and made me feel so completely desired and wanted.

It was so foreign to me to see that side of the bed used. I lifted the pillow and brought it to my nose. His scent lingered, and I closed my eyes to breathe him in. I'd been sleeping alone for many years, even before my husband's death. He had made the spare bedroom his own room shortly after he returned from the hospital that very first time. He claimed he could not sleep beside me because I moved "too much" in my sleep.

With a sigh, I made the bed and headed for the shower. I dressed in something professional looking yet still my style—dark jeans, a black tank top, and a white cotton cardigan. It was the closest thing to professional attire I owned. I knotted my hair into a messy but trendy bun and dabbed on makeup to hide my sleepless night.

The scent of coffee greeted me like a welcoming friend, and I found Rena and Scarlett waiting for me at the kitchen table. "Why does it look like you didn't sit at this romantic table setting?"

"We ate in a more informal manner." The memory of us naked and sitting in bed eating lasagna was still fresh in my mind. My cheeks burned, and I proceeded toward the coffee pot.

"Okay, I want to hear everything."

"There's not much to tell."

"Really? 'Cause those rosy cheeks and silly smile tell a different story."

"We had an enjoyable evening." My tone was coy, and that seemed to infuriate Rena.

"Come on..." She gave a squirming Scarlett a cookie. "I'm currently living vicariously through you."

"You're married," I said. "I should be living vicariously through you, not the other way around."

"Things are different with this little one." She wiped crumbs off Scarlett's face. "The spontaneity is gone, and I had that unsettling suspicion something was going on with that lady from his office, but I think it's just me being insecure."

I finished pouring my steaming mug and brought it to the table, making sure to set the hot liquid away from Scarlett's grabby hands.

"Did you confront him about it again?"

"No—I knew he'd just claim to not know her. But then I asked Mom who that woman was at the funeral, and she gave me the 411. Her name is Dalia, she's forty-two years old, never married, and apparently her mother is very sick and my husband is her mother's doctor."

"How did Mom learn all that?"

"Mom was pumping her for information because she wanted to hook her up with Niles."

"Didn't she learn to stay out of it after his first marriage or mine?"

"I don't think she can help it—it's a disorder. Anyway, quit distracting me. I want details."

I sighed. "It was wonderful."

"Did you have sex?"

"I don't kiss and tell." I wiggled my eyebrows.

"Did you wear the red and white dress?"

"Yup." My smile widened at the memory of how he tugged the tie open, and the hunger in his eyes as it fell to the ground.

"Oh, you had sex. And it was good, wasn't it?"

"The best sex of my life." I bit my lip. "I didn't even know it was possible for sex to be that good. Granted, I had sex with Nabil and a few casual encounters after, but nothing compares to last night."

"Because you have chemistry, history, and an emotional connection."

I sipped my coffee. "Yeah, I guess so. But we are both in places in our lives where we can't let things get messy. He has the kids and is going back to the Navy base in a few days. I have Tamara and a good life, a new business, and no man dictating how I should live. I like my independence."

"What business?"

"Don't tell Mom and Dad or anyone yet, but I'm buying half of the bookstore from Zaynab."

"That's wonderful. You have always loved that store. But what about the salon?"

"I'll still work at the salon while Tamara is student teaching, but after she gets a job, I'll probably quit. Or only keep a handful of clients."

"What about my hair?"

"I will do it, or you can have Noor do it for you."

"What made you decide to do this?"

"Well, for the first time in my life, I see a light at the end of the tunnel...a time when I can stop living life for other people. I'm free. My daughter is an adult and nearing graduation. My bills are minimal, and thanks to the life insurance that I was religious about paying throughout my marriage, I have enough money saved for retirement and this chance of a lifetime. I could help a friend and live out a dream all at once."

"That's all wonderful. I'm so happy for you, sis. But why would a relationship with Asher complicate anything?"

"I don't want to have to answer to anyone, ever again. We can have a friendship, a sexual relationship, but I will never allow anyone close enough to interfere with my life and choices."

"Not all men are Dad and Nabil. I want to kill my husband half the time, but he is incredibly supportive—he wanted to help me open my clothing store before this little one came. It was my choice to stay home with her—at least until she is in preschool. Then I'll reevaluate."

"It's different for you. You never had all your choices taken away from you." I took another sip of my coffee.

"I know, honey, but do not be closed-minded and judge Asher for the mistakes of another man."

"Maybe. But right now, can I just bask in the excellent sex?"

"Absolutely." She lifted her mug. "Cheers to excellent sex."

Chapter 29

Nuha

"Did you check on Juliette and George this morning?" Manni carried a cheese and tomato sandwich in one hand and a heaping, steaming mug of chai in the other. His unsteady hands shook, sprinkling droplets of chai all over my freshly mopped floors.

Nuha sighed. "Honestly, Manni, I just mopped."

"What?" He looked around, clueless. Then at the spots of chai trailing behind him. "That wasn't me." He flashed her a cheeky grin.

She stood and picked up the mop. "Right, because the boys snuck into the house and soiled my floor after they had already left for the day."

"No, you did it. You have chai in front of you—it could have easily been you."

"Oh, yes, it surely couldn't have been you." She traced over his steps with the mop. "I spoke to Juliette this morning. Asher took Bella to the hospital for her asthma."

"Asher is now responsible for three little children." Manni took a bite of his sandwich, dropping crumbs on the kitchen table.

Nuha reminded herself that this was a pointless argument. But how hard would it have been to place the sandwich on a paper plate?

"Hell has surely frozen if that boy has suddenly become responsible."

"The poor man is doing the best he can. Juliette mentioned he is doing wonderful with them despite the circumstances."

Suddenly, Nuha was protective of Asher. Maybe because for the first time, she considered his long-ago actions. Reading his love letter to Mariam, considering the girl he loved

CHAPTER 29

was forced to marry his cousin—a cousin his mother had mentioned on many occasions he did not "get along with back home." He'd felt betrayed by the people he loved. Yes, the boy was impulsive for just leaving for the Navy and staying away for so long, but if a person loves that deeply, they tend to feel all emotions strongly. The good and the bad.

Nuha, being an avid reader herself, had read many love stories and poems, but none resonated with her like the letter Asher had written to her daughter. His writing was fueled by admiration, kindness, and gratitude for just knowing Mariam. His sentiments were loving and hopeful. The letter was full of words and sentiments Nuha only dreamed her husband would say to her, just once.

Instead, she'd started a marriage to a basic stranger, moved to a new land, and had been forced to live in a house filled with people she didn't know. Not only did she have to get accustomed to a husband and "wife duties," but she'd had to navigate living with a mother-in-law, father-in-law, and her husband's four siblings.

His sisters would raid her closet, and his brothers believed her wifely duties included being their housekeeper. Even after Manni's siblings married and moved out, they were over constantly, their children terrorizing her children, stealing and damaging their toys.

Through it all, Manni never really took her side or supported his children when it came to his family. He was a good provider. The children did not want for anything. He gambled but always responsibly. He drank heavily in his younger days and could get confrontational, but he never laid a hand on her or the children. They had never feared losing their home or prosperity. But she didn't think he was genuinely in love with her or she with him.

He loved the idea of Nuha. What she could do for him, what true value they could bring into each other's lives. Mostly their children and stability. Yes, she loved him in the sense of a companion, a long-time constant in her life, the father of her children. But the love in stories and poems had never been a part of their lives and never would be.

She knew without any doubt why she'd kept that letter for so long. It reminded her that love could truly be beautiful. It could be something material, to taste and even touch. It could be tangible. It was rare and messy, but it was real and eternal.

CHAPTER 29

She put the mop away and returned to her bedroom to finish the translation of the letter after Manni left for the store. Asher's eloquently written words were going to take a bit of time to translate. She smiled when she logged into her computer and opened the translator application her grandson, Nicholas, had installed and taught her to use. Nuha was supposed to translate all her recipes for her grandchildren.

Her biggest issue was typing on the laptop in Arabic. The easy part was copying and pasting the text to ensure the beautifully written sentiments did not get lost in translation. Mariam, after all those years, deserved to read every syllable.

Chapter 30

ASHER

"Amoo Asher, can I sleep in my bed in my house?" Bella was finally released from the hospital at six p.m. after the antibiotics had time to work in her system and her oxygen levels had returned to normal.

I parked the car in the driveway of my parents' house. I was both mentally and physically exhausted.

"No, honey, it's late tonight, but I promise to bring all your things to your new room at

CHAPTER 30

Nana's house for you."

"I don't like that room. I want my pink room with the rainbows."

"I agree, you have a very pretty room." I watched her through the rearview mirror. The color had completely returned to her cheeks. "We can make your new room pretty too."

"Will you paint my room at Nana's house pink with rainbows?"

"Anything you want. We will spend the day tomorrow working on it, but you must promise to rest today."

I got out of the car and opened her door. "Pinky promise?" She stuck out her little finger. I sent a quick prayer in thanks to the heavens that she was okay. She wanted a pink room with rainbows. I'd even get her a unicorn. Anything to keep that girl happy.

"Pinky promise."

My list for tomorrow was getting longer by the second. Spending the day at the hospital had really thrown off my schedule. Davison had called earlier to tell me the house was going on the market next week and that I needed to sign some paperwork tomorrow morning. The house needed all personal items removed, which meant I needed to clear out my brother's belongings. The clock was ticking on my return to the base, but with one look at the little girl in my arms, I honestly didn't care if I was dishonorably discharged. All that mattered was being there for her and the boys.

Mikey and Alec greeted us at the door. They seemed pretty happy to see that their sister was okay. Even Alec was being extra nice to Bella. He sat beside her on the couch and put on a Disney princess movie for her.

"Ebni, you look tired." My mother inspected my face in the way only a mother can. "Why don't you leave Bella with me and go get some sleep."

"I could use a shower." I glanced at the kids, who looked pretty content together. "I won't be long."

"Go, take your time. They're fine right now." I headed up the stairs and into my bedroom. It hit me suddenly, I would have to move back into my parents' house, at least while I adjusted to the responsibilities of raising the children on my own. The idea of being in such close proximity to my father again gave me a little anxiety.

There was a soft knock on my bedroom door.

CHAPTER 30

"Come in."

Mikey, red-faced, and tear-soaked, stepped into the room quietly.

"Hey, buddy, what's wrong?"

"I heard Jidu and Nana talking this morning. Are you going to sell our house?"

"Yeah, buddy, I'm sorry. I was planning on telling you myself today. I hate you found out this way."

"Why can't we live in our house?" He was trying hard to hold back his tears, but every time he spoke, his words came out muffled.

"Because from now on, we are all a team. We are going to live together here so that we can all help each other. And Nana and Jidu will have to stay with you when I go back to the Navy."

"When are you leaving?" Fear danced in his red-rimmed eyes.

"In a few days, but I'm going to do my best to get back as soon as possible. For good."

"But why do we have to sell the house?"

"Because it doesn't make sense to keep if no one is going to live in it."

"What about all my dad's stuff? All our stuff. Are you going to sell it too?"

"The furniture, yes. But you and your siblings' bedrooms, all your clothes and toys will be brought here."

"What about my mom and dad's things?"

"Well, we will pack them up and I'll save all the important items for you guys, but their clothes should be donated to the church."

"Someone will get everything my parents owned?" Mikey couldn't wrap his head around this.

"Buddy, do you know what a will is?"

"No." He wiped his face with the back of his hand.

"A will is something adults have a lawyer write for them as instructions for what to do with all their belongings if something bad happens to them like your mom and dad."

"Did my dad have a will?"

"Yes, and he and your mom left me a detailed list of what they wanted me to keep and items to sell for your college fund."

"They did?"

"Of course. Your parents loved you so much and wanted to make sure you and your siblings were taken care of if anything bad happened."

He nodded. "Why did my parents have to die?"

"I don't know buddy, I guess God loved them so much, he wanted them to be with him." I

CHAPTER 30

gave Mikey the same answer I'd given Alec. I didn't have any other reasonable answer.

"I miss them." Tears pooled in his eyes.

"Me too." I took the boy and wrapped him in my arms. "I promised Bella that I would go get her bed and stuff tomorrow and bring them here. Do you want to help me?"

He wiped his eyes with the back of his hand. "Yes."

"Okay, you can come with me. We'll keep Thing One and Thing Two with Nana and Jidu."

"Okay."

"Why don't you wash up for dinner? I'm going to take a quick shower and meet you downstairs."

Chapter 31

TAMARA

The drive home to Bloomington Lake was long and quiet. Cross had insisted Tamara ride back with him, and she didn't have the mental fortitude to deny him. They'd been on the road for nearly three hours, and she could tell he wanted to talk, but she still wasn't ready. She'd woken up in the middle of the night and returned to the room she shared with her cousins while Cross was sleeping.

All she could think about was her mom. Her

CHAPTER 31

reaction. Her disappointment.

"I think we should get married." Cross was white-knuckling the steering wheel, his hands gripped at ten and two.

"You're joking."

"No." His tone was clipped.

"We are not financially ready to get married. Where would we live? How would we support ourselves? I barely make gas money at the salon and student teaching doesn't pay squat. Besides, we have only been dating for like two months." Her filter must have been muted by this pregnancy because, for the life of her, she couldn't stop the words that spewed from her mouth.

He reared back like she'd smacked him and glared at her for a moment before fixing his eyes on the road.

"You aren't financially secure, but I am. I've been working in the auto industry since I left high school. I have money saved and my new engineering position pays well. I can support us and a baby."

"I don't want you to support me and marry me out of obligation."

"Obligation? Are you kidding me?" Cross accelerated the car, made a quick right, then exited the freeway.

"What are you doing?"

He ignored her and continued driving into a Big Burger parking lot. Once he stopped the car, he stepped out without a word. Taking a deep breath, she followed him to the trunk where he rummaged around his duffle bag.

"What are you doing?" Tamara's blood boiled beneath her skin.

Cross didn't speak, but his lips glowered, his eyes narrowed, and his jaw clenched. His shoulders unyielding, he searched his duffle. Finally, he pulled something that fit in his palm behind him and turned to face her. "You think I'm proposing out of obligation? If so, why would I have this with me?" He handed Tamara a velvet box.

When she didn't immediately take it from him, he pressed it into her hand. Her throat tightened, and the box trembled within her grasp. Her chest constricted, and she struggled for air. The blood rushed in her ears, and the panic attack that had taken hold of her yesterday threatened to return. She closed her eyes and focused on her breathing. She swallowed hard. "What is this?"

"Open it." He crossed his arms over his chest,

CHAPTER 31

his nose flared, and his body went rigid.

Tamara's fingers trembled on the lid as she slid it open. A two-carat diamond ring sparkled back at her.

She opened and shut her mouth. "Your grandmother's ring?"

"I was planning on proposing this weekend. I knew you wanted to wait. I was okay with having a long engagement. But I wanted to be your man openly around your family, and I couldn't do that if our relationship was a secret."

"But—"

He cut her off. The intensity in his eyes halted her words. "Yes, we have only been officially dating for two months. We have been a couple since we were six years old. You are my best friend, my confidante, and my lover, now the mother of my child. I can't picture my life without you, and I don't want to. But you obviously don't feel the same about me as I do you."

"That's not true. I do love you with everything I am." Tears stung her eyes, and she struggled to find words.

"Then why not marry me?"

"What if ..." The words stuck in her throat, and she stared blankly at him. The question,

"What if you change your mind?" screamed in her head but wouldn't form on her lips. Her mouth opened and closed, and tears stung her eyes.

"Spit it out, Tamara. Just say it." His voice trembled. He was trying so hard to control his emotions, but hurt and disappointment shone from his tear-filled eyes.

"I don't know." Her voice cracked with tears.

He groaned and rubbed his face with both hands. "You keep that ring until you can give me a real answer."

Cross stomped away from her and into the Big Burger restaurant. Tamara stumbled back into the car and just gazed at the ring. The tears were no longer pooling in her eyes—they streamed down her cheeks in large droplets. *Why am I so afraid of marriage and commitment?* It wasn't like she wanted anyone else. Cross was it for her, always had been. She just hadn't admitted it out loud.

Cross returned to the car with a bag of food and handed it to Tamara. "You should try to eat. I brought you chicken and fries."

He unwrapped his burger and fries in silence. She expected the tension in the car to be thick with unspoken words, but it seemed like Cross had left his annoyance outside the car. He turned on the radio, and a calming tune swallowed the awkward silence and settled her raging anguish. She closed the ring box and placed it in the center console. The food smelled good for the first time in a week, and she devoured the chicken and fries.

Neither said another word the entire drive home. When he pulled up in her driveway he handed her the box. "I was serious. You keep that until you can tell me why you don't want to marry me."

"Cross..."

"Do you have an answer?"

She shook her head no.

"Then take it." He pressed the velvet box in her hand and opened the car door without another word. She wanted to stop him. Reach for his arm and curl up in his lap, reassure him of her love for him, but she sat shell-shocked in the passenger seat. Her mind whirled a million miles an hour, and speech seemed like a foreign concept. She couldn't verbalize the weight and the deep-rooted anguish surrounding words like marriage, future, and forever. Her entire body revolted at just the mention of those words.

Carrying her suitcase, Cross headed to her front door, and she found the strength to follow him. After she unlocked the door, he carried the bags up the stairs to what she assumed was her bedroom.

Moments later, he was back downstairs.

"You didn't have to do that."

He avoided her stare—keeping his eyes firmly on the wall above her head. "I'm going to go," he said.

He turned to leave, but Tamara gripped his strong hand. His fingers trembled in her own. "Cross." His gaze finally met hers. "I love you."

Cross's warm body engulfed her in a strong embrace. His muscular torso pressed against the softness of Tamara's body. The cologne of cherrywood and vanilla combined with a scent uniquely him covered her. She inhaled it, wanted to bathe in it, bottle it up, and mark her skin with the smell of him. She squeezed him a bit tighter—willing him to understand without words how much he meant to her. He pulled away far too soon, and a cold tremor slid up her spine. His stare burned into her tear-filled eyes. "I know."

He turned his back to her, strolled to the door, and locked it behind him. She sank onto the couch with the velvet box clutched in her sweaty palm until the front door burst open.

"Hi, honey." Her mom stormed into the house with her hands filled with grocery bags and thundered into the kitchen. "I'm so happy you're home," she called behind her.

Her heels click-clacked on the wooden floors and emulated the pounding of Tamara's rapid heartbeat.

"I have got amazing news." Kitchen cabinet doors slammed a few times. The animation in her mother's voice destroyed Tamara. How was she going to explain all the secrets she'd kept for the past few months? "But first, are you ready for movie Monday? I brought a bunch of snacks, and I was thinking we order Mexican even though it's not taco Tuesday. But if you want Chinese instead, I'll compromise."

A wave of emotions took over Tamara. Words had still abandoned her. First with Cross, now with her mom—she couldn't convey her emotions except by crying. Tears pooled and streamed down her face. Her body shuddered, and a full-on sobbing fest commenced. She sheltered her face with a throw pillow to lessen the sounds of her wails and allowed the misery and discomfort to release in all its glory.

"Tamara?" Her mom rushed to Tamara's side. "What's wrong? Are you hurt?"

Tamara's head lifted from the pillow, and she fell into her mother's arms. "I'm..." The word pregnant wouldn't come out. Instead, a loud sob escaped her lips. Her mouth babbled, but not one coherent syllable would form on her tongue.

"You're what, honey? You're scaring Mommy." Her mom's strong grip held her by the shoulders and her green eyes bored into hers, strength and love staring back at Tamara. She swallowed hard before uttering the two words that would forever change her life.

"I'm..." Her lips trembled. "Pregnant."

Chapter 32

MARIAM

The carpet was ripped from beneath my feet, and my world tilted. Tamara—pregnant? I stupidly believed she was still a virgin. I didn't even know she was seeing anyone. My mind raced with a ton of different scenarios. I wanted to yell, scream, and tell her I couldn't believe how irresponsible she had been. If she had talked to me, I would have guided her to get proper birth control. Oh my God, what if someone hurt her? What if this was rape?

I grabbed her by the shoulders and stared directly into her eyes. "Did someone force themselves on you?"

"No." Another sob escaped her lips, and my anger and panic deflated. I wrapped my arms around my baby girl, and we both sobbed. We stayed entwined for some time. I patted her back and rocked her until all her tears had dried. All the anxiety she'd been holding seemed to subside while mine accelerated.

"Who is the father?"

She lifted her head from my chest and wiped her eyes with her sweater sleeve. "I'm sorry, Mom."

"It's okay, I think." I brushed a strand of unruly hair from her face. "We will work this all out. But I need to get the whole picture."

"There's a lot I've been keeping from you."

"Oh my God, you don't know who the father is?" I stood and paced the room.

"Of course, I know who the father is... Mom, you don't think I knew who I had sex with?"

I stopped in the middle of the room and glared. "I thought you were a virgin, so Mommy needs a little catch-up session."

"Cross is the father."

"Cross?" I'll kill him. I trusted him to take

CHAPTER 32

care of my baby. I marched to the door, ready to kick his ass, but before I made it through, Tamara grabbed my arm.

"Mom. Where are you going?"

"I'm going to kill Cross."

"It's not his fault." She pulled me to the chair and nearly tossed me in it. "Cross is a good guy. Mom, for heaven's sake, he proposed."

"Marriage?"

"Yes." She picked up a little black box from the table and tossed it to me.

"Wait? How long have you guys been dating behind my back?"

"Two months."

"How many periods have you missed?"

"Just this one." She rubbed her face. "I can't believe we are having this conversation."

I rubbed my face with my hands. "Are you keeping the baby?" I cringed even uttering the words, but I needed to know where her head was at the moment.

"Of course." Her hand shifted to her abdomen.

She was already protective of the little bundle inside her. My grandchild. I was going to be a grandma. I shot up from the chair and headed for my liquor cabinet. I needed something strong and warm to ease the growing panic. I mean, she wasn't a child, though I treated her like a child at times. The girl in front of me was a woman. A beautiful twenty-five-year-old woman.

"So, you're getting married. We should make it quick, before you start showing. I'll see if I can reserve the Bloomington Club for next month. You might need to get married on a weekday because it's like a year wait for a weekend."

I babbled while I found the Brother's Bond bourbon and poured a nice full glass. The first gulp burned its way down my throat.

"I didn't say yes."

"What?" I took another pull of my drink. "But you have the ring."

Tamara sat back on the couch and curled her legs beneath her. "He gave me the ring to hold on to until I could give him a valid reason why we shouldn't get married."

I set my drink on the coffee table and picked up the ring box. The beautiful two-carat diamond sparkled so intensely that I was sure its shimmer could be spotted from Mars.

"Are you in love with Cross?"

"I love him. I've always loved him."

CHAPTER 32

"But are you in love with him?"

"Yes."

"Like how they describe in romance novels?" I knew the answer to this. They might have hidden their relationship from me, but I knew how they cared for one another. I'd seen firsthand the love in his eyes for my daughter and I'd noted her love for him for a long time.

"Yes."

"Then...what's the problem?"

"We have only been dating for like two months. I thought he was proposing because I was pregnant, but I just told him last night. He had the ring with him, Mom. He was going to ask me to marry him this weekend. Apparently, he was tired of our relationship being secret and wanted to openly be together around our family. I think Khalu Niles and Jidu scare him."

"You are making it hard for me to stay angry at the boy."

"It's hard to stay angry at him. He is one of the most thoughtful people I've ever known." She bit down on her lower lip and stared at her hands.

"So why don't you want to get married?"

"I have my reasons."

She abruptly stood and went to the kitchen, but I was quick on her heels. There was something she was avoiding telling me, and if I was going to hear shit from the entire community about my unwed daughter having a baby, I needed answers. Not to mention my parents, my siblings. Everyone would be horrified. They would accuse her of ruining the family name and mark her the Whore of Babylon. I didn't care about any of that shit. I would walk through hot coals and fire for my daughter. I needed the truth. Why would she decline a marriage to the man she loved if it would give her security and the proper family for her child?

"What are your reasons?"

"I don't want to talk about it." She opened a bag of potato chips and popped a chip into her mouth. Turning to the refrigerator, she dismissed me and pulled out a can of pop.

"Well, I do."

"Why? Are you going to force me to get married? Like Nana and Jidu did to you?" As though her questions were a mic drop, she retrieved a glass from the kitchen cabinet and filled the cup to the rim with ice.

"Wow. Really. What the hell is with that attitude?"

"I'm frustrated and dealing with a lot and you're just coming at me with a million questions."

"Are you fucking kidding me, Tamara? I've never been anything but *the cool mom*. The supportive mom. I think I deserve honesty and respect. And the fucking truth. Why don't you want to get married? It's a clear-cut question and should have a clear-cut answer."

"I don't know." She gathered her snacks and gave me her back.

The anger that had just been flowing through me deflated, and her reasons were suddenly clear. I placed a gentle hand on her shoulder. "Cross isn't like your dad."

She whirled on me and glared. I had hit the nail on the head. "I know Cross isn't like Dad. He is nothing like him. Why would you make that assumption?"

"My marriage was crappy, but you and Cross wouldn't have the same relationship. He is your best friend and I've known for a long time that someday you would be together. The love radiates from the both of you. Your dad and I were strangers who were not suited for one another. We never had or could possibly ever have what you two have together. You can't make your choices based on my marriage."

"Me not wanting to get married has nothing to do with you and Dad. I can't believe you. Do you have that little respect for my personal choices?" Tamara took a large gulp of her drink and gagged. "This pop tastes funny."

"I do have respect for your choices, but this is a big decision, and I think you are acting out of fear instead of using your mind."

"I'm not scared. I'm not you." Tamara slammed her glass into the sink.

I recoiled. "What's that supposed to mean?" My voice quivered. The anger I'd been trying to keep at bay resurfaced.

"You didn't fight for yourself and got sucked into a loveless marriage. You never got to go to school, get your degree. You never fought Dad for anything you wanted. You allowed the people around you to tell you what you were supposed to do, and you just obeyed."

"I did what I had to do. I had no choice. It was obey or be disowned."

"You were scared."

"And so are you. You are scared that Cross will turn out like your dad. He will one day wake up and become a stranger to you and this child you are carrying."

"Again, don't compare Cross to Dad."

"Admit it, that's the reason you don't want to get married."

"Don't toss your baggage on me, Mom. That's your reason for not dating and being the old, lonely widow."

"Wow. Are you really enjoying being bitchy to me or is it the hormones?"

"Whatever." She turned on her heel and left the kitchen.

"Fine." I stomped after her. "Go and ponder what is really going on with you. And just an FYI. The pop is fine. My grandchild is getting my revenge for me by not allowing you to drink soda at all."

I followed her to the foot of the staircase, and a wave of panic settled over me. "I hope my grandchild doesn't let you eat chocolate either. Or chicken." I listed all her favorite foods.

She didn't halt her forward progression at my words—just continued her march up the stairs without a backward glance. The last thing I heard was her bedroom door slamming shut.

My knees gave out, and I dropped onto the last step. My daughter was pregnant. I was going to be a grandmother. Tamara wanted to be an unwed mom by choice. So many emotions raged through me. I wanted to support her. But every fiber of my being screamed to force her to marry, secure her reputation and our family name. Of course, I wouldn't. I was nothing like my father. I wouldn't take her choices away from her.

I covered my face. "My parents are going to flip."

Chapter 33

ASHER

"Ready?" Mikey and I stood at the front door of my brother's house, the key trembling between my fingers. The day was going to be one long emotional roller-coaster.

He nodded. We had been to the house a few times, but something about this moment rocked me to my core. The same apprehension seemed to be emanating from my nephew, but he seemed determined and resigned to what we were about to do.

The little guy was trying to be strong, but packing up the home he lived in with his parents had to be terrifying. My mother tried to keep him in the house with the other two children, but I knew he needed this to feel some control over his own life.

"Let's do this." I patted his shoulder and unlocked the door. Mikey hesitated for a moment then followed me inside. The little guy was transfixed as he made his way into the living room and stopped dead at a leather recliner. He ran his fingers over the leather in a wistful caress.

"This is my dad's chair."

My brother's chair. If he were alive, I would tease him for turning into our father with his special chair. "Do you want to put it in your room?"

"Can we?" A little spark of joy danced in Mikey's eyes.

"Yes, of course you can."

"Thanks, Amoo Asher."

I smiled. "Sure thing. Do you want to pack up your bedroom?"

"Okay."

"Two Men and a Truck are here." Ragheed and Kal entered the house each with hands filled with flattened cardboard boxes.

It was a busy afternoon filled with packing. We each took a room. Mikey did his own room, Ragheed packed Bella's room and Kal worked on Alec's room. I tackled Bassam and Lydia's bedroom. It only took a few minutes and I realized I was in over my head. When every drawer I opened belonged to Lydia, I just couldn't get myself to rummage through her things. I dropped to the floor and pulled out my cell phone.

"Hello." Mariam's voice was like a comforting hug.

"Hey. It's so good to hear your voice."

"You too." There was strain in her tone. "You don't know how good."

"You, okay?" She had been my support since I'd been back, but I hadn't really done anything to return the kindness she'd shown me—besides the sex, which I thoroughly enjoyed myself.

"I can use a big hug," she said.

"My arms are always available for you."

"I'll hold you to it." She sighed. "What are you up to today?"

"I'm packing up Bassam's house, and I have a huge favor to ask."

"Sure, I could use a distraction. What's up?"

"Is everything okay? Is Tamara okay?" Lately, I felt like I was waiting for the next shoe to drop, and the sound of her voice made my stomach knot.

"Things are crazy, but I don't feel like talking about it." She sighed. "Please tell me what you need. I need to stay busy. I'm off on Tuesdays. I've already cleaned the house, the garage, and the car, but I'm still buzzing with energy. I need something else to focus on."

"Are you sure? You seemed stressed, and I really don't want to add to it."

"I'm asking you to," she persisted. "I really need something to do."

"If you're sure."

"Ash, yes."

"Okay, can you pack Lydia's things for me? I feel like I'm violating her privacy. It's just too personal, and she's a woman with woman things, and every drawer I opened had her intimate items."

"Asher, I get it. Of course, I'll do it."

"Thank you."

"You're welcome. Give me ten minutes and I'll be on my way. Do you have boxes and markers?"

"Yes, Ragheed and Kal are here with me and Mikey. They brought everything we need."

"Okay, see you in a few."

A sense of relief flooded me at the idea of having her with me. She seemed overwhelmed, and I hated taking advantage of her. But Mariam was one of the few people in my life I could ask. Packing Lydia's things seemed like it should be done by a woman who knew and cared for her. Her mother had already gone back to Germany, and there wasn't anyone else besides my mom, who would probably break down if she even entered the house.

The initial steps of packing up Bassam's clothes were torturous. His scent covered every inch of his closet. He still wore the same cologne by Hanae Mori. I brought a shirt to my nose and smelled my brother for the first time in a couple of years. My heart ached, but this time the tears didn't find their way down my face. Maybe I was all out of tears.

I packed all his shirts, slacks, and jeans neatly in the boxes, making sure to check all his pants pockets. It was a good thing I did. I found a total of five hundred dollars forgotten in various pants that I would be adding to the piggy banks of the kids.

Next, I started on his coats and jackets. Joy sparked inside me when I found the leather jacket. "Bass, you kept this?" The soft black worn leather jacket felt like butter against my fingertips.

"That's a really cool jacket." Mariam came into the bedroom carrying two coffees.

"It's the Christmas gift I sent him from France."

"I remember hearing about how instead of coming home to visit your family on one of your leaves, you and your friends took a European holiday."

"Bass was so mad I wasn't going to be home for Christmas. So I sent him this jacket. He was still pissed at me for not coming home, but I didn't think he saved the jacket."

"I can't believe he ever fit in that jacket."

I laughed. "He told me Lydia liked him soft and cuddly."

"You should keep it for Mikey."

"That's a great idea. He will fit in this in a few years."

After placing the jacket on the bed, I stretched out my arms. "I could use a big hug too." Her smile brightened all the dark places, but this smile didn't reach her eyes. Dark circles framed them as if she hadn't slept all night. She was still beautiful in a casual pink T-shirt and fitted torn blue jeans, but tension was clear in her slumped shoulders, and her demeanor seemed melancholy.

She placed the coffee cups on the dresser and wrapped her arms around my neck. Her soft curves pressed against my frame. Her face snuggled my neck, and I breathed in her tropical scent.

"What's going on, beautiful?"

"I...I can't talk about it right now. Just hold me. I needed this. I need you." I started to worry, but I knew Mariam well enough to know that she was used to holding on to her pain despite my attempts to help her share her feelings.

"Okay. Let's get started." She pulled away and plastered on a mask for me.

"I think you should find something like the jacket to save for Alec and Bella too. I'll do the same with Lydia's things."

We both worked quietly after that, and soon the room was covered in boxes filled with personal effects. We decided to donate all their clothes and shoes. But I found a cool suede jacket for Alec from Bassam's slim days and a wool Burberry scarf for Bella. We packed their more expensive personal items separately. Bassam's watches and jewelry, a diamond cross, a St. Michael charm, and a few other valuables along with all of Lydia's jewelry were packed carefully to be placed in a safe deposit box for when the kids were older.

"Her wedding dress." Mariam was on the floor of Lydia's closet in front of a cedar chest. "She had it preserved. Her veil, wedding shoes, and headpiece are in here too."

"She was stunning on her wedding day." I kneeled beside her and took in the layers of satin and lace.

"She looked magical in this dress. You know, she told me that it was love at first sight for her. She fell in love with Bass the moment she met him."

"It was the same for him. He said she stole his heart the moment she smiled at him."

"They were inseparable. Went everywhere together. Unlike Nabil. I was lucky if I got him to come to my parents' house for Christmas dinner." The disdain in her words was a new development. She typically used a neutral tone at the mention of his name. Never angry, sad, or happy. Just an even tone as though she

CHAPTER 33

were reading a passage from an engineering textbook. But now, something had shifted. She spoke his name with pure, unfiltered resentment.

I took her hand in mine. "That must have been frustrating."

"I didn't care. I dealt with all the questions about why he wasn't with me at weddings, family gatherings, even funerals. If it wasn't for me, no one would have even shown up at his funeral. He never paid respect or celebrated anything for anyone."

Her voice cracked with each word. "It didn't matter to me as long as it didn't affect Tamara. But lately, I've noticed how his behavior traumatized my daughter. He hurt her, Ash—and now, I'm pissed off."

"She's a great girl and that's because of you."

"Thanks. Sorry, today wasn't about my crazy life." She stood, and I followed, pulling her flush against me.

"I'm here for you. You know that, right?" Taking her face in my hands, I stared deep into her green eyes. "Anything. Anytime."

She nodded. "I think you should save this chest for Bella. Even if she doesn't wear it, she could take a piece of it and sew it into her wedding dress."

"Amoo Asher." At Mikey's voice, we broke apart.

"Hey, buddy. Are you done packing up your room?"

He stopped in his tracks at the sight of all the boxes. Eyes wide and mouth hanging open, he stood shocked for a moment.

"Mikey, you okay, honey?" Mariam made her way to him and brushed his hair from his eyes.

He nodded slowly. "Ragheed wants to know if the beds, our beds are coming to Nana's house."

"Bella and Alec, yes. Yours is up to you. You can bring your bed or keep the queen bed at Nana's house."

"I can keep the big bed?"

"If you want it."

"Yes. I can sleep like a starfish." He imitated a starfish with his arms outstretched.

Seeing a little joy in his face made everything okay. I got a glimmer of hope for the future. They wouldn't always feel so sad. They would one day find joy, feel security and hope again. And I would do everything in my power to make it happen.

Chapter 34

TAMARA

There was something so serene about the cemetery. A sense of peace always washed over Tamara whenever she visited her father's grave. Which wasn't often. Father's Day and his birthday were the only days her mom managed to convince Tamara to visit him. Tamara never voiced her truest sentiments out loud and worked hard on not acknowledging them. But today, she was volatile. Seething with a need to yell and scream at her father. The fight with her mom had hit a nerve. Her mom voiced the very thing she tried not to admit. Tamara was terrified Cross would be like her dad, but not for the reasons her mother believed.

It was a beautiful evening in Bloomington Cemetery. The sun was just setting in all its glory. Red and blue hues tinted the bright blue sky. Tamara sat on the green lawn before her father's grave and scoffed at the engraved headstone.

"You stopped being a loving father a long time ago." She ran her fingers over the cool grass and grabbed a handful within her fingertips. Her blood boiled beneath her skin, and she gripped the grass with both hands. "And I doubt you were a loving husband to Mom."

Her hands were covered in shreds of grass, and she chucked them at the headstone. The coils of tension and resentment she'd been holding for so long had reached their boiling point. She couldn't deny all her deep-seated insecurities revolved around her daddy issues.

"Why did you stop loving me?" A sob tore through her, and her body shuddered. "One day, I was your princess, and the next, I was nothing. No one. You just stopped loving me. You

CHAPTER 34

were no longer interested in me. My education, my friends, my life. You just shut me out."

The tears clouded her vision, and her voice echoed in the quiet cemetery. But it was like the gates had been swung open, and her feelings poured out without barriers. There was no stopping all the emotions she'd repressed, all the sentiments she'd been too afraid to voice or even acknowledge.

"Do you have any idea how that made me feel? It made me second-guess everything about myself and my relationships with men. I'm terrified he will stop loving me too. Just like you did. How crazy is that? Logically, I know that Cross is not you. But my heart." Her voice quivered. "My heart is scared to get broken again."

Tamara's hand moved to her abdomen, and her grief lightened at the thought of the little miracle inside her. The child had been conceived out of pure love. "You're going to be a grandfather, by the way."

She wiped the tears with the back of her hand. "And you know, I'm already in love with the life growing inside of me, and I can't imagine blaming them for getting sick. Or treating him or her like they're disposable, or they don't matter. I was barely a teenager and you just shut me out. I was so jealous of Lauren and Lena, the way their father loves them. Took them on father-daughter dates. He showed them how a dad is supposed to love."

Her voice quivered. "You showed me how easily a man could just stop loving me."

"Tamara?" The deep but gentle voice startled her. She peered up through the haze of tears to find Asher standing beside her. "Are you all right?"

The sun had set, and only the faint light of day lingered through the sky. She rubbed her eyes with both hands, too exhausted to pretend that she hadn't been crying. "Not really."

He sat beside her on the grass. "Do you want to talk about it?"

"I guess," she choked out between large sobs. "Everyone is going to find out sooner or later that I'm pregnant."

"Holy shit."

"Yup." She laughed at his wide-eyed and open-mouthed expression despite her anguish.

"Does your mom know?"

"Yes." Her body shuddered with tears.

"Well, that explains her mood today. Shit.

You okay?" He ran his fingers over his buzzed head.

"Yes. No. I don't know. Mom wants me to get married to protect my reputation."

He scoffed. "You would think since she was forced to get married by her father, she wouldn't try to do the same thing to you." There was bitterness in his tone, and she wondered if he liked her mom even back then.

"That's what I said. But she insisted it was different because Cross and I love each other. And you know what's crazy, I know that she's right."

Tamara was getting a second wind. The panic crept back into her chest. "Cross is not my dad and I'm not my mom. My heart is telling me getting married is the logical progression of my relationship with Cross, but my head..."

"It doesn't have to be," Asher said.

"No, my head is saying that Cross will change just like my dad did." Tamara covered her face with both hands, and mortification washed over her. Asher was essentially a stranger, so why was she telling him her deep, dark secrets? "Yes, I know how insane I sound."

A strong, comforting hand covered her shoulder. "I think your father always struggled with connecting with people, and from what your mom said, the sicker he became the harder it was for him to see past his own pain."

"No. He blamed me. He got sick because when I was twelve, he caught my flu. He was never the same after that. He never looked at me the same again." Tamara shuddered from head to toe, and her sobs came out of her in gasps of air.

Asher pulled her into a parental-type of a hug. The kind of hug she'd yearned to have from her father for many years. His embrace was strong but gentle and allowed her to lean into his strength to find her own. Finally, her meltdown subsided. She wiped her face with the sleeve of her shirt.

"I'm sorry for crying all over you." A sardonic laugh escaped her lips.

"It's fine. It's good practice for me for when Bella is older. I hope she won't ever cry to someone because I've screwed up so bad."

"No, I don't think you will. Something tells me you're going to be a great dad to her and the boys."

"I hope you're right. War wasn't as scary as

the prospect of raising those three monsters." He shuddered. "They truly are a handful."

Tamara placed her hand over her stomach. "I understand that."

"I think you and Cross are going to be excellent parents. Whether you get married or not."

"Thanks, but I think you are the only one that will think so." Tamara ran her fingers over the grass again and stared out across the cemetery.

"I've always been more progressive than most of my family." He shrugged.

"What about the Navy? When do you go back?"

"I'm supposed to be going back in a couple days. I've got another eight months for my enlistment, and I'll put in for retirement. But some things happened right before I left, and I might be home sooner."

"Well, I'm here whenever you need a babysitter. I'm probably not going to have much of a social life going forward."

"They love you," he said.

"I love them too. They have always been as close to me as Jax and Jordan. They never felt like third cousins."

Tamara's ringtone interrupted what had

turned into a nice conversation, and she sighed. "I better be getting home."

"You should really talk to your mom. She needs to know how you feel."

"I will, but I just need time to process everything I've discovered about myself first."

"Fair enough." He smiled.

"You like my mom, don't you?"

"You don't beat around the bush, do you?" His cheeks went a little pink.

"Nope. I always say what's on my mind even when I don't want to say anything."

"Yeah, I like her. A lot. I always have."

"I can tell. Are you going to ask her out?"

"If I did, would you mind?"

"Nope. I think you would be good for my mom." Tamara got to her feet. "Thanks for listening to me."

"Anytime."

She noticed he watched over her until she was safely in the car, and he moved down to the two piles of dirt that marked Bassam's and Lydia's graves. She watched as he got to his knees and did the sign of the cross over the dirt. She ached for him. Despite dealing with his own grief, he'd still sat and tried to comfort her. She made a mental note to do what she could

CHAPTER 34

for those kids while he was away.

With a sigh, she checked her phone. There were a ton of text messages from her mom and Cross.

Cross: You can't ignore me forever.

Cross: Just text me and tell me you're okay.

Cross: I love you. Whatever you decide.

Tamara's guilt increased with every message she read. She was hurting him, and he didn't deserve the turmoil she was putting him through. Her actions seemed to be out of her control. Her heart and mind were not aligned, and she couldn't face him until they were.

The next set of messages was from her mom. Tamara couldn't talk about her father with her mom. Any pain she would voice, her mother would blame herself, and that wasn't fair. She knew without a shadow of a doubt, her mother had done everything in her power to make Tamara feel loved and secure.

Mom: Where are you?

Mom: We need to talk.

Mom: So that's how it is? You're just going to ignore me?

Mom: Just saw Cross. You're ignoring him too?

Mom: Honey, I love you. Please let me know

you're okay.

Tears burned Tamara's eyes, and she tossed the phone on the seat. Started the car, but instead of going home, she parked her car at her grandparents' home. Tamara couldn't face her mom or bump into Cross. She needed time to evaluate her feelings for Cross and sort out her reservations about getting married without any interference from either of them.

She made the trek to the front door with a little apprehension. She couldn't tell her grandparents the real situation because they would lose their minds. Tamara could see Nana crying and falling to her knees in prayer to the Virgin Mary, Jesus, and Joseph statues while Jidu would yell and scream about how this was why girls could not have freedom.

She rang the doorbell, and Nana appeared. She was already in her night dress, her hair in a ponytail clasped at the nape of her neck, but her face lit up when she saw Tamara.

"This is a beautiful surprise." The excitement that was on her face only moments ago evaporated. "You have been crying."

She was so foolish. Why hadn't she cleaned up her face before knocking on the door? Her makeup must have been smeared and her face blotchy from crying. "It's nothing. Can I stay here tonight?"

"Come in." She stepped aside. "Does your mom know you're here?"

"No." Her stomach tightened.

"Come, let me make you some chai." Nana wrapped her in a warm embrace, and Tamara inhaled her scent of Poison by Christian Dior, but the once-comforting fragrance twisted Tamara's gut and made acid burn up her throat. A wave of nausea took hold of her.

She pushed away from Nana and bolted to the powder room. She barely lifted the toilet seat before losing the contents of her stomach. Since she hadn't had an appetite, it wasn't much.

Nana was behind her, holding her hair and rubbing her back. "Habibi. Are you sick?"

Tamara flushed the toilet and turned to the sink to wash her face and hands. The warm water eased the tender skin of her cheeks and eyes. "No, I just must have eaten something bad."

"Let me make you some newme busrra and chai. It will settle your stomach."

The thought of the dry lemon and tea made her mouth water, and a new wave of nausea rolled through her.

"No, I'm good. I just need to lie down. Can I go upstairs?"

Nana placed her hand over Tamara's forehead and cheeks. "No fever." She brushed her hair away from her face. "Of course. I just changed the sheets in the room."

"Thanks." She was making her way up the stairs just as she heard Jidu come through the front door. Relief washed over her. At least he didn't witness her spilling out her guts. What the hell was up with morning sickness—shouldn't it only be in the morning?

She finally made it up the stairs, exhaustion seeping into her bones. The moment her head hit the pillow, darkness followed.

Chapter 35

Mariam

My anger with Tamara had reached a new level of explosive. My hands trembled on the steering wheel while I turned down Bloom Lake Drive. When Tamara hadn't returned my calls and texts and Cross hadn't heard from her, my anger had changed to fear. What if something was wrong with her? What if she had gotten in a car crash? Every bad, horrid, and tragic scenario raced through my mind, and with each moment, my fear accelerated. I logged into my Verizon account and tracked her phone. That was the beauty of paying for your twenty-five-year-old's phone bill. I clicked on her "find my phone" and nearly fell out of my chair when the little blue dot was at 13571 Bloom Lake.

Out of all the places my daughter could find refuge—the girl chose my parents' house. I should have known. I was dumbfounded. If those two knew the reason she was hiding out, they would be at Cross's parents' house with a shotgun.

After throwing the car in park, I stomped up the front steps and banged on the door. My father looked confused when he saw me. He was wearing his black long johns and his readers were on the top of his head.

"Mariam." He stepped aside and let me in. "It's late. What are you doing here?"

I stepped past him and into the foyer. "Where's Tamara?"

"Tamara?" The confusion in his expression was convincing, and I wondered how clueless he could be sometimes for a man who'd controlled everything and everyone when I was growing up.

"Her car is in the driveway, and I tracked her

phone."

"I don't know." He scratched his head. "Nuha."

My mom came out from the kitchen with a tea tray in her hand. "Mariam, I was just going to call you."

"Where is Tamara?"

"She's upstairs but she's..." I didn't let her finish her sentence before I ran up the steps. My mother's steps echoed behind me. "Mariam, the girl is sick."

"That's what she told you?" I couldn't believe her. I had taken the news of her pregnancy well. I didn't blow my top, I respected her, I told her that I would stand by her side no matter what. When I said that, I meant stand beside her while the family freaks out about a pregnancy out of wedlock. But what did she do? Came to the one place I tried to protect her from.

"Mom?" Tamara came out of the bedroom, her hair messy and her face pale. Her eyes red-rimmed and swollen. My anger evaporated at the sight of my disheveled girl. I didn't care that she was an adult and about to be a mother too, she was still my baby.

"Why didn't you come home?"

"I just needed a break."

"A break from me?"

"I needed a break from everything. You, Cross, the situation."

"And you came here?" I pushed. Still trying to understand why she would seek refuge with her grandparents. Two of the most un-understanding people I knew.

"What's wrong with her coming to my house?" My mother had followed me up the stairs with the tray still in her hand.

"If you had to ask that, then you don't know why your granddaughter is actually hiding from the world."

"Don't be ridiculous." My mom rolled her eyes. "Tamara, habibi, I made you chai."

"Thanks, Nana," Tamara said.

Tamara moved past me and took the teacup. Then the minx turned around and went back into the bedroom.

"Seriously. You want kleicha with your tea, princess?" I stormed into the bedroom she was using as her retreat.

"I just made a fresh batch of shakar lama. I'll bring you some." My mother loved to cater to her grandchildren and headed to the stairs. "I'll bring you some chai too, Mariam."

CHAPTER 35

"No need, Mom. We are going home."

"But Tamara is sick." She was appalled.

"And she will be fine, in her own bed, in her own house." My tone rose with every word.

"I'm not coming. I'm staying here."

"The hell you are."

"I'm not leaving."

"Yes, you are. Put on your shoes."

"I'm twenty-five years old. You can't make me go anywhere with you." Tamara's tone matched mine. With every syllable, her voice got louder.

"What is the matter with the two of you?" My mother stood between us as a referee in a boxing match while my father started yelling, "What is going on up there?" from downstairs.

"No, I can't make you 'do' anything. But if you stay, we can sit and chat with your grandparents and tell them exactly why you don't want to go home with me. Get the chai, Mom, you might need the arak too. You will need something stronger to get through this conversation."

"Blackmail?" Tamara rolled her eyes. "You won't dare."

"Try me. I've had a shit show of a day and I'm not in the mood to bullshit." I crossed my arms and stared her down. Yes, she was grown, but I would not tolerate her disrespect or let her run away from her problems.

"What are you talking about? You know I don't drink."

I started feeling sorry for my mother. She was an innocent bystander in my rage, but I just couldn't stop myself.

"Tell her. Or wait—should I call my dad? You know he would love to be in on this conversation."

"Ugh. You're so impossible." Tamara turned back to the bedroom and placed the teacup on the nightstand. "You can't just leave me alone to figure this out?"

"You can have your moment. In your house."

Tamara slid on her sneakers and grabbed her purse. "I'm sorry, Nana. I better go." Anger radiated from her.

"I don't understand what just happened, but I know it wasn't your fault. Your mother has lost her mind."

"You have no idea." Tamara kissed her grandmother and headed for the stairs.

It was my turn to roll my eyes, but I reined my temper long enough to get the girl down the stairs and into the foyer where my father waited not so patiently for an explanation.

"Where are you going? I thought Tamara was sick."

"She's going home to be 'sick' in her own bed." The word *sick* was heavy on my tongue.

"That's ridiculous. She could have stayed here. We are her grandparents."

"It's not necessary. We are going home."

"Good night, Jidu." Tamara kissed his cheek.

"Good night, habibtiJidu. Maybe you can teach your mother some respect. Looks like she has forgotten all that we have taught her the older she gets."

"No, I haven't. Actually, I remember all too well, Baba. But maybe being obedient and respectful to you growing up didn't serve me well in the long run."

"Nuha, do you hear your daughter?"

"Let's go," I barked at Tamara, and this time she didn't dare say anything snarky. I walked out and locked the door behind me. I felt calmer with a locked barricade between me and my father's antics. I had always been the obedient daughter. I never really spoke back, and if I had it was always respectful until my father had tried to interfere with my upbringing of Tamara. The change happened instantly. My mama bear came out in full protective mode, and ever since, I always stood up to him on her behalf. Sometimes I wished I had the same fire for myself as I did for my daughter, but unfortunately, when it came to me, I couldn't find my voice. Maybe one day.

She got in her car, and I drove behind her, making sure this time she couldn't make a final escape.

It struck me at that very moment I was pissed off for not only her hiding out at my parents' house but for the entire situation. I was livid that she was irresponsible and had gotten pregnant. I never really thought she would keep her virtue for marriage—Lord knew technically I hadn't. But to get pregnant out of wedlock? The entire community was going to talk about her, and those not brave enough to say it to my face would be chewing her up and spitting her out behind our backs. The idea of anyone hurting her with a backhanded comment or an outlandish insult or by bad-mouthing my smart, beautiful, and amazing daughter behind her back fucking infuriated me. This mama bear didn't care her cub was all grown up and with a cub of her own on the way, I would cut a bitch if one nega-

CHAPTER 35

tive word out of their mouth hurt my girl. The problem was there would be too many people for me to take on my own.

When we finally got home, she stormed past me. "You got me home, but I'm not ready to talk. Just back off."

I watched her back as she climbed the staircase. Thank God she was home and safe. Everything else would be okay. It just had to be. I wouldn't accept anything less.

Chapter 36

NUHA

They really needed to move to a ranch-style house. Those stairs would be the death of Nuha someday. Her knees ached and her back groaned, but she took those stairs as fast as she possibly could the moment her husband talked down to her girls. She made it down the last step just as Mariam lost her temper with Manni, and Nuha cheered a little on the inside. He deserved it. She was always the meek one out of the four girls. Shy and timid, she kept her head in a book and always obeyed a request, even when it was the reason her life was ruined.

Yet, after she had Tamara, she became a she-wolf if she was protecting her daughter. Nuha admired her newfound strength, and after seventy-two years on earth, she was learning the power of her own strength because of the resilience of her girls.

Manni turned to her in a whirlwind of fury. "I've had it with your daughter's disrespect."

"I heard the comment you made to Tamara. You deserved what she said to you." Nuha wasn't in the mood for this rant. She limped past him and headed to the kitchen to wash the teacup and tray. But he followed her anyway and kept on ranting.

"I'm her father. I can say whatever I like to her or her child. Besides, I didn't say anything that wasn't true."

She slammed the tea tray on the counter and faced him. "This. This is the problem with you. You think you can say anything you want because you are their father. The king of this household. But you cannot. You are not exempt from common courtesy and human kindness."

His face was red, and on the Virgin Mary, steam came from his ears. "She was disrespectful. Coming here demanding to see her daughter, making that sick girl leave like this is a stranger's house. We are her grandparents. What was wrong with her being in our house? Why the attitude and rude remarks? I'll tell you. Because your daughter is an ungrateful and disrespectful woman."

"You surely couldn't be that clueless. Mariam was angry with her daughter. It had nothing to do with her being in our home."

"What's with you lately?" He stopped yelling and stepped closer, his eyes searching for something, but he blinked as though a stranger stood before him and not the woman he married. "You have been really hostile with me."

Nuha sighed. "I regret how we raised our daughters."

"I arranged good matches. And they had a choice. They could have said 'no' to the matches I arranged."

The laugh that came from her lips was a cross between "This is the funniest thing I've ever heard" and "Are you kidding?"

"Who had a choice? Mariam, Maryanna, Sara, or Rena? You told them. You didn't ask

CHAPTER 36

them if they even wanted to get married at such a young age. Rena was the only one you allowed to speak on the phone with the boy, but that was after you accepted the proposal."

"It's how you and I got married. It was how our parents did it and it worked for them. And it worked for our daughters."

"It didn't work out. We burdened them with those marriages. Maryanna and Rena are the only ones who are happy, though lately I worry about Rena. They were blessed with men who were smitten from the moment they met. Sara has had to deal with the worst in-laws and a husband without a spine. He has never taken her side against his controlling abusive mother for her entire relationship. It was you who insisted that Niles meet the woman who trapped him into marriage. And Mariam? Well, we know how her life turned out. Widowed in her thirties, when she could have been happy with the man who still adores her."

"What are you talking about? What man?"

"Asher."

He scoffed. "Asher. I didn't like him. Still don't. He followed Mariam around all the time. I didn't like it."

"Do you know why that boy joined the Navy?"

Manni shrugged and opened the refrigerator. "To hurt his parents. George told me so."

"He joined the Navy because he was in love with Mariam and you and his father arranged her marriage to his cousin."

He grabbed a water bottle and slammed the refrigerator door. "That's ridiculous. What did a young boy like him know about love?" He waved his hand dismissively.

"Let me show you." Nuha walked to the drawer that she had tucked Asher's letter into when the doorbell had chimed earlier. She had just finished translating the content when Tamara appeared on their doorstep. She pulled out the carefully folded letter and handed it to him.

"Asher wrote this love letter to Mariam twenty-six years ago and gave it to her the night you made your announcement of her pending marriage. She didn't have a chance to read it before I hid it from her. But the boy's words were so beautiful, I didn't have the courage to throw it away."

"What does a letter have to do with knowing what love really means?"

She placed the letter on the counter and looked him in the eyes. It was the first time

CHAPTER 36

she'd really looked at him in a long time. For the first time, Nuha saw something in him she hadn't before. Fear.

"I have been married to you for nearly fifty-five years and you have never shown me this kind of love. The kind of passion and devotion they write in books and poetry. Yes, you have been a good provider and head of house. Our children and I have never wanted for anything you couldn't provide. And that might be your love language, but you never learned mine. You have never whispered sweet nothings in my ear or written me something this beautiful. I don't think you even see me."

"I love you, Nuha. How do you not know this?"

Her soul ached for this old fool—he seemed truly perplexed by her feelings. "I love you too. You have been my companion for nearly forever. I couldn't imagine tomorrow without you. But I think you love the wife, housekeeper, and cook I've been throughout our marriage, yet you have never actually seen me. The person." She took his warm hands in her own. "I need you to see me, Manni. Maybe then I could see you too."

Chapter 37

ASHER

"Amoo Asher. Please, can I sleep in my new pink room?"

Bella danced around me like a butterfly. A noisy and energetic butterfly. It was so good seeing her running around again—I think I was still mentally shaken from seeing her little form in that large hospital bed.

"Not tonight. The paint must dry. Tonight, you will camp out in the room with your brothers, but tomorrow you can sleep in your pink room. We will set up all your toys. Promise."

"Pinky promise?" She stuck out her tiny pinky finger and batted her lashes at me. Did that little girl know she had wrapped me around that little finger of hers already?

I latched our fingers. "Pinky promise."

"Yay." She continued her circles around the living room. The nurse had said her medicine would boost her energy, and, boy, she wasn't kidding. I was exhausted—barely keeping my eyes open after an emotional day filled with moving and packing my brother's house, painting Bella's room, and setting up all the furniture in the boys' rooms.

Not to mention the interesting encounter with Tamara at the cemetery. If my cousin were still alive, I would have certainly kicked his ass for the crap he pulled with Mariam and her daughter. I had been an emotional wreck after packing up the house and needed a little break. I found myself in front of the cemetery. I wanted to be alone to yell and scream at my brother for leaving me with such a huge responsibility, but before I could get out my anger, I had heard Tamara shouting at the gravestone.

The pain that girl harbored was a punch in the gut. How could someone—not just any random person, but a father, hurt their child like that? Despite my father's mistakes and misguided ideas of raising "strong men," I never doubted he loved me and Bassam. Even Mariam's dad with all his talk about culture and traditions loved his children—his bad choices ultimately were due to his beliefs in old-school Chaldean values.

I understood Mariam's mood from earlier. She had been completely out of sorts today, and the news of her daughter must have been the reason. I wanted to be there for her, but I didn't want to violate Tamara's privacy. But boy, I couldn't wrap my mind around the fact that Mariam was going to be a grandmother at forty-four, and I'd never been a father.

"Amoo Asher." Bella had slowed down and found her way onto my lap with a book in her hand. "Will you read me a story?"

"Sure, but then it's bedtime."

She yawned. "Yes."

The book was pink, which wasn't surprising, and filled with princesses. But these weren't your average princesses with evil stepmothers. These were princesses with kindness and laughter superpowers. They lived double lives between their royal duties and saving the world with their powers of humanity.

"That was a great story."

Bella didn't even stir. Sometime while I was reading, she had fallen asleep. Happiness filled and warmed the dark places of my soul watching her slow intakes of breath. She still had that rattle in her chest, but her lungs sounded so much better.

I carried Bella to the nest of pillows and blankets my mom had made for her and tucked her into the folds of the blanket. I glanced at the other two snuggled in their beds, and a bit of hope ignited in my chest.

Maybe I hadn't gotten a chance to be a father in the traditional sense. I hadn't even considered fatherhood from the moment I joined the Navy, but now, after a horrific tragedy, I had been blessed to be the guardian of three amazing kids. That surely was the most rewarding gift ever bestowed on me.

They had to be the sunshine after the storm. The brightness after so much darkness. Through the love that brought us all together as a family, we would somehow find a way to heal from the grief.

Chapter 38

TAMARA

Tamara's cranium throbbed with every sound on the university grounds. What she once would have considered white noise blared like speakers between her eardrums. Her limbs ached, and her night of restless sleep had depleted all her strength. The fight with her mom the night before had gotten under her skin and followed her into her dreams, making sleep a treacherous state.

Out of breath and zombie-like, she succeeded

CHAPTER 38

in making it to her seat in genetics class but gagged at the potent whiff of aftershave coming from the boy seated beside her. He must have sprayed the entire bottle of cologne, or possibly bathed in a tub full of spicy musk, because her mouth watered and her stomach rolled. She covered her nose with the collar of her T-shirt in a desperate attempt to mask up from the toxic air around her. After a few moments, the acid lessened in her stomach.

She remembered the saltines she'd found on the kitchen counter next to the coffee machine this morning and searched her bag for the little bundle from her mom. Guilt washed over her as she reread the note that had been placed beside it.

Tamara, you might hate me, but eat the crackers. They will help with the sick feeling. Love, Mom.

Tamara nibbled on crackers and prepared to run to the restroom, but the salt on her tongue seemed to settle the volcano seething in her gut. Her mom always knew everything, from the reason the pop tasted gross and saltines working on morning sickness to the big life stuff. Could she be right about Tamara's reaction to marriage?

The classroom door closed but instead of the professor, his TA, Mason, came in holding a stack of white sealed envelopes. He was handsome in that dorky way, with messy long blond hair that framed an attractive unshaven face and black-rimmed glasses.

"Good morning, Professor Brothers will not be in today and has advised I give you your DNA results and set you free this morning," Mason said.

A series of cheers echoed in the lecture hall, and Tamara exhaled a sigh of relief that she wouldn't have to sit next to Cologne Boy for the next three hours.

"Be advised, he is giving you this extra time to really work on your presentations for next week. Remember, this assignment is worth forty percent of your grade. Any questions?"

A few hands were raised and questions about the assignment were asked, but all Tamara wanted were the results so she could get back to bed. Yet the last question drew her attention.

"I'm adopted. I tested the family members who raised me, but we know that there isn't a blood link between us. How can I possibly spin that into a worthwhile presentation?" Cologne Boy was kinda smart—who figured.

"Well, your question is valid." Mason adjusted his glasses and smiled broadly. "You can take the route of showing how your family is different, using inherited traits versus learned traits."

"Nature versus nurture. That's boss," Cologne Boy said.

"You can also use the origin part of the test—compare what your DNA test returns versus your adoptive family's heritage in percentages. Like you could possibly be two percent Irish and ten percent East Asian and your adoptive family fifty percent Irish and five percent Scottish," a feminine voice said from somewhere behind Tamara.

"There is always an angle. If you find yourself stuck, come look for me and we can toss around ideas. I'll be in Professor Brothers's office from now to noon today and tomorrow." Mason smiled brightly. "If there aren't any more questions, you can come and get your results."

Tamara's stomach dropped. She hadn't even thought about an angle for the presentation. She'd been so wrapped up with her personal crap, it had totally slipped her mind. Her family was dysfunctional but completely normal—with mom, grandparents, and first and second cousins to test but she didn't have much from her father's family except Asher and the kids. Tamara nibbled on another cracker.

"Had a late night of drinking last night?" Cologne Boy watched her chew on the cracker.

"Yup, late night." A late night of crying and restless sleep, but he was under the impression she had been out partying.

"Boss."

Tamara wracked her brain for an angle on her presentation all the way home from school after receiving the DNA results. If Cologne Boy could do nature versus nurture, she could gear the presentation around three generations of women in her family. How they were genetically related, but how each had their own quirks and habits. Maybe even tie in physical features—the Shammas family's green eyes and how many of the grandchildren inherited them. Tamara's mind reeled with ideas, but she struggled to compose a clear, thought-out presentation topic. The exhaustion of last night's restless sleep seeped into her bones, and the moment she stepped over the threshold, she climbed up the stairs to her bedroom and crawled into bed.

CHAPTER 38

It was nearly two in the afternoon when she woke, and her stomach rumbled with hunger. It was the first time in three days she'd craved any form of food. She just hoped she'd be able to keep it down.

There wasn't much to eat that appeared remotely appetizing, and she decided on basic cream cheese and a plain bagel. After toasting her bagel and slathering it with cream cheese, she went to town on the delicious morsel. Her stomach seemed to be okay. She was energized after her nap, and, feeling better than she had in days, it was time to tackle the presentation.

She prepared her workstation with her laptop, unsealed the test results, and smirked at the memory of the joke Lauren had made about Bianca and wondered if *big booty* would be considered an inherited trait. She was without a doubt going to find a way to tie that in somewhere.

She put on her reading glasses and dove into the packet. Her heart fluttered and her breath caught in her throat. Something wasn't adding up. The paper trembled between her fingertips. This must be an error, but how? She had followed the instructions thoroughly. She adjusted her glasses and reread.

Mariam Shammas: 50% Parent/Child
Asher George: 50% Parent/Child
Manni Shammas: 25% Grandparent/Grandchild/Aunt/Uncle/Niece/Nephew/Half Sibling
Nuha Shammas: 25% Grandparent/Grandchild/Aunt/Uncle/Niece/Nephew/Half Sibling
Sara Toma: 25% Grandparent/Grandchild/Aunt/Uncle/Niece/Nephew/Half Sibling
Maryanna Denha: 25% Grandparent/Grandchild/Aunt/Uncle/Niece/Nephew/Half Sibling
Rena Kalabat: 25% Grandparent/Grandchild/Aunt/Uncle/Niece/Nephew/Half Sibling
Niles Shammas: 25% Grandparent/Grandchild/Aunt/Uncle/Niece/Nephew/Half Sibling
Bianca Denha: 12.3% First Cousin/Great grandparent/Great Grandchild
Lauren Denha: 12.1% First Cousin/Great grandparent/Great Grandchild
Lena Denha: 12.3% First Cousin/Great grandparent/Great Grandchild
Thomas Toma: 12.2% First Cousin/Great

grandparent/Great Grandchild

Nicholas Toma: 12.5% First Cousin/Great grandparent/Great Grandchild

Jaxson Shammas: 12.4 % First Cousin/Great grandparent/Great Grandchild

Alec George: 12.6% First Cousin/Great grandparent/Great Grandchild

Bella George: 12.5 % First Cousin/Great grandparent/Great Grandchild

Michael George: 12.8% First Cousin/Great grandparent/Great Grandchild

Jordan Shammas: 0.5 % Fifth Cousin/Distant cousin

Asher should be appearing as 6.25 percent with a range of 2%-11% for the first cousin once removed category. He was her father's first cousin. Not 50%. And the kids, Mikey, Bella, and Alec should be in the 3.13% with the 2%-6%. The blood rushed to Tamara's ears. How was that possible?

Then, Jordan. He appeared to be a distant relative—when he should be listed in the 12.5% with a range of 4%—23% with the rest of Tamara's first cousins.

This had to be a mistake. The room started to spin. The rug was pulled right from underneath her feet. What if this was true? What if

Asher was her biological father? Did he know? Was that why he was so kind to her yesterday at the cemetery? *I have always liked your mother.* What if there was more to their story no one else knew? *What if...* She couldn't even finish that idea. But she had to know if there was any truth to these results. Asher couldn't be her biological father...

Tamara's brain zeroed in on the box of her mom's journals Cross had found last week, and she bolted to her feet. The journal of the year her parents got married was up there. It was the same year she was conceived. Every fiber of her being told her the answers were in that journal. She made the trek to the attic in record time and searched for the box of journals. Right on top, the journal was labeled 1997. She hesitated, not completely sure she wanted to know what secrets lay between those pages. She sank onto the dusty floor of the attic. The blood rushed to her ears, she tugged on the silk ribbon that marked a section on the journal, and an envelope tumbled onto her lap.

The white letter-size envelope fell face-up, and her father's neat scroll stared up at Tamara. *"Mariam."*

She stared at the letter in the same way

as she would look at a bomb ready to detonate. Her shaking finger traced her father's handwriting. She turned the envelope around and traced the seal. It had never been opened. Whatever her father wanted her mother to know had been hidden here for many years. These could have very well been his last words to her mother. With a sour taste on her tongue, she eased the seal open and slid out the letter. Her hands fumbled to unfold the letter. With a heavy chest, she adjusted her reading glasses and began to read. She inhaled a jagged breath when she read the first sentence on the page.

Mariam,

Did you know that I have what is called a cystic fibrosis gene mutation? Along with all my other health problems, apparently, I can't have a child. But I have a daughter. How could that be possible? My questions were answered when I read this journal.

On our wedding night, you came to my bed pretending to be innocent and pure. I was angry with myself for being intoxicated that night. I felt horrible that I might have hurt you. But your journal proved you were just a wolf in sheep's clothing. Through your incessant need to document your life, your secrets were unveiled to me and made me the fool in your world.

I wondered many times if I should tell you that I've learned of your deep, dark secret. I've spent many nights thinking how despicable you truly are to live this large of a lie. To let me fall in love with a child you claimed to be mine but is actually my cousin's daughter.

From the moment I learned of your deceit, I couldn't even look at the girl without seeing his eyes staring back at me. Her dark eyes, so much like his, mocked me from a face I used to love. But your betrayal stole the only person I truly loved away from me, and I wanted you to pay. You are probably wondering why I never exposed the truth. Well, I'm a sick man and need someone to pay my bills, cook, and clean for me—that is what you are to me, a means to an end. But I also didn't want you to be free to be with him. Why would I ever give you the chance to be happy when you made me so miserable?

The doctors say that I might live out the rest of the year and I wanted to be sure you knew that you didn't fool me. When I'm dead and gone, I want you to know that I saw the lies and *secrets underneath the sweet mask you put on for the world.*

You didn't fool me, Mariam.

Nabil

The letter dropped from Tamara's shaky hands. All along Tamara had blamed her father for allowing his illness to take him away from her, but really, it was him just trying to survive after he was betrayed by her mother. He must have seen Tamara as a betrayal too. The person he loved the most turned out to be the biggest betrayal of all.

Tamara had to know what he had found in those journals. The need to get answers consumed her. This letter and the DNA test had stripped her of her identity. Only by reading her mother's private thoughts would she understand the true scope of the lies she'd been fed her entire life. The journal quivered between her fingers as she flipped to the passage with the red ribbon in the center. Her vision blurred from tears, she read. Her mother's deep-seated turmoil over her marriage and her horrible wedding night. Her emotions raw and pained. She described in detail the pressures of pretending for the world that she was happy in her loveless marriage.

The only times she seemed truly happy were her entries of Tamara and the one passage of her night with Asher before she got on the plane to Iraq. Journal after journal, her mom would mention Asher. The memories of him and the love she had for Tamara were her only true joy.

Tamara was startled by her mom's voice calling at the foot of the attic stairs. Her blood began to boil from all the things she'd just learned. Despite feeling empathy for her mother based on her heartfelt sentiments in the journal, she couldn't look past what her mother's actions had cost her. A real relationship with a father. Apparently, she had two fathers, but due to her mother's bad judgment, she didn't have either of them in her life.

Snatching up the letter from Nabil and her mother's journal, she charged down the attic stairs where her mother waited.

"Hey, honey." Her mom's eyes widened, and the smile on her lips froze when her gaze dropped to the journal in Tamara's hands. "Tamara, what... What do you have?" She stuttered on her words. Her face turned as white as a ghost.

CHAPTER 38

Tamara ignored her questions and stomped right past her to the kitchen where she had left the DNA test results.

Her mother followed. "Tamara, why do you have my journal? You know that this is a violation of my privacy."

With every step Tamara took, anger simmered beneath her skin, and it took every bit of control for her not to explode. "I got my test results for my project today. And you know, at first, I didn't think it could be possible. It had to be wrong."

"What are you talking about?" Her mom looked truly confused.

"What would be wrong? It should have been a simple, straightforward test." The laugh that escaped Tamara's lips scared even her. "Simple, maybe." Tamara lifted her chin. "If there weren't secrets in my family tree."

"What are you babbling about? What secret?" Her mom was a great actress. She continued with her lies.

Tamara tossed the results of the DNA test at her mom. "Asher is my biological father."

"What?" She gaped at Tamara. She opened and closed her mouth—her green eyes wide and panicked.

"Oh, and if you're wondering, Dad—or Nabil—for fuck's sake, I don't even know what to call him anymore. He knew, he learned all about your relationship with Asher. He left this letter for you." The letter hit her mother's chest and fell to the floor.

Tears streamed down Tamara's face, and her voice trembled with every word. Her mom scrambled to the floor and retrieved the discarded note—her head down, she skimmed Nabil's last words with a horrified expression.

"He never stopped loving me because of something I did. He stopped caring about me because I looked like my biological father." Something between a sob and a wail exploded from Tamara. "He said I had Asher's eyes, and you know, now I see it. The same black-as-night irises. No one else in the entire two families has them except Asher and Amoo George."

"But I don't understand. We used a condom."

"Condoms are only 99% protection."

"I never believed you could have been his child. If I had known, I would have—"

"You wouldn't have done anything, Mom. You know as well as I do, especially back then, you didn't have the balls to stand up to your

CHAPTER 38

family, especially your dad. Nothing would have been different because it was easier to obey than have your own mind."

"No, I would have fought." Tears streamed down her mother's face, and she just stared in disbelief at the letter Nabil had left her.

"Well, it's too little, too late now." Tamara picked up her keys and walked out the door. She had no idea where she was headed, but she couldn't stand being around her mother for another second.

"Tamara, wait."

"Mom, I'm broken. I didn't trust Cross not to hurt me. I couldn't say yes to marrying him because I worried he would stop loving me, just like Dad."

"Tamara, please come here. Let's talk."

Her mother had gotten off the kitchen floor and followed Tamara to the door. She clasped Tamara's arm, and she recoiled. "Don't touch me."

Tamara's body trembled from sobs, and she ran for her car. Her mother called after her, her own wails following behind. But when Tamara shut the car door and pulled into reverse, her mom's voice was only a distant murmur.

A horn behind blared a little too late. It was less than a second before the crash of metal on metal. Tamara's head slammed on the steering wheel, and everything went dark.

Chapter 39

Mariam

Watching the cars collide was an out-of-body experience. I saw the pickup approaching, and I kept waiting for Tamara to hit the brake, but she wasn't looking—just whipped out of the driveway without a glance to her left or right. It all happened in the blink of an eye. The black truck slammed into the passenger side of Tamara's little sedan. The screeching of tires and the sounds of metal crushing and glass breaking blended with my screams of terror and filled the quiet street of Rosebud Drive. My legs buckled beneath me, and the wind was knocked out of me. Her little car was bent in half in the center.

I staggered but found my footing and ran to her side of the car. She was unconscious, blood trickled down her face, and her head rested on the inflated air bag.

"Tamara." I tried to open her car door, but it was jammed. "Help. Someone, help. Call 911." My tears blurred my vision.

"I'm dialing." The tall, black-haired man had jumped out of his truck and met me beside Tamara's window. "I'm so sorry. I thought she was going to stop."

He was a wreck himself, pacing back and forth in front of the car. "Jesus. Yes, there's been an accident. A young woman is unconscious, looks like there's bleeding on her head."

The man spoke to the emergency operator, but all I could do was press my head to the window and try to reach Tamara.

"Tamara honey, can you hear me?" I knocked on the glass, choking on my sobs. But she didn't even stir. I pulled at the door handle, but it was still either locked or jammed due to the impact.

CHAPTER 39

"Tamara. Oh my God." Cross appeared out of thin air. His skin was ashen, and tears streamed down his cheeks. "Tamara. Is she okay? What happened?" He yanked on the door, but it didn't budge for him either.

"I have the spare." He dug through his jacket pockets and pulled out two key fobs. He unlocked the car and grabbed the handle. It opened this time.

We both scrambled to grab her, but a voice stopped us in our tracks.

"Sir, don't move her, we could do more harm to her injuries." The tall dark-haired man had returned. "The 911 operator said the ambulance is on its way."

We both eased away, terrified of hurting her.

"What happened?" Cross weaved on his feet.

"Man, I'm so sorry. I thought she was going to stop reversing out of the driveway as I approached, but it was like she didn't see me or even look to see if I was coming."

"That's not like her. Tamara is a cautious driver."

"I tried to stop, but it was just too late." The man hung his head in regret.

"Auntie, what happened? Tamara wouldn't just peel out of the driveway without looking." Cross clasped my shoulder, and I lost any self-control I had moments ago.

A renewed set of tears pooled in my eyes, and I brushed them with the back of my hand. "We got in a fight, she was angry at me and took off. I followed her out, and it just happened really fast."

Cross hugged me, and I sobbed into his shirt. "What were you arguing about? Me? The baby?"

"No..." I cried harder. I couldn't even formulate words. "She...learned something about her father and..." I choked on my words. I was a coward. My daughter was in a car crash because of my secrets, and I was still unable to admit the truth.

The sirens blared from around the corner and parked in front of the house, saving me any more inquiries. Cross's mother, Deena, and the rest of the neighborhood had all gathered to see and pray for Tamara.

Ameera appeared beside me and handed me my purse. "I brought you your purse and locked the house for you."

I blinked in surprise. The woman lived ten houses down from me and was as old as Jesus. "Did you walk here?"

CHAPTER 39

"I drove my car to Deena's house and walked over." She placed a hand on my shoulder. "Don't worry, she will be fine. Let us pray together."

I wiped my face with the back of my hand. Ameera clasped my hand, and together we prayed the Our Father and Holy Mary prayer out loud and in Chaldean. I hadn't prayed for quite some time with so much urgency. But with Ameera's hand in mine feeding me her strength, I was able to reach out to my faith for support. Maybe she wasn't the black cloud, after all.

Tamara was loaded into the ambulance, and Cross appeared beside us. "Why don't you ride with her, and I'll follow in my car."

I nodded. "What about all this?" I pointed at the heap of metal that used to be my daughter's car. The sight alone made the acid churn in my stomach.

"Auntie Ameera, can you call Amoo Faris and have him tow it to his shop? I'll call him later to make arrangements with the insurance company."

"Of course, anything you need. Our family is here for you." Ameera turned to me. "God be with you and that beautiful girl. I will light her candles and pray the rosary for her safety."

"Thank you," I said.

Cross helped me into the ambulance, and I was finally able to put Tamara's hand in mine. She felt cold to the touch, and her skin was so pale. I looked at the IV they had attached to her, and I realized I hadn't told them anything about her medical history.

"She's pregnant and allergic to Penicillin," I blurted out to the paramedic working on her vitals beside me. She was a young woman with dark red hair, big blue eyes, and a kind smile.

"Yes, the gentleman told me," she said. "We have everything we need."

"Are my daughter and the baby going to be okay?" I whispered.

She placed a gloved hand over mine and her striking blue eyes bored into my own. "We are going to do everything we can to ensure they get the best treatment possible."

The paramedic worked on the head wound and the blood that caked Tamara's bruised face. Renewed tears streamed down my cheeks, and I just held her hand and prayed for my daughter and my unborn grandchild.

Chapter 40

Nuha

Nuha hadn't spoken to Manni since last night. This morning, when she awakened, he wasn't sleeping beside her. Figured. He was angry about the things she'd said to him. But if voicing her emotions after fifty-five years of marriage drove them further apart, so be it.

It was late in the afternoon, and she had spent most of the day upstairs organizing clothes and finally made it back down to start making dinner to find a surprise on the kitchen counter. Nuha's favorite flowers, a beautiful arrangement of pink peonies wrapped in lovely white tulle had just been left there. It wasn't Mother's Day or her birthday—Niles always brought flowers on those days. Sometimes the girls brought over an arrangement, but they never brought them on off holidays and never peonies. She wasn't sure any of them knew they were her favorite flower.

Where had they come from? The scent was divine, and the sweet floral fragrance radiated throughout the kitchen. She ran her fingers over the soft petals and noticed the little envelope peeking through the two dozen flowers. Manni's neat scroll in Arabic peered back at her.

Haiyti,
Your favorite flowers are pink peonies. You told me once at the farmer's market when we were first married. I remember telling you they are the most beautiful flowers I've ever seen. But as beautiful as they are, they do not hold a candle to you.
All my love,

Chapter 40

Manni

Tears welled in her eyes. Manni never, ever brought her flowers. She was surprised he even remembered the time at the farmer's market and the conversation about pink peonies. Honestly, she was shocked he hadn't confused them with roses. Maybe the old fool wasn't as clueless as she always assumed.

After she arranged the flowers in a vase, there was a little pep in her step, and she decided to make Manni his favorite meal—beef kabab and hummus with Iraqi salad. She took her time grinding the onions, garlic, tomatoes, and parsley. Next, she combined them with the ground beef and spices like her mother and grandmother had shown her as a young girl. They had made sure that Nuha and her sisters knew how to cook for their husbands. She smiled fondly at the memory of all of them being schooled and put to work in the kitchen. Her grandmother always insisted that when they got married, the family recipes were to be passed down from mother to daughter and granddaughter to keep the legacy and traditions alive.

Nuha laughed. Her daughters might have

learned to cook, but the granddaughters—while they had reasonable housekeeping skills and might be able to fry an egg or two, cooking Arabic food would be a challenge for them.

Except for maybe Bianca. She seemed to always be interested in what Nuha made and what spices belonged in each dish, and she was even excellent at distinguishing the different spices in food. Nuha added a teaspoon of allspice, a pinch of salt, a dash of black pepper and combined the mixture gently before molding the meat onto metal skewers for grilling.

Cooking had always been comforting to Nuha. Maybe because it made her feel closer to her mom. Her daughters should have that experience too when she was gone, and she vowed to start the cookbook for her girls. It would be a way to share her grandmother's recipes with her grandchildren. Even her daughters needed to call and verify seasoning or directions for the more traditional dishes. Maybe a mandatory cooking class with the ladies. Her grandsons could join too, but something told her they would eat way more than cook anything. But with a cooking class, she could recreate her time with her own mother, grandmother, and sisters. That would make this house feel less lonely.

Lost in thought and with steadfast work, it wasn't long before the hummus and Iraqi salad were in the refrigerator, and she was outside grilling the kabob.

"Nuha." Manni had joined her outside. He always liked to steal a piece of fresh food off the grill.

"Perfect timing. Dinner is ready." She removed the last kabab from the grill and turned off the flame. She closed the lid on the grill to minimize the smoke from the grease and smiled brightly. "Thank you for the flowers and beautiful note."

"That was Ameera on the phone."

Disappointed that he dismissed her "thank you," she winced. "She's probably calling to gossip. I'll call her back after we have dinner."

"Nuha." He shook his head no, but it looked like he was struggling with his composure. "Sit down."

"Just help me get the tray inside and we can sit at the table."

Nuha picked up the tray and headed into the house. Manni followed her inside, took the tray from her hands, and set it on the countertop.

"Tamara was in a bad accident. She's in the hospital." Tears glinted in Manni's eyes.

Jesus, Mary, Joseph. Nuha's knees weakened. "What happened? Is she okay?"

"Ameera said she was hit coming out of the driveway, but she hit her head and was unconscious when the ambulance came."

Mother Mary, protect us. The world tilted, and she lost her balance, but Manni caught her around the waist. "You never listen, sit down." He steered her to the chair at the kitchen table and kneeled beside her. "Calm down. We need to be strong for Mariam."

"We have to go... Mariam will be losing her mind."

"I know, but you cannot go out in your nightgown. Get dressed, I will put away the food."

Nuha looked down at the sheer house dress—no slip. It would have been scandalous. She nodded and stood. "Manni, I'm scared."

"I know. But everything is going to be okay. I will not accept anything else." He kissed her forehead. This was the man she married and depended on. He may need reminding to be more romantic, but he provided her with what she needed most—strength. The stern, stubborn, hardheaded man who always moved through every moment with confidence. Right now, she needed his confidence like she needed air to breathe.

Chapter 41

ASHER

With only two more days until I would be heading back to base, I had spent the entire day preparing for my departure. My brother's house was completely packed up, except for the furniture the realtor suggested we keep to "stage" the house for buyers. The kids' rooms were set up at my parents' house and all the important papers were signed with Davison. All that was left was to find a nanny capable of doing drop-offs and pick-ups for school

CHAPTER 41

and afterschool activities. Since my future in the military was still up in the air, I had to be prepared to not return for at least another eight months.

When Ameera had called my mother to tell her Tamara had been in an accident, I didn't hesitate, just picked up my keys and drove over. I wanted to repay Mariam for being by my side since I'd returned, but I'd also bonded with Tamara at the cemetery and had grown fond of her.

When I stepped inside the hospital, I didn't know what to expect. I didn't even know if I would be welcomed since our relationship was under wraps. Cross leaned against the wall, his head down, arms crossed, and the weight of the world on his shoulders.

He glanced up at my approach, and I noticed his red-rimmed eyes and how his boy-band hair was standing on the side at the roots from running his fingers through it.

"Hey." He clapped my hand.

"How is Tamara?"

"She's still unconscious. They are running tests. They can't tell us much until they see the extent of the head trauma."

I looked around making sure I wasn't in

earshot of any of Mariam's family and lowered my voice. "And the baby?"

Cross's eyes widened and he glanced around too, nervous we would be overheard. "That's one of the tests they're running."

I placed a hand on his shoulder. "The waiting sucks."

"Yeah, it's the worst."

"How is Mariam holding up?" I watched her pace the waiting room, and her entire family was there with her. Head down, her hair a wild mane, her clothes disheveled, and her arms wrapped around her torso.

I assessed the mood in the room. Auntie Nuha, Sara, and Mary were sitting beside each other, rosaries in hand, their heads down in prayer. Amoo Manni had his eyes closed, probably asleep, and all Tamara's cousins were huddled together, their normally bright smiles gone and replaced with sadness.

"Not good. She's kinda freaked out."

"Asher." Sara was the one who noticed me first.

Mariam froze in mid-pace and recoiled when she heard my name.

"Asher." Her gaze didn't meet mine, and her tone was panicked. "What are you doing here?"

Instantly, I realized I had overstepped, and my presence wasn't welcome. "I'm sorry to intrude, I just heard and wanted to know if I could help with something."

Tears ran down Mariam's face, and a sob escaped her lips. Her family erupted with comforting words. "She's going to be okay," "Let's just pray." But the more they tried to comfort her, the wilder she'd become. Her hands in her hair, she paced and sobbed.

"It's all my fault. She got in the accident because she was angry with me."

"No. Things happen, honey." Mary stood and tried to settle her down with her motherly soothing tone, but Mariam wasn't having any of it.

"No. No. It's because of me. My secrets and my lies…" Another sob exploded from her, and her body trembled.

I wanted to hold her, tell her everything was going to be okay, and I figured with the current circumstances no one would look too deeply at me holding her.

I stepped closer. She jerked back and waved her hands at me. "I can't. I hurt you too. I hurt Nabil. He hated me. You should hate me too.

Everyone has suffered because I was stupid and too scared to stand up for myself." She turned on her father. "I was too scared to stand up to you."

"What are you talking about?" Auntie Nuha walked over to Mariam and grabbed her by the shoulders. "This isn't the time for this talk. Your daughter needs you to be strong."

She pulled away from her mother, hands shaking in the air. "You don't understand, Mom. This is me being strong for her." She wiped her face with the back of her sleeve. "I have to confess all my sins to all of you, maybe then God will forgive me."

"What did you fight about?" Cross stepped up. "You said it wasn't about me."

"No." Her eyes met mine for the first time since I entered the waiting room, and I held my breath, unsure where all this was headed. I sensed everyone's gaze on me, and a sheen of sweat covered my back.

"Auntie, why was she so distracted that she backed out of the driveway without looking for oncoming traffic?" Cross had taken hold of her shoulders now, and his face was serious, but he bore a calm mask. His voice was even and soothing.

Her stare found mine again with renewed tears, but her freak-out had evaporated. "I'm so sorry."

I moved toward her and took Cross's place in front of her. My chest ached. The blood rushed to my ears. She was scaring the shit out of me.

"What is it, Mariam?" I whispered.

"She received her DNA test results for her assignment and we learned that... That..." Her lips quivered. "That you're...her father."

Aunt Nuha's voice. "Jesus. Mary. Joseph. Help us," filled the otherwise silent room.

I reared back. It was like I was sucker-punched in the gut. I bent over to catch my breath. "How? It was only once. We used a..."

"I know." Her voice was just barely a whisper.

"What are you talking about? You were married to Nabil when you had Tamara. He wasn't even in town?" Her father had stood and circled her—fury in each of his strides.

"The night before I left for Iraq with you. Asher and I had..."

"You guys had sex before you went back home to marry his cousin." Mary covered her mouth.

"Jesus. Mary. Joseph." Auntie Nuha did the

sign of the cross.

"I'm oddly not surprised," Sara said. "It should have been Asher they arranged the marriage to. You guys always had feelings for each other."

Amoo Manni pointed his finger in my face. "I always knew you weren't any good. I should..." He raised his fist, and I reared back.

"Manni." Auntie Nuha grabbed his arm. "Don't be ridiculous."

"What did I miss?" Niles had entered with Jordan and Jax, and all three stood at the entrance of the waiting room, bewildered.

"I'm not sure you want to know, khalu." Bianca was the one who answered.

"Why was Dad about to punch Asher? Did he find out they're together or something?" Niles stepped farther into the room and looked between the two of us. The room fell silent. If a pin dropped, you would hear it in the stillness. Nausea rolled through me, my legs buckled beneath me, and I staggered against the wall.

"The family for Tamara George?"

A woman in scrubs broke the most intense moment of my life, and I welcomed the distraction. Me, a father. Tamara, my daughter. My head spun with this revelation. The car-

CHAPTER 41

pet was pulled from beneath my feet, and I was free-falling. My stomach twisted, and acid burned in my throat.

"Yes." Cross stepped up while Mariam and I had a staring contest.

"It was a nasty blow to the head. She has a concussion, and her face is pretty bruised up from the impact of the air bag. But she and the baby are fine."

There were audible gasps and sighs from the entire room. And the word "baby" was repeated a few times.

"Thank God." Lauren's voice was audible over the muttering of the entire family.

"There must be a mistake. She can't be pregnant, she's not married," Auntie Nuha argued with the nurse.

"Whoops." Mariam had that maniacal laugh again that I hadn't heard from her before today. I wondered whether she was having a full breakdown, and honestly, I couldn't blame her. I was holding on by a thread.

"No, it's not. You're going to be a great-grandmother. Cross is the father, and…oh, and she doesn't plan on getting married." She whipped her head and faced her brother. "Niles, you missed my earlier announcement. Asher is actually Tamara's father. We just found out today—before all of this. And, yes, we were dating, as you all know, I've loved him my whole life, but that was before we learned I've kept a child from him for twenty-five years."

Mariam turned to me. "I wouldn't blame you if you hated me for the rest of my life, I hate me right now too. I hate how stupid I was not to think there was any chance that you were the father. I'm truly sorry."

She stomped toward the exit and whipped around again to face her family. Her finger pointed at all of them one by one. "Don't you dare insult Tamara, or actually, don't even mention the baby unless it's to congratulate her." Her wild mane flipped behind her, and she stormed off.

"Well, shit? Did someone body-snatch Mariam?" Niles's voice broke the eerie silence.

"Jesus. Mary. Joseph. What is happening in this family?" Auntie Nuha raised her arms in the air like she was waiting for the answers from the heavens. "Manni. Do you hear this?"

Amoo Manni growled. "This is why you don't give girls freedom. And you had the nerve to defend her to me yesterday."

It was as if I'd watched the entire interaction

through a camera lens. It didn't feel like it was actually happening in front of me. Like I was just behind the camera recording the moments without feeling or reacting. Just on record. My insides were numb. My hands shook. Maybe I was in shock?

I was Tamara's father.

Suddenly the numbness was replaced by hurt and anger. Grief even. Grief for a loss of time I could never get back. It was all truly sinking in. I bent over, trying to catch my breath. But no air seemed to be entering through my lungs. Every single inhale burned my chest, and it was as though a knife stabbed me in the center of my ribs.

"Asher." It was one of the twins—Lauren, I think. "You don't look so good."

I closed my eyes and counted backward from ten in an attempt to calm down. When I got to ten, I was calmer but still really disoriented.

"Should I get a nurse?" The concern she had for me was really sweet and it helped me gather my wits.

"No. I'm okay. It's just been a long day."

The room had cleared out and she led me to a chair. "I think you should sit. Not everyone finds out they are a dad and grandfather in one day."

Holy fuck, I was going to be a grandfather and I never had the chance to be the girl's dad. I didn't understand this feeling brewing inside my chest. It was a mixture of shock, hurt, and fury, and it seemed to be directed at Mariam. She was right—this all was her fault. Had she not gotten married to Nabil, I would have known the child was mine. Why hadn't I questioned it before? Why hadn't I seen it before? She had my eyes. She looked like Mariam with the same delicate features, but she had my black eyes, my black curly hair, and my naturally tanned skin. My temper and directness.

"Everyone went to see Tamara. Did you want to go in there?"

Suddenly it all seemed pretty real. I needed to get the hell out of there. "I have to go."

My words were choked, and my eyes burned with the restraint of tears.

She placed her delicate hand on my shoulder. "It's going to be okay."

I nodded and stood. My legs were heavy, but I gathered myself a bit longer until I made it outside and in my car. I picked up the phone to call Bassam. I needed my brother. I needed his big-brother encouragement. His advice. The moment I started looking up his name in the favorites in my contacts, the realization he was gone hit me like a ton of bricks. The tears came in thrashing sobs and didn't stop for some time.

When I finally made it home, I hadn't expected anyone to be awake, but Baba was sitting in his chair quietly watching something on the Shahid Network in the dark. He looked as wrung out as I felt.

"How is Tamara?" His voice was hoarse and raspy as though he had been crying.

"She's—uh, my daughter." The words were out of my mouth before I could catch them. I was spiraling and falling all at once. Bassam was gone, he left me his kids, and now I'd learned I had a twenty-five-year-old daughter. Despite the resentment I had for him the majority of my adult life, I just needed my dad. I dropped onto the couch adjacent to him and covered my face with my hands.

"What did you say?" His tone was more alert than before.

"Baba, Tamara heya Benti." Sobs raged through my body, but I sucked them back. "Not Nabil's daughter. Tamara is mine."

"How?" His hand clasped my shoulder. "That would mean..."

"Mariam and I... It was only one night. The night before she left to get married." I sucked in a jagged breath.

"This is all my fault." Baba moved back to his chair, choked up by his own tears. "If I would have listened to you and stopped the engagement, this wouldn't have happened. You wouldn't have a daughter you barely knew."

My father's confession and crying made me realize that I'd forgiven him a long time ago, but it seemed like he hadn't forgiven himself.

"Baba. It's okay, no one knew this would happen." I tried to console my father, but he continued in between shaky breaths. "No, I need to say this. You wouldn't have moved away and never wanted to come home. Your brother blamed me. Your mother blamed me. And I blamed myself. Abni, I'm so sorry for what my choices took from you."

I fell to my knees in front of him and clasped his hand. "It's okay. It's over now. I'm home, and even if I have to leave, it will only be for eight months."

"It's a shame. I see you with the kids. You are excellent with them—you would have been an excellent Baba to Tamara. You will be an excellent father to her now."

"But how do I become her father now? She is a grown woman." This was the question that plagued me the most.

"You can be her friend."

"Does she even want me to be a part of her life?"

"Abni, there is only one way to find out."

I nodded, my chest feeling a little lighter. The anguish that had been brewing inside me eased. My father squeezed my hand.

"She has your eyes. The same as mine."

Chapter 42

TAMARA

Tamara's eyes fluttered open. The stench of anesthetic and sterilization reached her, and she blinked away the glare of fluorescent lights to see white sterile walls. The sounds of machines and the tubes on her nose sent a cold chill down her spine. Hospital. Car crash. Her hands clasped her abdomen, and she attempted to rise from the bed, but her head throbbed.

"My baby." Her voice was hoarse to her own

ears.

"Easy, honey. Your baby is fine." A woman in scrubs and a white coat clasped Tamara's shoulders and eased her back onto the pillow. "I'm Doctor Nelson. Do you remember your name?"

"Tamara." Her voice quivered. The baby was okay. The doctor's confirmation eased the panic brewing in her chest. Her reckless behavior had nearly killed the baby. Tears welled in her eyes.

"You banged up your head pretty badly though, so you have to take it easy." Doctor Nelson adjusted the tube plugged in Tamara's nose. "You have a concussion, and a few bruises. I would like to monitor you and the baby for a couple of days, so you will be here with us just a bit longer."

"Okay." The tightness in Tamara's chest unraveled, and tears streamed down her face. She wasn't sure if it was relief that the baby was all right or fear of what could have happened, but the tears turned into choking sobs.

"It's okay, you are fine. The baby is fine." Doctor Nelson patted her arm. She had a kind face, honey-brown eyes, and a long, braided ponytail. "Your family is all in the waiting room and are really excited to see you."

The fight with her mom, the letter from her dad—who wasn't her biological father—Tamara irresponsibly pulling out of the driveway without looking for oncoming traffic...it all hit her like a ton of bricks. She wasn't ready to see anyone—especially her mom. She wasn't over all her mother's lie had stolen from her life.

"Here they come now." Doctor Nelson smiled. "There is a whole lot of them, and we asked them to take turns."

"Hey, babe." Cross's warm hand wrapped around her own.

"Cross. I'm so sorry." The stupid tears started again.

He kissed her hand. "Nothing to be sorry about."

"Tamara, honey. I was so worried." Her mom had stepped up to the other side of the bed, but Tamara couldn't shake the anger that simmered beneath her skin every time her mom spoke a syllable.

"Tammi, thank God you are okay." Auntie Maryanna strode in followed by her sons, saving Tamara from having to engage with her mom. "Another car crash. I'm so thankful

CHAPTER 42

you're okay."

"If you wanted to play bumper cars, all you had to do was ask," Nick said.

"Yeah, we could have taken you to a great spot." Thomas snickered.

"Funny guy, this one," Auntie Maryanna said.

Despite Doctor Nelson asking the family to take turns visiting, four aunts, one uncle, seven cousins, two grandparents, one mom, and one boyfriend all crowded her hospital room. The air was thick with tension between the grandparents and her mom. Tamara's suspicion was solidified when before Nana left, she turned to Mom. "Do not think your display out there was the end of our conversation."

Tamara made eye contact with Lauren, lifted her brows, narrowed her eyes, and glanced in the direction of Mariam. Lauren understood her "What was that about?" Since they were teens, they could have whole conversations using facial expressions, and the older they became, the better they communicated with just their eyes.

Lauren signaled "Later" by looking up quickly and pursing her lips. Tamara was relieved when her aunts gathered their things to follow the grandparents out the door—taking her cousins with them.

"You should leave too." Tamara turned to her mother.

"I'm not leaving you alone." Her expression was shocked and her bright green eyes were kind of wild. Open, intense, and unyielding.

"Cross will stay with me." Tamara clasped his hand.

"Sure." There was so much she needed to say to him. To apologize for her actions the past few days. He didn't deserve her wrath or the mistrust. It wasn't his fault she was screwed up because of her parents.

Her mother looked between them, and tears formed in those big eyes. Tamara hated the guilt that crept inside her chest, but she wasn't going to yield. She needed space from her mom to process everything, and her head wasn't clear enough for it at the moment.

"Fine," she said.

"You want to take my car?" Cross reached into his pockets and retrieved his keys for her.

"No." Her eyes met Tamara's. "You don't want me in the room and that's fine, but I'm not leaving the hospital."

Without another word, she walked out and

CHAPTER 42

closed the door behind her, leaving Cross and Tamara alone.

Cross sat in the chair beside her and clasped her hand. "You scared me. You scared everyone."

"I'm sorry. Sorry for everything. Sorry for how I treated you." She brought their joined hands over her chest. "I love you. I want our forever. I know that now. I was just afraid you would be like my dad and stop loving me. But now I know, he didn't stop. He just knew the truth about me. Cross, he wasn't my biological father. And he knew the truth."

"I know." Cross kissed her hand.

"How? I just found out before the accident."

"Your mother. She had a full-on meltdown the moment Asher showed up at the hospital. Everyone knows everything. Even him."

"She had a meltdown?" That was so unlike her. She was always in control of her feelings and emotions. Always prim and proper. But Tamara guessed it was a mask—it seemed she wore many masks to disguise her truths.

"She was scary. She just told everyone that Asher is your father and you learned it from the DNA test. That Nabil knew and hated her, and that Asher should hate her too."

"I can't believe it. Why would she do that?"

"She kept saying if she confessed her sins maybe God wouldn't take you away from her."

His words hit Tamara right in the gut. Was her mother really to blame? Maybe her mom should have figured out sooner that Asher was Tamara's biological father. But maybe it was too late. Tamara remembered all the angst in her mom's journal. The grief she described in being forced into an arranged marriage. The passages of how her marriage was loveless, lonely, and brutal. Her own eyewitness accounts of how she'd shouldered the burden of being the only breadwinner and providing a loving and safe home for Tamara. Suddenly all Tamara's fury at her mom evaporated to be replaced by remorse.

"And she announced you're pregnant, I am the father, and you don't want to get married." Cross laughed. "It's funny now, but at the time, even your grandfather was dumbstruck."

"Well, that explains the reason my grandparents were being distant with me."

"It was a lot for them. Your mom hit them with all the whammies. Then threatened them not to mention the pregnancy if they weren't going to congratulate you."

CHAPTER 42

"What did Asher say?"

"The poor guy, he was completely shocked. He looked green. Oh, and apparently, they've started dating too."

That must have been a sucker punch for Asher after all he had been through. Learning he had a daughter when she'd just been in a car crash after he lost his brother and sister-in-law in a car crash two weeks ago. He and Tamara had become friends after her own meltdown in the cemetery, and she wondered if he was happy or saddened by the news. What if he didn't want a relationship with Tamara? What if her mother's actions had damaged another relationship with a father?

"Hey, don't worry." Cross caressed her bruised cheek. "He just needs a moment to process."

"I know."

"Rest now."

"Cross."

He kissed her hand again. "Yeah."

"I do want to get married. But I don't want to do it like we are ashamed of this baby and are getting married to hide our mistakes. This child was created out of love with two parents that adore it."

"I told you, I want to marry you, today, tomorrow, next year, in five years. You want to wait? We wait."

"I just want to wait until after the baby is born."

"Then we wait until after the baby. But who is going to tell your grandparents and mine?"

"I don't know," she said. "I honestly don't care. If they love us, they will have to get over it."

He laughed, and the tension he had been holding in his shoulders seemed to float away. "Maybe your mom will scare everyone into submission."

"I still can't believe it all happened."

"I know where you get your fire from." He brushed a wild strand of hair from her face. "Do you need anything?"

"Can you hold me?"

He gifted her with that lopsided grin and climbed into bed with her. She cuddled against his chest. The feel of his warm body combined with his spicy scent comforted her spirit. There had been one constant truth in her life: Cross. Always kind, endlessly loving, and forever in her heart. He embodied the sincerest meaning of love.

"I love you, Cross."

"I love you."

She closed her eyes and let the comfort of his arms carry her into dreamland.

When she awakened the room blared with sunlight, and Tamara's mom was sitting in the chair beside her bed. Tamara's body ached, her head pounded, and her mouth was dry.

"I sent Cross home to shower and get some food. He will be back later."

Tamara nodded. "Can you hand me some water, please?"

The water cup trembled in her mom's hand, and Tamara grabbed it before it fell from her shaky fingertips.

Tamara sipped the water and noted her mom's red-rimmed eyes, disheveled appearance, and face swollen from crying. Tamara's own tears welled in her eyes. "Mom. I'm sorry."

"Oh baby, this isn't your fault. It's all mine." Her mom placed the cup back on the side table and sat at the edge of the bed.

"I just saw the results, read the letter from Dad, and lost it."

"Shh." Tamara's mom hugged her. "I didn't know. I swear, I didn't know."

Tamara let the scent of Chanel Chance wash over her as she held on to her mom and let the tears flow. "He didn't hate me, Mom. He just saw Asher in my eyes. All these years, I thought he hated me because I got him sick with the flu and it gave him pneumonia."

"Oh, honey. I'm to blame. I'm so sorry. If I had known all those years ago that I was pregnant with Asher's baby, I wouldn't have gotten married. I've never had the strength to fight my family for me, but I have never had a problem telling anyone to fuck off for you."

Tamara's sob turned into a wet laugh. "I heard you scared the crap out of everyone yesterday."

Her mother climbed onto the bed, and Tamara tucked her head on her shoulder. "The car crash so close to losing Bassam and Lydia... I turned into the Hulk, and the need to protect you gives me strength I didn't realize I possessed."

"You're going to need it. Cross and I aren't getting married until the baby is born. I don't want to act like we were shamed into getting married."

"What about Cross?"

"He is just happy we are getting married."

CHAPTER 42

"Well, I learned my lesson from my parents' mistakes with me. I will support whatever you want."

"Thanks." Tamara glanced up and looked at her. "Mom, have you talked to Asher?"

"No. Not since my ridiculous outburst yesterday. He is probably hurt and confused. I can't blame him."

"Do you think he is going to want a relationship with me?" Tamara felt like a little girl asking her mom that question, but the little girl inside her truly yearned for a relationship with her dad.

"Yes, I do. Me, on the other hand—it's more complicated."

"How do you feel about him, Mom?"

"I love him. Never stopped, and I will probably love him until the day I die."

"You need to tell him. You need to explain—you need to do a grand gesture like in a romance novel."

"I don't know—he probably hates me. I would hate me. For the love of God, you should hate me." She covered her face.

"I don't hate you. And as for Asher—there's only one way to find out."

Her mom picked up the remote and started

flipping through the channels. "*The Price Is Right* or *Three's Company?*"

"Terry, Cindy, or Chrissy?" Tamara snuggled deeper into the pillow. "Chrissy episodes are the better ones."

"Let's see." Her mom flipped to the channel, and in unison, mother and daughter groaned when Terry appeared on the screen.

"It always annoyed me that they made Terry a nurse, but she still was an airhead."

"Me too. Like I'm smart enough to be a nurse, but I still have the common sense of an ant."

"Still, I love the show," Tamara said.

"Me too."

"We own a bookstore, by the way. I signed a couple of days ago, but you mic-dropped the whole baby thing and stole my glory."

"Really? That's amazing. I'm so happy for you, Mom."

"I'm a little nervous now, but if I've learned anything lately, it's to follow your heart."

"Yes, follow your heart right to a pile of books," Tamara teased. She was so proud of her mom. She was fighting for what she wanted. Fighting for Tamara, and she couldn't ask for a better mom and best friend.

"Oh, I love this episode. It's when Jack finds

CHAPTER 42

the quiz in the magazine, and he thinks that either Janet or Terry filled it out." Her mom raised the volume on the TV.

"Me too. My favorite scene is when Jack falls in the lake."

"Serves him right." Mom laughed.

They dropped the big topics and spent the rest of the afternoon watching reruns of '70s sitcoms, leaving the stresses of the past couple of days in the real world behind while they indulged in the make-believe.

Chapter 43

Asher

My hands trembled around the arrangement of flowers—white roses for my daughter. My daughter. The more I thought about it, the less it sank in. My brain struggled to wrap around the idea, but my heart fluttered at the concept.

My mouth dry, I softly knocked on the hospital room door, praying Mariam wasn't inside. I wasn't ready to tackle that subject. The betrayal from Mariam seemed much too great,

CHAPTER 43

despite my head telling me she had no idea the girl was my daughter.

"Come in." Cross's voice came from the other side of the door.

I slowly opened the door and eased inside. A battered and bruised Tamara lay on the hospital bed, and Cross was perched beside her in the adjacent chair.

"Hey." Cross's gaze traveled between Tamara and me with an expression of unease. "Come in."

"Hi." I fidgeted, not sure what to do. "These are for you." I handed her the flowers, and she brought them to her nose.

"Thank you. They're beautiful." She handed the bouquet to Cross. "Can you see if you can put them in water?"

"Sure thing." He gestured for me to take his seat and walked out of the room, leaving me and Tamara alone. I sat in the chair beside her bed and studied her face. She did most certainly have my eyes, my complexion, my black curly hair. It was strange seeing the resemblance now that I knew the truth.

"God, how didn't anyone realize that you're my father? I look so much like you."

"So, we aren't going to beat around the bush,

huh?" I grinned. That's what I liked about her the most. Her frankness. She was confident, smart, and strong. A little hint of pride sparked in my chest.

"What's the point?" She smiled. "I'm not really good at filtering my thoughts before they come out of my mouth."

"I like it. Takes out the guesswork on my end."

"So I'm the daughter of Asher George and the granddaughter of George George and Nuha George."

"Yes," I said. I feared the joy that flourished in my chest at her words. What if she didn't want a relationship with me?

"Are you disappointed?" Her tone had dropped, almost like she was afraid to ask me.

"Shocked, yes. Disappointed, absolutely not. I'm happy. I just wish..." I struggled with my words. My anger at her mother and myself shouldn't be directed toward her.

"Wish you could have raised me?" She finished my sentence for me.

"Yes. After what you told me about Nabil, I wish I could have saved you from all of that. It's my job as your father to protect you, and without knowing the truth, I wasn't able to do

CHAPTER 43

that." My skin pricked with a protectiveness I didn't think was ever possible two weeks ago. The more I remembered the things Tamara had said, the angrier I became.

"He knew," Tamara said. "He left my mom a letter in her journal from the night you guys spent together. Apparently, he learned when I was twelve that he couldn't have children. That's why my parents couldn't have another child after me."

Her tears rolled down her cheeks, and I wanted to bring him back from the dead just so I could kill him myself for hurting her.

"Why didn't he say anything when he found out?"

"To hurt my mom and probably you too."

Her last statement hung in the air between us. "Are you disappointed that I'm your father?"

"No. You know, after my meltdown at the cemetery. I wished my dad would have been more like you. Turns out, I got my wish in a way."

I exhaled a sigh of relief. "You are obviously an adult and about to become a parent yourself. I know you're not a child and don't need a father. But can we get to know each other?"

"I'd like that." She gave me another smile, and my anxiety eased with her answer.

"Me too."

Chapter 44

MARIAM

My mother's steel blue Jaguar parked in the driveway was the last thing I expected to see outside my house after my all-nighter in the hospital. She was sitting on my front porch, her hair down around her shoulders, wearing a modest navy summer dress with a book in hand. I'd always loved that Tamara and I shared the same love in romance books as my mom.

"Hi, Mom."

"Mariam. How are Tamara and uh, the baby?" She hesitated on the word *baby*. I knew it was a miracle she hadn't fainted upon learning about the pregnancy. I couldn't be angry or surprised. For our culture and combined with the Catholic religion, it was a blow. When relatives and people in the community heard about the indiscretions of me and my daughter, our family's name would be tarnished.

"Both good. They will probably release her tomorrow." I unlocked the front door. "Want coffee?"

"Yes, please." She put a bookmark inside her paperback, tossed it in her purse, and followed me inside.

It was a good thing that my mom was with me. The moment I walked into the kitchen and noticed the letter, my journal, and the test results on the counter, tears welled in my eyes. The sequence of events that followed hit me like a runaway train. Tamara might have forgiven me, but I still needed to see Asher, and honestly, I needed to forgive myself for my mistakes and the lives I'd ruined.

"Mariam." She placed a hand on my back. "She's fine."

I turned and collapsed into my mother's

CHAPTER 44

arms. "Mom, when that car hit hers, after losing Bassam and Lydia…"

"I know. But habibi, she's fine. The baby is fine. Thank God we were lucky." My mom held me, and I let her. I needed her comfort and her to remind me it was going to be okay.

"Yella, sit down. I'll make us Turkish coffee."

I watched her bustle around my kitchen. She knew it pretty well, and I remembered all the times she would come here and care for Tamara while I was at work and Nabil was locked up in his own room.

"Mom, Nabil knew Tamara wasn't his. He knew and didn't tell me."

"What? How do you know?"

I handed her the letter that was on the kitchen counter. "When Tamara got the DNA results, she went looking for my journals and found this letter from Nabil in the journal from the year we got married. It was tucked in the passage about my night with Asher."

"Jesus. Mary. Joseph. Forgive us." She made the sign of the cross. "Why would he not say anything? How long did he know?"

"Apparently for a very long time."

She leaned against the kitchen counter and started reading. Open-mouthed, eyes wide, she seemed just as horrified by Nabil's letter as I had been. "I feel sorry for him. I feel sorry for all of you. You all suffered for our mistakes."

She dabbed her eyes with the tissue she always tucked in her bra. "Sit. Sit. I'm going to make us coffee."

I sat at the kitchen table and stared at Nabil's words. They were so pained, and I deserved what he had done to me. But in his attempts to punish me, he hurt Tamara, and for that, I couldn't give him a pass. That girl had believed she had gotten her father sick and he hated her for it. She grew up thinking a parent could one day stop loving their child.

"Have you talked to Asher?" My mother placed a steaming coffee cup in front of me.

"No. I don't know how to face him, especially after my meltdown yesterday."

"You were in rare form." She snickered. "Your father was terrified of you."

"Oh my God. Baba. What did he say after all of that?" I covered my mouth.

"He ranted a little, but I helped him realize it was all his fault. If he would have allowed you to make your own path in the very beginning, none of this would have happened."

"And he agreed?"

CHAPTER 44

"If he knows what's good for him." She winked. "Anyway, how do you feel about Asher?"

I looked down at my hands. "I love him, Mom. I've always loved him."

She nodded, took a sip of her coffee, and her eyes searched my face. "I brought you something. But before I give it to you, I need you to know that in this whole situation, I acknowledge my own mistakes. And I'm deeply sorry for my part in the pain I caused you."

She pulled out an aged paper that was folded into a square and handed it to me. "I found this with all your gifts after your graduation party. After your father had announced your engagement, I knew I couldn't give it to you. I was selfish. I was trying to keep the peace in my family, but what I should have done was fight for you with the same fearlessness you fight for Tamara. For this, I'm very sorry."

I gently unfolded the withered paper and saw the neatly scribbled words in Arabic. My stomach dropped to my feet. "Asher's letter. But I thought I lost it."

I remembered the hurt in his eyes when I told him that I misplaced it before reading it. It matched the look on his face the moment I told him that I couldn't stand up to my parents and then last night when he learned about Tamara. He was heartbroken, and it was me who kept hurting him. The letter was in Arabic, but after that summer, I didn't have any interest in learning to read and write the language anymore.

"I can't read it."

"I know. I could read it to you, but I want you to be able to truly appreciate his words on your own, so I translated it for you." She pulled out another letter and handed it to me. My fingers trembled against the page. "It sounds a little formal in English, but that is because the Arabic written language is a little formal."

The lovely Mariam,
Did you know your eyes aren't just green? They are like a chameleon. The colors in your eyes shift with your mood and the brightness of the light around you. The moment sunlight bathes your enchanting features, the green dances in shades of golds, blues, browns, and I could stare into them forever. Your smile brightens the darkest of days, and your laugh is the melody that speaks to my soul. Your body—that you often ridicule—rivals that of

Greek goddesses. But it is your mind that completely enthralls me.

If you haven't figured it out yet, I am head over heels for you. You have captured my heart, invaded my thoughts, and are the starring role in my dreams. I fell in love with you the moment we met. I know it sounds like a cliché, but it's true. We were moving into the house across from yours, and you were sitting on the back porch, your nose in a book and ignoring the world around you. I was captivated by your concentration, and when the sun showered you, you radiated like a beacon of light, and I have never been able to look away from you since that moment.

There are times when you look at me and I'm lost for words. So in love, I'm tongue-tied around you. So enchanted, I can't look away from you. Unable to express my devotion out of fear of losing you. But then, there are moments when you grace me with your shy smile, you bite your lower lip and bat those luscious lashes at me, and hope ignites my very soul. And I think, just maybe, you feel the same way.

This letter may be too forward and my confession of love and devotion unwelcome. But I will never be sorry for expressing my senti-

ments. I would rather play the fool than one day regret not telling you just how much I adore you.

If you feel even the smallest of romantic affections toward me—I would be the happiest man.

All my love and deepest devotion,
Asher

Tears stained the page in my trembling hand. "Mom. That was so beautiful."

"Yes. One of the most beautiful love letters I've ever read. And he was just a boy."

"He told me he loved me—that night—but I never dreamed his feelings were this deep for me."

"The boy deserves better than what we have all done to him. Anyone able to love that deeply and that beautifully is an incredible soul."

"I know." I wiped my face with a paper napkin. "But how do I make up for all that I've done to him?"

"I don't know. But you have to be as vulnerable as he was in that letter. You owe him that much."

Buzzing with adrenaline, I leaped from the chair and busied myself by making my mother

CHAPTER 44

and myself glasses of ice water to go with our Turkish coffees and noticed the journal on the table. I knew instantly the only way he could see the depth of my love for him all those years was for him to see it for himself.

Chapter 45

Asher

"Well, I'll be damned." Ragheed and I were sitting on my back porch drinking beers on our last night in Michigan before we had to face our fate at the hearing. I'd just finished detailing the entire scene with Mariam and her family at the hospital. I was still raw and reeling from the entire thing.

"Yup."

"So, you have a daughter and you're about to be a jidu?"

"I'm still wrapping my head around it all."

"We are leaving tomorrow—have you at least had a chance to talk to the girl? Tamara."

"Yeah, yesterday afternoon." I remembered our conversation and laughed. "You'll like her. She's smart, funny, and right to the point. She told me we could get to know one another, and we plan to email while I'm away."

"What about Mariam?"

"I'm not ready to see her. My mind tells me she didn't do it on purpose, but I feel completely betrayed that I never got to experience raising my daughter."

Ragheed pressed his hand over his chest. "That's rough. But you should talk to her. We are leaving again—with this crazy world we live in, we don't know if we have tomorrow. You shouldn't have any unsaid words."

I stared up into the clear dark sky and marveled over the radiance of the bright stars. Despite the warm summer night, ice flooded my veins at the mention of speaking to her. "That's the thing. I don't know what to say. I've got nothing to say to her. Not now. I'm not sure I'll ever be able to look at her face again and not be angry."

"Well, shit. I can't really blame you, Akhi."

Ragheed stood and stretched. "I better be going. I'll pick you up at 0400 hours."

We headed back into the main house while Ragheed said his goodbyes to my parents and the kids.

Bella strolled over and looked between us and clasped my leg. "You are leaving with Amoo Asher tomorrow?" she asked Ragheed.

"Yes, beautiful."

"You take care of him, okay?"

"Oh, sweetheart, I always have his back."

She nodded and reached up for me to carry her. "I believe you."

"Well, looks like you finally won her over." He laughed.

"All it took was blood, sweat, tears, and a pink bedroom."

When we walked out onto the porch, I nearly tripped over a large gift box. After gathering my bearings, I noted the parchment with my name on the envelope. I only knew one person who made their As with a smiley face in the center. It was from Mariam. After Ragheed and I said our goodbyes, I picked up the box and went to my room but didn't get a chance to look at the letter or the contents inside until I'd read Bella the same story three times and refereed two fights between Mikey and Alec—of course each fight was started by Alec, because Mikey was still an angel.

When the house was completely quiet, I finally locked myself in my room and closed the door. I hesitated at first, not sure I wanted to know what was written inside the letter or what was in the box.

But curiosity finally got the better of me, and I opened the letter.

Dear Asher,

I can't begin to express how sorry I am, for everything. You deserved so much better. All I can do is offer my deepest apologies for the pain I've caused. I need you to know that from the moment you sat beside me on the swings and asked me about the book I was reading, I've been deeply and completely in love with you. Back then, I was scared to fight and scared to express my feelings, but I'm not afraid anymore. My love for you and my love for our daughter gives me strength. I think you saw a little of that in the hospital the other day.

If you never want to see me or hear from me again, I understand. But I couldn't let you leave tomorrow without telling you just how much you set my heart on fire. You are the very best man I know. You amaze me with your strength, wisdom, courage, and your ability to love so very deeply.

I love you, Asher. Yesterday, today, tomorrow, and always, I love you with my entire mind, body, and soul.

I hope one day you will find it in your heart to forgive me.

Love always and forever,

Mariam

My hand trembled on the lid of the gift box as I eased it open. My heart fluttered at the sight of the baby album. This had to be Tamara. I might be biased, but she was the most beautiful baby in the world. I flipped through the pages. Each one had an update on what she liked and disliked eating. Her favorite toy or game and her new words. Tears burned my eyes when her first word was *baba*, and I laughed out loud when her first phrase was "big booty dance," and a picture showed a little Tamara, who looked a lot like Bella, dancing. The album went on for eighteen years. Just one page for each year, but it was like Mariam had given me a glimpse of Tamara and a morsel

CHAPTER 45

of the childhood I missed. I placed the album in my duffle bag beside the picture of Bassam, Lydia, and the kids at Christmas.

I was so distracted by the pictures I hadn't realized there were also three notebooks inside the box. I recognized one of them at once—it was the beautiful leatherbound journal Mariam carried around with her everywhere. I couldn't forget it, because I'd given it to her for Christmas one year.

I flipped through the pages. It was her thoughts and fears all neatly scrolled in delicate handwriting. I wanted to dive in and devour her words, crawl around in her head, but my mind wouldn't let me. I didn't want to soften toward her. I wanted to hold on to my anger at her. It was just safer that way.

Four a.m. came too quickly, and before long Ragheed and I were in San Diego and driving to the base. My heart and mind were still arguing about reading the journals the entire flight home. I knew I was going to cave soon—I just wanted to torture myself a little longer—but I busied myself memorizing Tamara's baby book.

Now another war raged inside me as we parked the Mustang and marched into the base. The need to be home with the kids and now to get to know my daughter was all-consuming, but everything I'd worked for in the past twenty-six years might just be flushed down the drain. Our hearing was tomorrow morning, but we received a message to report to Martin's office after we landed.

My pulse raced as we greeted seamen, officers, fellow senior chiefs, and lieutenants as we moved through the halls.

"I don't understand why he wanted us to report here, now," Ragheed mumbled under his breath for the third time.

"I'm just glad we wore our uniforms on the plane." It would have been awkward walking around these hallways dressed as civilians. "We would have wasted time having to get changed, and you know he hates being kept waiting."

From the moment we received the message, Ragheed had been an anxious mess. A sheen of sweat covered his brow, and his tanned skin held a greenish hue.

"Finally," Kal said.

He and Basher looked like two worried hens pacing in front of Martin's office door, and if it didn't feel like two dragons were head-butting inside my stomach, I might have laughed out loud.

"You landed over an hour ago. Let me guess, Charming drove?" Basher asked.

"What's wrong with my driving?" Ragheed lifted his chin.

"You drive like a khala." Kal laughed. "My great aunt, Ama Evelyn, drives faster than you."

Ragheed rolled his eyes but before he could retort, the office door opened, and Lieutenant Commander Martin walked out. We all stood at attention, and the two clowns quit their banter.

"At ease. Charming. Pan. Welcome back." He turned to me and gripped my hand. "Son, I'm very sorry for your loss."

"Thank you, sir," I said.

"Okay, come into my office. We need to talk." He stepped back into his office, and we followed him inside.

I entered and Ragheed followed, but I was surprised to see Kal and Basher enter and close the door behind them.

Martin took his seat behind the desk and grinned. "The charges against the two of you have been dropped, and you can thank the filming skills of Beast and Tarzan."

"How? Did the girl come forward?" Ragheed fell into the seat in front of the desk.

"Go on and tell them, Beast. I get so much joy in hearing this story." Martin leaned back in his chair and held his cigar. He looked at me. "Son, you look like you might need to sit down."

I took the seat beside Ragheed and turned to Kal. "What happened?"

"Well, when I came back from Detroit, me and Basher were having drinks at the pub and there he was, boasting about taking what he wants from women—whether it's consensual or not. I recorded it"—Kal grinned—"just in time to capture the details of how he followed the bartender into the bathroom."

"Show them the video," Basher said.

"Oh yeah," Kal said.

He reached for his phone, but Martin spoke. "No, let's watch it on my bigger screen." He flipped on his computer and tapped a few keys. Soon, the jerk's voice blared from the speaker. He was intoxicated, which was probably why the idiot didn't realize our buddies were seated in the booth right next to his.

I couldn't believe my ears—well, I could. He was a sorry piece of trash demeaning woman with his locker-room talk. He bragged about grabbing her fat ass and called Ragheed and me camels for breaking up his fun.

"This video has been submitted, and he is under investigation. Even if the girl will not testify against him, I don't think he has much of a career with the Navy anymore," Martin said.

"So that's it? We are free and clear?" The shock in my voice was palpable.

"Yes. And just in time—you four have an assignment," Martin said.

My heart fell. I had been sure I would be returning home after this hearing. Though technically, I had prepared to not return until my time ended, I wasn't ready to leave the kids. Leave the daughter I just met. As Martin detailed our task, all I kept thinking was I had people depending on me. Counting on me to come back home. For the first time in my life, I wanted to plan my life for someone other than myself.

Chapter 46

Mariam

It had been fourteen days, eight hours, twenty-four minutes, and thirty-six seconds since the moment I left the package with my journals on Asher's doorstep. I didn't expect him to just forgive me, but I hoped I'd hear something. Maybe a text message or email informing me that I was indeed a horrible human. I'd take his rage and anger. Any emotion would give me hope he still cared for me, but his silence gnawed at my heart, mind, and in-

CHAPTER 46

securities.

I yanked my journal from my purse and prepared to pour my thoughts onto the empty page—a judgment-free safe space where I didn't have to filter my words and hold back any feelings. It was the form of info-dumping tactic I'd used my entire life to free all the things I kept bottled up inside, but my pen froze after my usual salutation of "Dear Diary."

I skimmed through the words I'd written these past two weeks. There were a few mentions about the salon, the bookstore, and my family, but everything seemed to revolve around Asher. *I wish Ash...*and *I hope Ash...*and *I miss Ash.*

Pages and pages of things I wanted to say to him, but Dear Diary wasn't the intended audience for my journal. They were sentiments and acknowledgments meant for only one man. Every passage from the moment Asher entered my life thirty years ago was a sort of love letter to him. Sure, I had expressed my hurt and the pain of my marriage and my family's interference in my life, but Dear Diary was an alternative to Dear Asher. I flipped to a clean page and allowed all my emotions to pour onto it.

Dear Asher,

I know that in the letter I left you two weeks ago, I said that I would understand if you never wanted to speak to me, but I take that back. I will never stop trying to make things right between us. I've wasted too much time pushing back my feelings and accepting that our being apart was fate. It wasn't destiny. It was the horrible choices that led me to lose the man I love. Fear that kept my daughter from knowing an incredible father. It was my need to please my family that broke your heart and robbed you of a child. Not anymore. I don't choose to be compliant. I can't lose you again, Ash. I won't. I need you to know that I'm going to fight for you. Fight for us. Fight you for us if I must. I should have done that twenty-six years ago, but I didn't have the courage. I have the bravado now, and I will do everything in my power to convince you to give me another chance.

I noticed my journal entries all start with Dear Diary, but they should have been addressed to you all along. So read them, send them back, or burn the letters, but be prepared to receive one letter every single day for the rest of my life.

I'm sorry.

I know those two words seem simple and don't express the extent of the sorrow, shame, and remorse for how I've treated you. I guess there's a bit of truth in the saying, "You hurt the ones you love," because I love you, Asher. I miss you. It's been fourteen days since you left, and seventeen since you last held me. If I close my eyes, I can remember the feel of your arms around me, and it takes my breath away.

So, to fill you in on the past two weeks, the bookstore is starting construction this week. Tamara had her first ultrasound. She and Cross got to hear the baby's heartbeat for the first time. Cross recorded it on his phone and let me hear it. I'll tell Tamara to send it to you. I met the new nanny you hired to help your parents out with the kiddos. Maria is super sweet and the kids like her. Even Alec didn't have any complaints. She's off on Saturdays, and I've volunteered my highly sought-after babysitting skills in her place. Since you had such great success with karate classes, I've enrolled Niles's boys along with Bella, Alec, and Mikey. We go to karate class, pizza, a movie, and ice cream. By the time they're home, they're usual-

ly whipped from the activities. I've taken over bedtime on Saturdays too. Bella insists we read the princess book she read with you every night, and I can't seem to get Mikey to sleep in the bed. Your mom says he sleeps in Bassam's chair every night. Alec has become more of a jokester than angry—I guess that's progress. Your parents seem tired, and I'm hoping that the break on Saturdays gives them time to rest. They do light up around the kids, though. Auntie Juliette thinks the entire troop of kiddos reminds her of our crew. Makes me wonder, will Bella fall in love with Jaxson in the same way, I fell in love with you?

I wish you were with us. The kids miss you. I miss you.

All my love,
Mariam
P.S. Look out for another letter tomorrow.

"What are you doing back here?" Zaynab peered into the office of Books and Bites. "Eddie is here."

I carefully ripped the page from the worn leatherbound journal. "Who?" My mind was still on the babbling words I'd just spilled all over the paper.

CHAPTER 46

"Eddie, the hot construction foreman? He is here to go over the renovation blueprints."

"Sorry, I forgot all about the meeting. My mind is completely elsewhere."

"Are you regretting this business venture now that you're going to be a grandma?"

"What?" I came around the desk. "No, after becoming a nana, the store is the best thing in my life."

"Okay, good." She brushed her hair behind her ears. "Then why did you look so sad when I came in here?"

"I'm wooing Asher." I handed her the letter.

She smiled as she skimmed the writing, but as she read, worry danced behind her big brown eyes. "You are really exposing your feelings. You sure about this?"

"I'm at the all-is-lost moment of my story." I ran my fingers through my hair. "I have already lost my heart...shouldn't I try to get it back?"

"Yup. And I'm going to help you." Zaynab hugged me. "Between the two of us, we will knock down his barricade with all our grand gestures. What perfume were you wearing the night you had sex?"

"What I always wear—Chanel Chance." I

folded the pages of the entry neatly and placed them inside the journal. I planned on mailing it right after the meeting.

"Okay, make sure you spray this page with it before you send it out. And every other letter you send. We are going to attack all his senses."

"You're the best friend ever." I squeezed her shoulder. "Now let's go meet Hottie Foreman."

"Is it bad that I want to do really bad things with him?" Zaynab asked.

"If I wasn't in love with Asher, I would want to do really bad things with him too." I dropped the neckline on her fitted T-shirt. "Better let the girls do some talking."

"Well, if they are gonna chat, I might need to take off the shirt altogether. My ladies don't have the same stage presence as yours do."

"Yeah, well, at least yours don't need to be attached to earrings to stay upright."

"There isn't enough there for them to reach my ears." She chuckled.

"Well, you know what they say, more than a mouthful is wasteful," I teased.

"Well, I'd love to give him a mouthful." Zaynab covered her mouth. "Lord help me. I'm so attracted to him. But I refuse to get involved until this reno is finished."

CHAPTER 46

"Then you'll jump his bones?" I asked.

"Absolutely."

She brushed her long mane over her shoulder and winked before sauntering out of the office with a little bounce in her step. I followed her out, hoping Hottie Foreman wouldn't crush her like her ex-boyfriend.

After a very productive meeting with Hottie Foreman, I got the impression he was just as fascinated with Zaynab as she was with him. They looked cute together too. She was this tiny thing who barely reached his torso, and he was a broad-shouldered hunk of muscle with dark brown hair and honey-colored eyes. He was sampling the café's pastries, and I took it as my chance to mail the letter to Asher. I returned to the office, retrieved the letter from my purse, and sprayed it with my perfume before sealing it in a pink envelope from Zaynab's stationary stash. I pulled out my cell phone and texted Farrah. She was a surefire way to get his address without too many questions. I knew Tamara had it, but I didn't want to involve her in my attempts to woo him.

Mariam: Hello, beautiful, do you think you can get me an address for Asher from Kal?

My phone buzzed with a text instantly.

Farrah: Hey, doll, absolutely. One sec, he's on the phone with me.

Mariam: Thanks.

Once I sent this letter, I was committed to possible rejection my entire life. Because I meant what I'd written—I wouldn't stop trying to get him to forgive me. My phone buzzed with two text messages back-to-back from Farah.

Farrah: 306 Memory Lane, San Diego, CA 92101

Farrah: Are you flying out for a visit? You know I'm down. *Heart emoji, eggplant emoji. Laughing emoji.*

Mariam: Not yet, but I reserve the right to ask later. Thanks! *Wink emoji.*

After addressing the envelope, I made my way to the post office box, and before I slid the envelope into the mailbox, I prayed I wasn't making matters worse.

Chapter 47

ASHER: FOUR MONTHS LATER

"Amoo Asher, can you show us the ocean again?" Bella's beautiful smile lit up my laptop screen. "I want to see the dolphins again."

"I'm still at home, but I'll get you some videos of them and you can watch them whenever you like." I'd wanted to escape Bloomington Hills for the majority of my adult life, but in the last four months, I'd wanted nothing more than to go home. Facetime calls had become my lifeline to the kids, my parents, and Tamara.

"Cool. Alec wants to tell you something."

She slid over, and Alec's serious face appeared on the screen. "Amoo Asher, I'm a yellow stripe, look." He flashed a white belt with two yellow strips on the screen.

"That's amazing, bud. I'm so proud of you. Did you earn that yesterday?"

"Yeah, Auntie Mariam took us out for ice cream and cake to celebrate. Mikey and Jordan moved to a blue stripe belt but Jaxson and Bella are still a white belt."

"Hey, where is Mikey?" Mikey was always the one in the background, and I had to work hard to get him to open up—this online communication was complete crap.

"Hi, Amoo Asher." Mikey was wearing glasses, and it crushed me that I hadn't been there to help him get them. Apparently, *she* had taken him for my mom. She was doing all the things I couldn't do until my retirement.

"Congrats on getting the blue stripe, I'm proud of you."

"Thanks. It's no big deal." He glanced down at his hands.

"It is a big deal. Always celebrate your wins."

"Okay."

CHAPTER 47

"Hey, Asher." Tamara wrapped her arms around Mikey's shoulders and peeped into the camera. Her face radiated happiness, and I couldn't believe this grown woman was my daughter. She called me Asher instead of Dad. I understood why but hated her mother for stealing that title from me.

"Hey, Tam, you look great."

She beamed. "I'm going to be huge." She eased around Mikey and gave me the side view of her growing baby bump. My grandchild took over the entire screen.

"You still don't want to know if it's a boy or girl?" I couldn't believe she was waiting. I know she didn't get her patience from me.

"Nope. Healthy baby, that's all that matters." She smiled. "Okay, I'm filling in for Maria. Amoo Niles is taking the boys to an NBA game, and me and Bella are going to get manicures with Mom and shop until we drop. Don't make that face, Asher." Her tone was stern but her voice playful. She glanced down at Mikey. "Can you make sure Alec packed all his soccer gear? Khalu Niles had to come back last week."

"Okay. Bye, Amoo Asher." Mikey waved at the computer screen.

"Have a great game, bud." But Mikey was

already out of his chair and Tamara had taken his place.

"So, are you going to hate Mom forever and ever?" Tamara pinned me with a what-the-hell stare, and I hated disappointing her.

"It's complicated," I said.

"It's not. You still care about her. If you didn't, you wouldn't flinch every time I mentioned her."

"Listen to your kid, she's smarter than you." Ragheed stepped into the kitchen freshly showered and ready for a relaxing day of sailing on a Navy buddy's boat. "Hey, beautiful."

"Hi Ragheed." Tamara laughed. "See, even your friends think you need to at least try to forgive Mom."

"Don't you have kids to look after?" I wasn't going to have them team up on me.

She glanced at her watch. "Yup. I better get them ready. Khalu will be here in a few minutes for the boys, but this conversation isn't over, Mr. George."

Logging off the call, it irked me that both Ragheed and my daughter were against me. Mariam's actions had stolen a child from me. Before knowing Tamara was my daughter, I

CHAPTER 47

never even considered having a kid. But after getting to know her and memorizing her baby albums—I realized how much joy Mariam had robbed from me when she didn't fight for me.

"I'm going to stay behind. You and the guys can go without me." I dumped my coffee cup in the sink.

Ragheed rolled his eyes. "Quit being a punk. The woman made a huge mistake—she knows it too. Just look at the unopened letters piled in the front hall closet. Brother, you need to learn forgiveness or stop caring because you have been an unbearable prick since we returned from Detroit."

"Fuck you." I turned my back on him, stormed into my bedroom, and slammed the bathroom door shut behind me.

After stripping out of my clothes and stepping into the hot, steamy shower, I couldn't get Mariam's face or body out of my mind. The woman was engrained on my skin and flooded through my veins. Despite how hard I tried, I couldn't shake her hold on me. I craved her in ways I couldn't put into words. I missed her laugh, her scent, and the way she lit up a room with her mere presence. I ached for her body beneath my own. The taste of her skin, the swell of her breasts, and the sweet spot between her legs. Like my mind, my body betrayed me and my cock yearned for her. My attachment to her fueled my anger, and I transferred that fury onto her. It had been months, and the only time I could get off was when I pictured *her*. Angry, filthy sex, where I punished Mariam for all her transgressions against me—and today it was no different, except despite imagining her chastised for her wrongs, my mind drifted to that night four months ago when we made love in her bedroom.

When I was finally dressed and out of the bedroom, I half expected Ragheed to be waiting in the living room for me with a sour look on his face. Instead, only silence and a coffee table piled with letters and packages from *her* greeted me. The letters had started to appear two weeks after we returned to San Diego and continued to come every day. Besides the letters, there were a few packages too. I had refused to open any of them, but my resolve was fading quickly.

I headed to the kitchen, made an Irish coffee, and strolled out to the balcony. The morning air was still crisp, but the sun was warm on my skin. I picked up my phone to dial Bass and remembered he was gone. I'd done that exact thing so many times. The pain and grief crawled to the surface and knocked me backward. I needed my brother. He would know what I should do, but in my heart, I knew he would tell me to man up. Bassam would say forgive Mariam because I still loved her. Forgive Mariam because it takes two to make a baby. Forgive Mariam since she didn't have the choice to refuse the marriage to Nabil. She would've been disowned and that would have been too scary for an eighteen-year-old.

I returned to the living room, picked up a letter, unsealed the envelope, and started to read.

Dear Asher,

Today was a great day. Books and Bites is nearing the completion of the renovations. We have a grand reopening scheduled for October 1st, just in time for spooky Halloween. It's going to be magical. I wish you were here to share it with me.

Tamara went for her latest ultrasound yesterday, and they still refuse to know the sex of the baby. What's wrong with them? I don't even know where she and Cross get their pa-

tience. Definitely not from me.

I'm shopping and planning for the baby shower. My mom and yours have tagged along for some of the planning, and I see a little of the sparkle in your mom's eyes these days. Her great-grandchild is a blessing after so much tragedy, and I think it's helping her heal just a little bit.

In other news, Ameera ambushed me the other day wanting all the details of our past and Tamara's pregnancy out of wedlock. It was the first time I told her it was none of her business. I think I channeled your big dick energy because I've never been able to have boundaries before—I guess having you back just to lose you all over again changed me. Made me tougher.

Miss you. Love you.
All my love,
Mariam

The tension pressed hard against my chest for months loosened, and I chuckled at her big-dick-energy reference. I could hear her voice in my head while I had been reading the letter, and her scent radiated from the page. My tight limbs relaxed. I needed more of her words. Her thoughts and humor. I grabbed the next letter and started reading.

Dear Asher,

Last night I had a wet dream. I haven't had one this powerful since I was a teenage girl—and just like back in the day, you were the main attraction in my dirty dream. We were at a wedding. I don't even know who was getting married, but I followed you outside and tried to kiss you, but you pulled away. You still hadn't forgiven me, but I was relentless, and you gave in. You pressed me against the brick wall and kissed me like you needed me as much as I need you. Your hard body against my curves, your hardness against my stomach, and your hand was inside my panties rubbing me in the way only you know how. My climax was fast and intense. But when I awoke it was my own fingers between my legs. Not yours. I'm not ashamed to say I cried myself back to sleep. I miss you, Asher. My body misses you too.

All my love and desire,
Mariam

After reading the last letter, I was completely

hooked and had to admit I was ashamed of my behavior. It wasn't until late in the evening that I finished reading every single letter. I hadn't eaten anything, and sometime between morning and afternoon, I switched from Irish coffee to whiskey neat. I moved on to the packages, and I smiled at the picture of all the kids in their karate gear. The other packages were more of the same. Each had a little note attached.

Pictures of the kids, a book of love poems, and a framed picture of Tamara and Cross holding the 3D image of the baby. It was the last package that made my insides stop, drop, and roll. It was a photo book filled with sexy pictures of Mariam. She was dressed in lingerie and posed in a very provocative way. Her breasts barely contained in tiny leather cups, her hair fanned out on a silk sheet, her thick thighs clad in black garters, leather covering the triangle between her legs. Her face flawless and her green eyes hypnotizing. Not that I was complaining, but what the hell was she thinking? I searched the package and found a note.

Asher, I can't make you forgive me and give me a second chance, but I need you to know all of me will forever be only yours. I had vowed after I became a widow to never share my life with another man, but I know now it's because that place in my life has always belonged to you. No one else will ever compare to you.

All my love, yearning, and desire.
Mariam

I was a selfish prick. There wasn't much more to it. She had been pouring so much into these letters for four months. I hadn't even bothered to open one. One thing was made clear, she'd finally fought for us, for me, and it was time I let her know all her fighting was worth it. Her attempts weren't in vain.

I picked up my cell phone and texted Tamara.

Asher: Are you still with your mom?

I watched the little three dots as she compiled her reply.

Tamara: Nope.

Relief flooded my veins.

Asher: I need your help to surprise your mom when I come home for a visit.

Tamara: When are you visiting?

Asher: I'll request a few days of leave for next week. Prob Fri–Sat.

I watched the little three dots as she composed her reply and tried to formulate my plan. One thing was for sure—I needed to use that big-dick energy she mentioned in her letter to me. The three dots appeared and disappeared. My phone rang instead.

"Hey." It was a little awkward asking my new-to-me daughter to help parent-trap Mariam, but there wasn't anyone else I trusted more to help me right now.

"Does this mean you forgive Mom?" Tamara's voice was high-pitched and elated.

I laughed. "Yeah, I guess it does."

"It took you long enough."

"I know…but I want to make it up to her. You game?"

"Heck, yeah. I've been preparing for this for like months."

I took another pull of my whiskey, and warmth spread throughout my chest. "Good, here's what I need from you…"

Chapter 48

MARIAM: ONE WEEK LATER

Between the expansion of the bookstore, my work at the salon, assisting Tamara not only to prepare for a new baby but planning a wedding, and helping Juliette when the nanny had her off days—I was physically and mentally exhausted. My mind was in a constant state of worry, wondering if I'd drop something with all the balls in the air.

I missed Asher. I craved him day in and day out. The feeling only grew stronger over time.

The hole he left inside me seemed to expand every single day. I hadn't heard anything from him after sending a letter every day for four months. I don't know if he read my letters. For all I knew, he might have burned them, along with those scandalous pictures I sent him. I was convinced he hated me more after receiving them because otherwise he surely would have reached out.

It was time to write the last letter. I had said I would write to him forever, but my pride couldn't take any more hits—even if I deserved it. Besides, he was coming home on leave tonight. Even though his mom had invited me to the gathering at their house, I didn't have the guts to face him. At least his parents didn't hate me. They both said that Tamara had always felt like their granddaughter despite believing she was a great-niece for all these years.

The tears clouded my vision, but I took out the last page of the stationery set I'd been using for his letters and began to write.

Dear Asher,
This will be the last letter I send to you—going forward, all my thoughts and feelings will

be directed to Dear Diary. I'm sorry I've bothered you the past four months. It was my desperate attempt to get you to forgive me. I thought if I displayed my heart on the page, you would maybe forgive me. Maybe even love me again. I know now that was a foolish effort, and I'm sorry for any added inconveniences my letters and parcels have caused you.

I'm not mailing this letter, since you should be in the sky and on your way home, but I want you to know that I will still be here for you and the kids. I've always loved them, and after spending so much time with them these past months, I've grown extremely attached. If it is still all right, I hope you will allow me to keep my Saturday adventures with them.

Welcome home, officer.
Love always and forever,
Mariam

Sealing the letter, I scribbled his name on the front of the envelope. A teardrop smeared his name. I glanced at the time—according to his mom he wouldn't be home for another couple hours. I wanted this over with—it was my closure.

The drive was quick, and I slid the letter into

the mailbox without anyone seeing me. When I returned home, exhaustion seeped into my bones. The emotional strain of waiting for any sign from Asher had crushed me.

I poured a large glass of rosé, cuddled in my favorite chair, wrapped myself in a fluffy blanket, and grabbed my newest romance from my military men subscription box. It was the newest collaboration project at Books and Bites. For obvious reasons, I'd been consumed with every single military hero romance novel. I was halfway through when I heard a knock at the door. I glanced at the time—it was a quarter past twelve. Tamara must have decided to come home after the party, after all.

I shuffled to the door and unlocked it while I shouted loud enough for Tamara to hear me from the other side of the door. "How do you plan on living away from me if you can't even spend a night without your mommy?"

No one was at the other side of the door, and a cold chill traveled down my spine. I prepared to close and lock the door, but then I noticed the suitcase on my porch, open and filled to the rim with all my letters.

My words halted on my lips. My mouth went dry. Asher had returned my letters. Fresh

CHAPTER 48

tears filled my eyes as I closed the suitcase and wheeled it inside, locking the door behind me. When I returned to my chair, a large muscular body occupied it. *Asher.*

"This letter was in my mailbox when I got home today." He lifted it to his nose. "But it didn't smell of your perfume."

He was a sight for sore eyes. My mouth gaped open, and my heart was in my throat. "How did you get in here?"

"Tamara gave me the key to the back door."

"Why are you here?" I raised my chin. I couldn't take any more bullshit. He either needed to forgive me and love me or get the hell out.

"I don't accept you bowing out. You promised me a letter a day." He flashed me a wicked grin, and my stomach fluttered.

His eyes roamed my body, and he licked his lips. I was suddenly too aware of how see-through my white cotton tank and shorts were, I wasn't wearing a bra, and it was cold without my throw blanket. I lifted my chin. "You didn't seem like you cared either way, so I thought it was time to stop chasing someone who doesn't want me."

"I read every letter multiple times, and do you

know what I realized?"

He stepped close, and I swallowed hard. The blood rushed to my ears. "You'll hate me forever?"

"No." He brushed a loose strand of hair behind my ear and caressed the side of my cheek. I closed my eyes to the feel of his touch, and my body swayed.

"I'm your mortal enemy?"

He chuckled. "Look at me."

My eyes fluttered open, and fire burned in his dark gaze. "I realized that no matter what I do, how far I go, I will always love you. I can't and I don't want to live another day without you."

My lips trembled. "Then why did you not respond to any of my letters?"

"I didn't open them until last week. And once I did, I answered every single one of them."

"You waited all this time to open them? You are so stubborn...wait, you wrote me back?"

"I responded to every letter, gift, trinket, and delicious picture you sent me. They are outside in that suitcase."

"Really?"

He caressed my jaw, his nose so close to mine. The warmth of his breath teased my cheek, and I trembled as I relished the feel of his hands finally on my skin. The tension I'd carried in my body for these long months eased with every stroke of his hands on me.

"I'm sorry I allowed my wounded pride to take over my common sense," he said.

"Apology accepted." I leaned into his frame with my curves.

"I come with three little packages. They are cute, sweet, dramatic, and complete terrors. Does that bother you?"

"I love those monsters, and I'm kind of attached to them now."

"They love you too. All I heard about while I was gone was Mariam this and Mariam that." He laughed and pulled me into his arms. His hard body pressed against mine, and his hands teased the curve of my hips.

"In fact, Bella and Tamara picked this out for you." He reached into his pocket and pulled out a black velvet box.

I gasped when he got on one knee. My vision blurred from tears. I covered my mouth with trembling fingers.

"Will you marry me and make us one big, wildly unconventional but incredibly happy family?"

I got on my knees before him, laughing and

crying all at once. The tightness and ache of longing in my chest eased. I hadn't breathed properly for four months because I believed my childhood foolishness had cost me the love of my life once again. "Yes, let's build the family we should have had together a long time ago."

He placed the ring on my trembling finger and clasped my face. "I love you. I love you, Mariam."

"I love you, Asher."

His lips covered mine, and I sighed in relief at the contact. We moved in a whirlwind of arms, hands, and mouths. The sound of clothes tearing and fabric flying, the crash of something breaking in the background. Probably my wine glass.

I pushed Asher onto the sofa and cradled his hips with my thighs. His hands heated a trail from my neck to my core, and I bucked against his fingers. His lips tasted and teased my mouth, my neck, and my breasts. Each touch drove me deeper into his spell.

"Mariam." His gaze found mine, and in the depth of his shimmering black eyes, a lifetime of love and longing mirrored the fire in my soul.

He clasped my hips, and I guided him inside

me. He filled me in a way I didn't think was possible. He possessed not only my body, but my heart, my soul, my entire being. Everything was right in the world for the first time in my life.

We finally got our happily ever after.

Chapter 49

Tamara: Another Four Months and One Week Later

Tamara was grateful for her family and friends, but she was pleased when her baby shower was coming to an end and it was almost time to pack up the banquet room at A Taste of Iraq. Her back and feet ached, but she didn't regret wearing the adorable yellow heels and matching sundress.

"This is a wand?" Asher pointed the toy wand at Tamara's mom like it was a sword.

CHAPTER 49

"That's not just a wand, it's the Elder Wand," Mom clarified.

"A wand for old people?"

"Mr. George, you have much to learn about our buddy, Harry Potter," Mom said.

The party Tamara's mom had arranged for her baby shower was freaking impressive. With Tamara student teaching, preparing for motherhood, planning a wedding, and looking for a home for her growing family, her mom had insisted on hosting a baby shower.

"What's Harry Potter?" Asher inspected the wand.

"Life," Mom and Tamara said in unison. Mom high-fived Tamara. The baby picked that moment to kick, and Tamara stumbled back.

"Are you okay?" Asher came to her side, wide-eyed.

"I'm fine, just need to sit for a second." The little one inside her wasn't due for another two weeks and could be a kicker for the NFL.

Asher helped Tamara into the chair, and he and her mom had a seat at the table beside her.

"So, what's with the suitcases and witch hat? I don't get it," Asher said.

"Those are Hogwarts school trunks and the school sorting hat," Mom said.

"It's getting lost in translation." Asher smirked, and Tamara loved watching the exchange between her parents. Her biological parents. Her baby would have both sets of grandparents and great-grandparents to spoil him or her. She still couldn't believe Cross had talked her into not finding out the sex of their baby.

Her mom beamed, but Asher still seemed confused by the décor. Each table had mini traveling trunks and a sorting hat. Little bubble bottles disguised as potion bottles were placed at each table setting. The cake was an adorable stack of Harry Potter books with a picture of baby Harry at the center—scar and all. All the tablecloths were dark blue with little gold stars, and the chairs were adorned with ties of all the house colors. Big, golden-winged keys hung from the ceiling, and it felt like they were sitting in a scene from the book.

"You can't be serious." Mom clasped her hand with Asher's, and tears of joy pricked Tamara's eyes. Her mom's engagement ring sparkled between their joined fingers. Tamara couldn't remember her mom ever being so happy and carefree.

CHAPTER 49

"Hey, non-magical folks." Khalu Niles plopped in the seat beside Tamara.

"Non-magical? Don't tell me you know what all this"—Asher waved his hands in the air—"is about."

"You do too. It's that funny-looking kid with glasses and a scar." Khalu Niles pointed at his forehead. "There are movies, books, and a theme park with a fire-breathing dragon."

"The theme park at Universal?" Asher asked.

"That's the one. Jordan and now Jax are obsessed with the movies, and Jordan started reading the books thanks to that one." He pointed at Mom.

"I had all the kids last week and we watched the first movie. Even Bella was completely invested," Mom said.

"Jordan just gave Mikey the first book in the series to read. Brother, you're about to be sorted into your Hogwarts house," Khalu Niles said.

At the mention of Jordan's name, Khalu Niles's eyes met Tamara's. She was the only one who held his secret, and due to her own experiences with hidden truths, her stomach knotted. She didn't want this secret hanging over Jordan's head.

"Sorted?"

Asher's bemused expression was priceless. "Mom, why don't you give him a tour and explain the phenomena of our magical world?"

Khalu Niles and Tamara were left alone, and he shifted his stare from her as if that would stop Tamara from voicing her thoughts. Did he even know his bigmouth niece?

"Khalu, can we talk for a second?" His green eyes met hers again, and he nodded. She noted the darkness beneath his eyes and the stress in his shoulders. He even seemed a little disheveled—his black polo shirt and dark denim slacks were slightly wrinkled, and his hair was untidy, like he could use a haircut.

"So, you took another test, right?" She lowered her tone for only him to hear.

He ran his fingers through his unruly hair, making the brown strands stand on end. "Yeah. Yours was accurate."

"I'm so sorry." She placed her hand on his arm. "What are you going to do?"

"He is mine. My boy, despite the results."

"Of course. You are his father in all the ways that count."

"I love him, and I'm worried if I start searching for answers, I might..."

CHAPTER 49

"Might shake the wrong tree."

"Right. I still need answers, though. I must know the who and why." His face darkened. "With how accessible DNA results are now, I don't ever want Jordan to find out the way you did. You were lucky. Asher is a good guy, but what if by looking, I invite danger to our door?"

"It's scary. There's so much we don't know. Like why Auntie left."

"She's not your aunt." Khalu startled her with his tone.

"Sorry." The little one decided to give Tamara a double kick and do a skillful backflip in her belly. She buckled and clasped her side.

"You, okay?" Khalu noticed her discomfort, but she waved him away.

"Yes." The pain subsided just as quickly as the hit had come. "Why did Rula leave? Where is she? And why would she marry you and stay for eight years if there was someone else in her life at the time?"

"I couldn't care less where she is, but I need to know because she's the one who has the answers I need."

"That's where we should start looking."

"We?" Khalu smirked and raised a brow. "You think you're helping me?"

"Yup, unless you want me to tell my mom. You know she loves to help."

"You promised you wouldn't tell anyone."

"And I won't, but I didn't promise to stay out of it."

"Right now, I'm going to focus on my boys. I have the new nanny, and the kids love her."

"She's really pretty, the nanny." Tamara wiggled her brows.

"You are worse than your grandmother." He rolled his eyes. "She's been trying to make more out of my working relationship with Dalia."

Tamara laughed and reared from another kick from the active baby. This one was sharp, and it made her leap from the seat in pain. The pain faded, but something wet slid down her thighs. For a moment, she assumed she had lost control of her bladder. "Khalu, I think my water broke."

"Holy hell." Khalu leaped from his chair. "Baby. It's coming. Her water broke."

Cross was at her side in seconds. Followed by her mom and Asher. Soon everyone was around them.

Nana was the one who took control. She was wearing a blue skirt and matching blazer with

CHAPTER 49

a bright pink peony corsage on the lapel. She had blushed when she admitted Jidu had gotten it in honor of her first great-grandchild.

"Everything is fine. Give the girl some room." She inspected Tamara's stomach. "I was worried this would happen. The child is sitting low in your belly."

"But we have two weeks." Cross's complexion had turned a pale green.

"It happens sometimes." Nana patted his arm. "This is normal." She clapped her hands. "Mariam, call the doctor and tell him that Tamara is on the way to the hospital. Cross, get the car and bring it out front. Remember, calmly. Don't drive fast."

Cross kissed Tamara's forehead and ran out like the building was on fire.

"What part of calmly didn't that boy understand?" Nana nodded her head and turned to Asher and Niles. "You two help Tamara outside."

"What should I do?" Jidu said.

"You go pay the bill with the manager."

"Mom, no, I'm paying," Mariam said, on hold with the doctor's answering service

"Don't be ridiculous—this is our first great-grandchild," Nana said.

"Right." Jidu peeled off in the other direction, and Tamara noted he was wearing a matching blue tie to Nana's suit and the mini boutonniere to Nana's corsage. What was going on with those two?

"The rest of you, party is over. Pack the gifts and decorations. Take them to Mariam's house." She clapped her hands together like a coach would do, and everyone went to work.

Asher and Khalu Niles helped Tamara out the door and into the passenger seat. Her mom hopped into the back seat while Asher stood beside the car, not sure what to do.

Tamara peered up at him. "Asher, are you coming?"

"If you would like me to. I don't want to overstep."

"I want you there."

His face lit up. "Okay."

He turned to Niles and clasped his shoulder. He seemed to need to steady himself. "Can you please help my parents get the kids home?"

"Absolutely, Jidu."

Asher barked out a laugh and got into the back seat with her mom.

Cross clasped Tamara's hand and brought it to his lips. "Ready, Mom?"

"Let's meet our little one," she whispered.

Little kicker punched again, letting Tamara know he or she was ready to meet them too.

"Holy shit, Asher, we are going to be grandparents," Mom squealed.

Tamara's thoughts turned to Nabil—the man she'd believed was her father for her entire life. She prayed he was looking down at her today, happy he was a grandfather too.

Epilogue

ASHER

In a matter of months, I'd become a father and grandfather, and now I was about to become a husband. My insides were in knots, my hands trembled, and an electric energy hummed through my body.

Cross dusted the shoulder of my black tailored jacket. "Looking sharp, Father-in-law. I must step up my tuxedo game for my wedding now."

I shoulder-bumped him. "You don't look so

EPILOGUE

bad yourself, Son-in-law."

"I think Alec and Mikey are the best-dressed among us. Then me, and you gentlemen come in last," Father James teased. He wore a long white robe, red sash around his shoulders, and a Bible in his hands.

I chuckled. "How could I argue with a priest?"

The boys did look handsome in the suits and reminded me a lot of Bassam and me at their age, even as they were shoving each other with their shoulders beside Cross.

"Knock it off." Cross tapped Alec's back. "Remember what Tamara said: No surprise if you guys fight inside the church."

I wanted to elope—just me and Mariam on a beach somewhere, but she wanted our families to share in our special day. Looking out at the small group of family and close friends we'd invited to the wedding, I was happy they were here to share it with us. Especially the kids. Our marriage joined us all together as one family unit in the eyes of God, but legally, the adoption of the children wasn't official yet. Mariam and I were adopting them together.

The traditional melody of the wedding march echoed through St. John Church, and

Bella came down the aisle looking as cute as a button in what she called her "pink princess dress" while pushing my grandson, Grayson, in his decorated stroller. They were followed by Tamara in a beautiful floor-length gown that matched Bella's in color and was less princess and more queen in its fit and shape. I still couldn't believe she was my daughter. That I was a grandfather and about to adopt three more children. Love and terror gripped my chest all at once. How could something bring so much joy and fear at one time?

The tempo changed and "Here Comes the Bride" played. Our family stood and blocked my view of Mariam coming down the aisle. My pulse raced, and my legs were lead. I swallowed hard. The anticipation was killing me. But then, I saw her. A vision in a pale pink dress that swayed with each step she took toward me on her father's arm. Our eyes met across the aisle, and the tension in my body eased. My heart swelled, and I knew that if we were together, everything was going to be all right.

She finally reached me, and Amoo Manni took my hand. "You are a good man, Abni. I'm sorry I didn't see that before."

EPILOGUE

It was the first nice thing Manni Shammas had ever said to me.

"Thank you."

He kissed both sides of my and Mariam's cheeks as was customary and placed his daughter's hand in mine. "Be good to each other."

When Mariam's gaze found my own, she beamed up at me. "You look so handsome."

"Me?" I kissed her hand. "You look incredible."

A throat cleared behind me, and I turned to see Father James pretending to be impatient, but his expression was amused. I led Mariam to our places, and she handed her bouquet to Tamara to hold.

Father James did the traditional prayers in Arabic and a few in English before he had Mariam and I face one another and join hands. "These two have gone through a lot to get here and they might not have gone the normal route—dare I say it was a more scandalous way—but they have created a beautiful, strong foundation for a loving family." This earned a few chuckles from everyone.

"Asher and Mariam, please join hands."

Mariam's fingers linked with my own, her

eyes filled with tears and a smile curving her lips. I mouthed, "I love you."

"These are the hands of your partner, your best friend, the love of your lifetime. The person who will encourage your hopes, dreams, and faith in God. These hands will hold you during times of struggle and joy. They will provide strength, courage, and comfort through good and bad times. They will tenderly hold your children and grandchildren. In your case, sooner than most."

Glancing at Father James, I laughed.

Mariam whispered, "We have a priest with jokes."

"He's not lying," I whispered back.

Father James cleared his throat. "Asher, do you vow to love, honor, cherish, and protect Mariam until death do you part?"

He placed the microphone below my chin.

"Absolutely," I said. When he didn't move the mic from me, I looked up at his amused expression. "Yes?" I asked. He motioned for me to continue, and I realized I'd missed my mark. "I do."

Laughter and a few *aw*s erupted in the church. I shrugged and sheepishly grinned down at Mariam.

EPILOGUE

"Mariam, do you vow to love, honor, cherish, and protect Asher until death do you part?"

"Absolutely, yes, I do."

More laughter came from the crowd. It wasn't time to kiss my woman yet, but I ached to kiss that beautiful mouth. We exchanged rings and the ceremonial crowns were placed on our heads as more prayers blessed our union. I escorted my wife to pray before the Virgin Mary and I shot a little prayer of my own for Bassam and Lydia. I hoped Mariam and I had their blessing to raise Mikey, Alec, and Bella together as one family.

Mariam returned and clasped my hand. Father James pronounced us husband and wife, and we faced our family and friends. Pure joy and a feeling of contentment filled my heart and soul. Cross stepped beside us with the microphone. "I'd like to introduce Mr. and Mrs. Asher George."

Mariam tugged me closer. "Kiss the bride already, Mr. George."

I eagerly pulled her against me. Her arms wrapped around my neck, and I kissed my wife before God, our family, and friends.

The halhala echoed in the church and mixed with cheers. I released Mariam's lips, and she raised our joined hands in triumph as I led us out of the church and to the waiting limo.

We took pictures with Cross and Tamara holding our champagne flutes, and then I finally had my wife alone during the short ride to the Bloomington Golden Hotel for our reception.

"Are you happy?" Mariam caressed my cheek.

"Never been happier." I kissed her hand. "I just wish..." My voice trailed off.

"That Bassam and Lydia were here to share it with us?"

I nodded. "I prayed for them today and hoped we had their blessing to adopt the children together."

"I think we do." Her finger teased my lips.

"How do you know?"

"I dreamed of Bassam and Lydia. Mostly Lydia. It was my bridal shower in the dream, and she and I were dancing with Bella. Then she thanked me for looking after the kids and asked me to always watch out for them." She shrugged. "It might be my subconscious working out the past year of events, but I choose to believe it was Lydia giving me her blessing."

I clasped both her cheeks. "I believe that too."

EPILOGUE

When our lips crashed together, I knew Mariam's dream was the blessing I needed from my brother and sister-in-law.

Sign-up for [Reem Kashat's newsletter](#) to receive a FREE novella. The Letters is a collection of Mariam and Asher's love letters mentioned in the story. Visit https://mailchi.mp/reemkashat.com/forgive_and_remember_readers to join this exclusive mailing list and receive, The Letters novella and other exciting perks only for Forgive and Remember readers.

Acknowledgments

This book contains character references to subjects that might be difficult for certain readers. *Forgive and Remember* includes themes of depression, emotional abuse, mental health, illness, death, adult and child grief, and neglect. To anyone that has gone through or is currently dealing with any of these topics, I want you to know that my heart sees you and I'm sorry.

To my cover designer, A.J. Norris, at Delicious Nights Cover Design, thank you for making me the most beautiful cover and family tree! I really appreciate all the time and effort you spent on making my vison a reality. To my editor, Jennifer Haymore, words can't describe how grateful I am for all your hard work in making my story shine.

A very special thank you to Synthia and Jennie. You showed me great kindness and answered all my questions regarding Navy life. I really appreciate all your generosity and patience. Thank you so much for your years of service.

To Aliza, thank you so much for taking time out of your busy life to beta read this story. Love you to the moon and back!

About the author

Reem has a bachelor's degree in English and Creative Writing and co-manages a YouTube channel called Book Harlots. She is a first-generation Chaldean-American with a unique perspective on storytelling steeped in the cultural traditions of her upbringing. Growing up in a home with immigrant parents and navigating a strict Catholic and cultural background of a small Indigenous group from Iraq, her narrative voice is rich and unique. In addition to English, she speaks both Arabic and Chaldean. She is a foodie with a huge extended family and loves highlighting those aspects in her work. She describes herself as the perfect archetype for a heroine of a romcom - quirky, a little clumsy, and looking for the love of her life inside of a romance novel. Reem is a Potter-head, Supernatural fanatic, BDB Harlot, a fashionista, and a believer in love at first sight. You can find more stories by Reem under her other Pen name, Sage Spelling.

Asher and Mariam

High School

Asher and Mariam

Wedding Day

Family Tree

Shammas and George Family

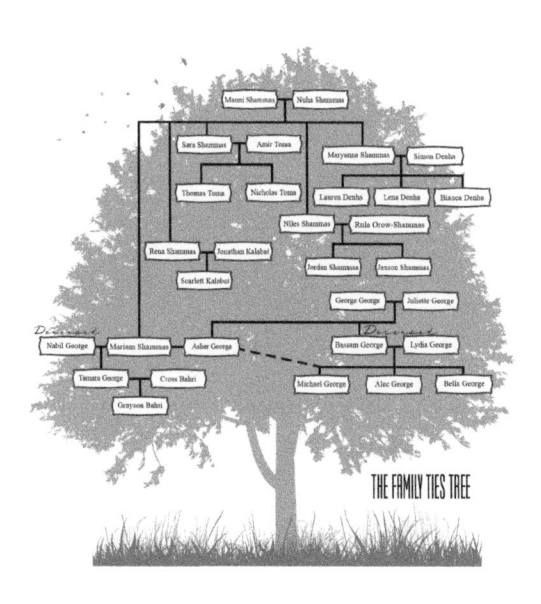

Manni Shammas — Nuha Shammas

Sara Shammas — Amir Toma
- Thomas Toma
- Nicholas Toma

Maryanna Shammas — Simon Denha
- Lauren Denha
- Lena Denha
- Bianca Denha

Niles Shammas — Rula Orow-Shammas
- Jordan Shammas
- Jenson Shammas

Rena Shammas — Jonathan Kalabat
- Scarlett Kalabat

George George — Juliette George

Divorced: Nabil George — Mariam Shammas — Asher George ---- Bassam George — Lydia George
- Tamara George — Cross Bahri
  - Grayson Bahri
- Michael George
- Alec George
- Bella George

THE FAMILY TIES TREE

Milton Keynes UK
Ingram Content Group UK Ltd.
UKHW011814120624
444110UK00001B/34